AFTERMATH

Mary Beth pointed her fork at her daughter. "There'll be no swearing in this house, young lady."

Her stern rebuke earned her a raised chin and tightened mouth that was so much like Stephen's, Mary Beth winced.

"I know why you haven't cried. You don't love Daddy!"

"Of course I do! Did." Aurora's hostile expression demanded an explanation. Mary Beth sighed and decided to tell the truth—some of it. "I want to cry more than anything," she admitted, silently imploring her daughter to understand. "But I can't," she finished in a low, pain-filled voice.

"Why not?"

Because your father is a cheat and a liar and I despise him. Oh, how she wanted to say the words aloud. But this was the wrong time. So she crumpled her napkin and swallowed back the words. "There are things you don't know," she said, sounding remarkably calm.

"Like what?"

"It's complicated."

"This has something to do with why Daddy was in Seattle, doesn't it?"

"I can't talk about this, Aurora." *Please, not yet.* The mere thought of how Stephen's betrayal would upset her daughter made Mary Beth ill. She nudged her plat [illegible] "I promise I will, but [illegible]

ANOTHER LIFE

Ann Roth

ZEBRA BOOKS
Kensington Publishing Corp.
www.kensingtonbooks.com

ZEBRA BOOKS are published by

Kensington Publishing Corp.
850 Third Avenue
New York, NY 10022

All Kensington titles, imprints, and distributed lines are available at special quantity discounts for bulk purchases for sales promotion, premiums, fund-raising, educational, or institutional use.

Special book excerpts or customized printings can also be created to fit specific needs. For details, write or phone the office of the Kensington Special Sales Manager: Attn. Special Sales Department. Kensington Publishing Corp., 850 Third Avenue, New York, NY 10022. Phone: 1-800-221-2647.

ISBN-13: 978-0-8217-8034-3
ISBN-10: 0-8217-8034-4

First Printing: April 2007
10 9 8 7 6 5 4 3 2 1

Printed in the United States of America

In loving memory of Karl Schuessler.

Special thanks to Sophia Bell Lavin and Andie Scoggins,
whose legal expertise helped with this book.
And to Mr. Thuong-Tri Nguyen,
who took time from his busy schedule to answer questions.
Any mistakes or misinformation are mine.

PART ONE

Horrendous Surprise

Chapter One

Mary Beth Mason was running late because she couldn't find her keys. Where had she left them? Standing in the middle of the kitchen where she'd spent the past hour preparing a chicken-broccoli casserole for dinner, she tried to recall.

She remembered the cell phone ringing as she'd pulled into the garage after the garden club meeting—Susan Andrews wanted to discuss the upcoming ballet guild fundraiser. Absorbed by the conversation Mary Beth had wandered inside and tossed the keys . . . somewhere. She drew a blank.

Nerves thrumming, she chewed the pad of her thumb, which wasn't as satisfying as biting her nails but protected her bi-weekly manicure. Good thing Stephen wasn't here, because he considered any kind of finger or nail chewing "coarse."

What was it he said last week when she couldn't find her sunglasses? "Forty years old and senile already."

It was a joke but also a jibe. Stephen, who was nearly sixty and neurotically organized, never misplaced anything and didn't understand people who did. Especially his wife.

The minute-hand on the art deco kitchen clock stuttered forward, and she was later still. As breathless as if she was in the middle of a tennis lesson, she rapidly searched the kitchen, the den, the dining and living rooms, and even the powder room reserved for guests. No luck. The keys weren't in any of the bedrooms or bathrooms upstairs, either, or in her purse, sweater, or coat pockets.

"Oh, dear," she muttered, back in the kitchen. Maybe she *was* getting senile.

It was her day to drive carpool. Aurora didn't like to be kept waiting after swim-team practice, which ended exactly fifteen minutes from now. Mary Beth pictured her daughter's pretty young face tightened into the same scowl Stephen used to convey disapproval. Father and daughter also shared the same intolerance for those who weren't as organized and punctual as they were.

But then lately, Aurora found fault with Mary Beth no matter what she did. At fourteen the world revolved around her, and she expected her mother to bow to her needs no matter what. Teenagers!

Worse, Aurora would whine about this to Stephen tomorrow night when he called from Singapore. Then the chiding would begin.

"There are only three of us in this family, Mary Beth. How hard can it be to run the household smoothly and efficiently?" she mimicked, lowering her voice in imitation of Stephen's. "Surely even *you* can do that."

"I'd like to see you juggle Women's Club and PTA meetings, the garden club, symphony, art guild, and opera fundraisers, *and* sit through every one of Aurora's swim meets and clarinet recitals," she muttered under her breath.

Not loud enough for anyone to hear, because Mary Beth preferred to avoid conflict. Of course, at the moment there was nobody around to hear.

Stephen never drove Aurora anyplace, and he rarely attended her activities. He was too busy making money and traveling to Asia to work with clients. He paid the bills and handled the investments. Mary Beth's job was to run the house and care for their daughter, and that meant picking her up *on time.*

The phone rang—not the cell but the land line. She ignored it. Friends and family would know to try the cell. Anybody else could leave a voicemail message. After five rings, the machine picked up.

There was one last place to check for the keys. By the time she reached the foyer, the phone was ringing again. Her gaze homed in on the marble-top console inside the entry. Though she couldn't recall using the front door or the adjoining coat closet today, her keys lay there, a tangle of silver and gold.

Wouldn't you know they'd be in the last place she looked. At least she had them now. They jingled as she snatched them up.

The phone went silent. Almost immediately it rang again. Odd. She checked her watch, then rushed into the kitchen and picked up.

"Hello?"

"Is this Mrs. Mary Beth Mason?" asked a sober female voice.

Too clipped and businesslike for a salesperson.

"Yes, it is," she replied, tapping her toe impatiently on the floor. *Hurry up, hurry up.*

"This is Barbara Collins for Dr. Suzanne Frank at Harborview Hospital in Seattle. Please hold."

Seattle? Aside from a family vacation years ago, Mary Beth didn't know the city or anyone living there. This call made no sense, but while she waited on hold she ran through the possibilities. Couldn't be family, because Stephen and Aurora were her only living relatives. Stephen had a frail brother twelve years older, but he lived in England. There were business associates all over the world, but all their friends lived here in San Francisco.

The line clicked. "This is Dr. Frank," said a soft female voice. "I'm afraid I have bad news. Your husband has suffered a massive coronary."

The words didn't penetrate. Mary Beth frowned. "There must be some mistake. Who did you say you are?"

"Dr. Suzanne Frank at Harborview Hospital," the woman repeated. "You *are* the Mary Beth Mason married to Stephen Edward Mason III?"

"I am, but—"

"Your husband is in the ICU under my care, Mrs. Mason."

The keys slipped from Mary Beth's fingers, clattering onto the tile. "But that can't be." She sank onto a bleached-wood kitchen chair. "Stephen is a partner at the law firm of Jones, Westin and Hawkins. He specializes in international law. That's why he's in Singapore." Though no one could see her, she shook her head. "He's definitely not in Seattle."

The doctor cleared her throat. "Look, I don't know anything about your husband's travel itinerary.

All I know is, if you want to see him alive you'd better get up here right away. I don't think he's going to make it through the night."

Mary Beth slumped in the hospital-beige lounge chair outside the Harborview Hospital Cardiac ICU. It was nearly one in the morning, eight hours since she'd received the call that had brought her here. She'd arrived at the hospital only twenty minutes ago, but it felt like days.

Stephen had suffered a second coronary, the nurse at the ICU desk had informed her, and the doctors were working to save him. So here she sat, numb and waiting. Yet nagging questions hummed through her brain like irritating gnats.

For starters, what was Stephen doing in Seattle when he was supposed to be in Singapore? Why hadn't he told her where he was?

Mary Beth hugged her Prada handbag close. It was cold and hard when she needed warmth, a comforting touch, or at least a sympathetic smile. But at this late hour she was the lone visitor.

If only she'd brought Aurora. Her distraught daughter had begged to come along, but Mary Beth hadn't wanted her to see her daddy this sick. So she'd called Ellie Saunders, her oldest and dearest friend, and asked her to stay with Aurora. Stephen didn't approve of the never-married Ellie, whose father once had served time for passing bad checks and who worked as a paralegal at a non-profit law firm specializing in immigration. But the woman was like a sister to Mary Beth and a godsend of a friend, and she lived in nearby Oakland. She'd packed a bag and come at once, offering to stay with Aurora until Mary Beth brought Stephen home.

The elevator pinged and a weary-looking but beautiful woman stepped from the cage, balancing a large cup of Starbucks coffee and a jumbo Godiva chocolate bar. She wore strappy heels that had to hurt her feet, and shimmery off-black stockings. Her legs were long and shapely, and she walked like a woman used to high heels, an art Mary Beth had never mastered.

Blowing a strand of thick, blond hair from her face, she took a seat across from the white coffee table in the same waiting area. Her hair was shoulder-length, wavy and glamorous, and the color looked natural. She set down her things and shrugged out of her black dress coat, which looked to be cashmere.

The coffee smelled good. Mary Beth tucked her limp, brown, chin-length hair, which she dyed to hide the gray, behind her ears. She and the blonde exchanged weary, sad smiles.

The woman was a good ten years younger than she. Judging by the slinky black cocktail dress clinging to her body, she was slimmer and shapelier than Mary Beth had ever been. She put on weight just thinking about candy, but this woman probably ate all the chocolate she wanted and never gained a pound.

Mary Beth envied her. She also felt frumpy and fat. She tugged her gray cardigan over her ample hips and wished she'd changed out of her old gray wool trousers, striped blouse, and loafers before rushing to catch the plane.

Not that different clothes would help. She was and always had been on the chubby side of petite.

The woman ignored her coffee and tore open the candy bar. Mary Beth couldn't help but notice her nails. Short but not chewed, and no polish. Mary Beth's were acrylic, moderately long, and a tasteful sea-shell pink. She flexed her fingers proudly. She definitely had this woman in the nail department.

Her companion noted Mary Beth's open study and quickly swallowed a mouthful of candy.

"I'm Caroline."

Shamed by her petty, vain thoughts when her gravely ill husband lay fighting for his life down the hall, Mary Beth flushed. "That's a lovely name."

"Thank you." Caroline held out the candy. "Would you like some?"

Hugging her purse to her waist, Mary Beth shook her head. "Thanks, but I'd better not. I'm Mary Beth."

"Nice to meet you," Caroline said. "I feel so silly wearing these clothes to the hospital," she gestured at her sheath and shoes, "but my husband and I were about to celebrate our tenth wedding anniversary. We live on Bainbridge Island, and he was supposed to pick me up at the dock and take me to dinner and dancing. But he never made it. Apparently he collapsed while waiting for me in the parking lot. Massive coronary." Frowning, she absently rolled a corner of the wrapper around her finger. "I never did get dinner, so I guess this is it. I'm not really hungry, though." She tossed the candy bar onto the table, then picked up the coffee, raising it as if in toast. "Cheers."

"I'm so sorry," Mary Beth replied. "You seem much too young to worry about old-age diseases like heart attacks."

"Actually, my husband is quite a bit older than I am. He was a widower when I married him. I was a baby, barely twenty, but I knew he was the man I wanted."

Mary Beth knew about marrying young, and nodded. "We have a lot in common. I was also twenty when I married. My husband, too, is older, by twenty years. He'd been divorced quite awhile and couldn't wait to get married. Neither could I."

Remembering, she smiled. She and Stephen had been so much in love that nothing mattered but sharing wedding vows and setting up house. "He was starved for feminine attention."

"I know exactly what you mean. Taking care of my husband was so time-consuming, it took me three years to get the fifteen credits I needed for my graphic arts degree."

"At least you got it." Mary Beth had wanted to earn her bachelor of arts in history, but Stephen had said she didn't need a degree because he would take care of her for the rest of her life. Wanting to please him, she hadn't argued.

"I not only graduated, I run a successful graphic design business from home," Caroline said proudly. "What do you do?"

"Compared to you, not much. I'm a housewife and mother. Lately though, I've been thinking about going back to school—I'm not sure what field—and then getting a job. Our daughter's nearly grown and I need to find something to fill the time."

Mary Beth shut her mouth. She'd never admitted her dream aloud, and here she was, telling a stranger.

Caroline threw her a thumbs-up. "Good for you, Mary Beth. I say, go for it."

"Maybe I will." Though Stephen wouldn't like the idea of her working. He was old-fashioned that way. "But not right now." Mary Beth glanced at the closed doors of the ICU. "Like your husband, mine also suffered a massive coronary. The weird thing is, I don't know what he's doing in Seattle." She massaged her temples, which had started to pound. "We live in San Francisco. He was supposed to be in Singapore on business."

"You're a good eight hundred miles from home." Caroline's big, blue eyes filled with sympathy. "If God forbid it had to happen, it should have happened in your own city. My husband travels to Singapore, too. He's a lawyer."

"No kidding. Mine too, specializing in international law. Who knows, maybe they know each other. Who does he work for?"

"He's self-employed. Wouldn't that be a sad coincidence." Caroline's mouth hinted at a smile. "They could talk business through their oxygen masks."

Mary Beth grinned. Given the gravity of their situations, an eavesdropper might be appalled at their light banter. But talking with this friendly stranger helped keep her from drowning in worry, and she clung to their conversation like a lifeline.

She liked this woman and her dry sense of humor, and wanted to know more about her. "Any children?" she asked.

"One daughter, Jax." Caroline caught a lock of her wavy hair between two fingers and absently tugged it. "She's seven, and the apple of her daddy's eye. How many do you have?"

"Same as you, a daughter. Aurora's fourteen, and a lot like her father. He's her hero, the man who can do no wrong." Mary Beth glanced at the forbidding ICU doors and bit her lip. "If anything happens to him . . ."

"I know." Caroline leaned forward, caught Mary Beth's hand and squeezed it.

Mary Beth squeezed back, then let go to hug herself. For a moment neither of them spoke, each lost in the grip of fear and uncertainty. Sharing the pain with someone who understood was a great comfort.

"So Aurora puts her father on a pedestal," Caroline said after a while. "Are you up there, too?"

"I wish. Her dad's gone so much that I get stuck with the discipline and the unpleasant stuff. You know what I mean. Making sure the homework is done, and keeping an eye on the amount of time she spends on the computer. If I didn't limit her phone and TV time, too, she'd fritter away her life on them. That makes me the evil mother."

"Jax isn't into chat rooms or cell phones yet, but like you, I'm the disciplinarian." Caroline sighed. "Why do husbands do that to their wives—force them to be the mean taskmasters?"

"Isn't it obvious? To make themselves look better."

"Huh. I never saw it that way, but I think you may be on to something."

"Took me a while to figure it out, but I've got ten more years of marriage than you. I'm sure you'd have figured it out sooner or later. You think you have it rough now, just wait 'til Jax reaches puberty," Mary Beth added. "Then life gets *really* fun."

"I'll just bet." Caroline wrinkled her nose. "Is it as awful as they say?"

"Worse."

They smiled at each other as if this were a mundane conversation at the dentist's office.

Suddenly the ICU doors swung open and a slender, fifty-something woman in blood-streaked scrubs strode toward the waiting room. Mary Beth caught her breath.

"I'm Dr. Suzanne Frank." She glanced at Mary Beth. "Mrs. Mason?"

Her heart in her throat, she jumped up. "Yes?"

Caroline also rose. "I'm Mrs. Mason," she said, shooting Mary Beth an odd look.

As if she were crazy.

"Now this really *is* a coincidence," Mary Beth said. "Both of us with the same last name, with husbands who travel to Singapore and are here in the ICU."

The doctor frowned from one to the other. "There's only one patient with the last name 'Mason' here—Stephen. Which of you is Stephen Mason's wife?"

"I am—"

"That would be me—"

Mary Beth and Caroline replied at the same time.

Clearly the blond woman was delusional. Mary Beth gaped at her. "I ought to know who my husband is. We've been married twenty years."

"Who your husband *was*," the doctor gently corrected, her expression both grave and sympathetic. "I'm sorry, but he died on the operating table."

Chapter Two

Mary Beth stared down at Stephen's prone, sheet-draped body. He was so white. So still.

Dead.

She waited for grief to flood her or her heart to break. But she couldn't feel anything, couldn't think, couldn't cry, as if her body, brain, and heart were shrouded in thick cotton. She observed this as if from a great distance, curiously detached, yet deeply interested in her surroundings and in everything she said and did.

A shiver shook her, causing her to tremble violently. She chafed her arms, a useless motion given that her very core was frozen. Too cold to feel.

Maybe she was in shock. If she could just crawl into her and Stephen's king-size bed and burrow under the cashmere blankets, maybe she'd warm up and awaken from this nightmare.

But the woman standing on the other side of Stephen's body was no dream. Nor were the big, silent tears rolling down the perfect, smooth skin of her high cheekbones.

Caroline Mason, my foot. How dare she claim Stephen as her husband!

Suddenly fury pierced through the cotton, as razor-sharp and jagged as lightening. Mary Beth narrowed her eyes and drew herself up tall. At five feet three she was a good four inches shorter than Caroline, but she managed to look down her nose at her.

"I don't know who you are or what you want. But if you have one shred of decency or compassion, you'll leave me alone with my husband."

The younger woman's watery gaze skittered to Mary Beth's face, the grief now laced with anger. Her chin raised and she swiped her eyes with the backs of her hands. "Stephen is *my* husband."

The gall! Mary Beth crossed her trembling arms over her chest and let her low opinion show. "That's a lie, and you know it."

"What I know," Caroline retorted in an equally heated voice through clenched teeth, "is that Stephen and I were married exactly ten years ago today—no, yesterday. January fifteenth. Here." She slipped off her wedding band, a flashy platinum affair encircled with a row of baguette diamonds. "Look at the inscription."

The ring felt hot in Mary Beth's icy palm, but she barely registered that fact. She squinted at the etched lettering. *Stephen and Caroline—Two Bodies, One Heart*, it read. The date was as the woman had said, January fifteenth, ten years ago.

Her wedding ring bore the identical inscription, except with 'Mary Beth' instead of 'Caroline,' and the date July eleventh, ten years earlier. Her heart lurched painfully. She tugged the braided, fourteen-carat gold band from her finger and silently handed it to the other woman.

Caroline studied the engraving, sniffling but without comment. In silence they traded back, each slipping her ring onto the third finger of her left hand.

"Apparently we're married to the same man at the same time," she said. "Our inscriptions should read, 'three bodies, one heart.'"

Under different circumstances the quip might have been funny. Right now, Mary Beth wanted to slap the stupid woman. "This is no time for jokes."

"You think I don't know that? Stephen is—*was*—a bigamist. Dirty, stinking rat-bastard."

Caroline fished a wadded tissue from her bag and blew her nose. A shred of tissue flaked off, landing on his colorless cheek. There it stayed, a damning tribute. She balled up the remains and stuffed it back into her bag. "I'd kill him if he weren't already dead."

Mary Beth did not smile. She forgot that a short while ago she'd liked Caroline, had thought her beautiful, comforting, and funny. Now she despised her.

However, she did second the murder sentiment.

For ten years Stephen had lived a dual life, and she hadn't so much as guessed. Fueled by anger and pain, her mind began to whir. Had she been so blind and naïve? How could he do this to her and Aurora, and why? What an unpleasant, ugly, hurtful mess. Thank heavens Stephen's parents were gone, because this would have destroyed them. Lord knew what his ailing brother would think, but this just might finish him off. Mary Beth's father had died while she was in high school. Her mother had followed two years later, shortly before Mary Beth had met and married Stephen.

She'd always regretted her parents hadn't known him or seen the easy life he'd made for her and Aurora. Now for the first time ever, she was thankful they were dead.

Aurora however, was alive and beside herself with worry. For all Mary Beth knew, she was clutching the phone, waiting for word of her father's condition.

How am I going to tell her about Caroline?

She couldn't deal with that right now. Ellie would know what to do.

What will I tell our friends? Does anyone know?

Hunching her shoulders under the harsh weight of Stephen's deception, she released a heavy breath.

Dear God.

Though the kitchen clock said midnight, to Mary Beth it felt later. Slumped over the table, chin propped between her palms, she cast a weary eye at Ellie, who sat across from her.

"I feel like I'm in hell," she said. "I probably look it, too."

Ellie's brows arched. "I won't lie, you have looked better. But after the week you just spent . . ." She shook her head.

The tragedy had taken its toll on Ellie, too. Fatigue had leached the color from her slender face, and behind her chic, rimless glasses her brown eyes were bloodshot from lack of sleep. She'd been with Mary Beth since picking her up from the airport six days ago, and knew the whole, sordid truth about Stephen. Shocked and appalled, she'd stayed close by, ready to listen and console whenever Mary Beth needed her.

"You're the best friend ever, Ellie. I don't know how I'd have made it through the last few days without you."

Ellie waved off the thanks, her no-nonsense nails and ringless fingers slicing the air. "You'd do the same for me. I could use a stiff drink, though." She nodded at the bottle of Jim Beam she'd retrieved from the well-stocked bar off the dining room. "How about I fix us both a bourbon on the rocks?"

The last thing Mary Beth needed was alcohol. She'd always been a cheap drunk, and a drink would loosen her self-control. She might do something crazy, like storm through the house cursing Stephen. With Aurora upstairs and likely to hear, it was not a good idea. She shook her head. "No thanks, but you go ahead."

"How about a snack? You've hardly eaten a thing today, and goodness knows, there's a ton of food in the house."

Throughout the day friends and acquaintances had dropped by with condolences and food. Mary Beth glanced at the cakes, pies, and breads piled on the granite counters. The refrigerator was full, too, bulging with casseroles, salads, and more pies. But the thought of eating sickened her. Again she shook her head.

Ellie shrugged. She mixed her drink, then lifted the glass. "Here's to better days."

"Ha-ha," Mary Beth replied tonelessly.

Her friend regarded her with concern. "No

matter what Stephen did, you loved him. It's okay to grieve and cry."

On a rational level that made sense. Yet Mary Beth's heart remained frozen in her chest, the same as when she'd stared down at his lifeless body nine days ago.

He'd cheated on her and had played her for a fool. Shamed her and hurt Aurora beyond what any person, let alone an adolescent struggling with her own problems, should have to bear. Though Mary Beth hadn't told her daughter the awful truth about her father. Not yet. The knowledge would further devastate the grieving girl.

How could you hurt us like this, Stephen?

"I can't grieve or cry," she said. "I'm too damn mad." Her fingers gripped the smooth edge of the inlaid mahogany table in the center of the spacious kitchen. "He told That Woman he was a widower," she seethed, refusing to use Caroline's name. "A widower!"

The fury that shook her voice didn't seem to faze Ellie. "Anger's healthy, too." She swirled the golden contents of her glass. "At least he left you well-off. A big insurance policy and a gorgeous home with no mortgage is nothing to sneer at."

"Throwing money at the problem doesn't absolve him." Mary Beth narrowed her eyes at the recessed lighting in the cedar-plank ceiling and raised her fist, shaking it ominously. "Hear that, Stephen? You're a real shit, and I hope you rot in hell!"

Ellie's mouth quirked. "You tell him, sister." She lifted her glass. "Here's to venting."

Despite Mary Beth's fury, the brief outburst had

exhausted her. She released a tired sigh and rubbed her bone-dry eyes.

"You should get some sleep, hon," her friend advised. "We both should. Tomorrow will be rough."

She meant the funeral, which started at one, after the regular Sunday services. Then a big reception here at the house.

Considering what Stephen had done he didn't deserve a funeral. Of course he'd get one, both for Aurora and the community. Mary Beth had made the arrangements with Reverend Smigel at Calvary Presbyterian, the Pacific Heights church the Mason family had attended for generations. She'd wanted no part of planning the reception and had supplied Ellie with the caterer's name and a credit card.

Mary Beth cringed just thinking about tomorrow. All those people at the funeral and then in her house, invading her privacy. Watching her, and she couldn't even cry.

Dread settled like a lead ball in her stomach. Her nerves already were stretched so thin, she was afraid they'd snap. What if she lost control and embarrassed herself and Aurora?

With that distressing thought a rash of worries flooded her mind, the same ones that kept her awake at night.

She gnawed the pad of her thumb, caught herself, and dropped her hand to her lap. "Do you think anyone knows about Stephen?"

It wasn't the first time she'd voiced the question to Ellie. She must be sick of hearing it, but good friend that she was, she didn't show it. Just shook her head.

"If they did, believe me, you'd know."

Mary Beth thought about her and Stephen's friends—the Whitakers, Jacksons, and Andrews. They were a conservative bunch, four of the six Stephen's friends since childhood. The men were his partners at Jones, Westin and Hawkins. When Mary Beth had married him, their wives had become her friends—even though Marsha Jackson and Susan Andrews were twenty years older with grown children. Pam, who was forty-six and had married Kevin Whitaker after he lost his first wife to cancer, knew the others, since all of them came from the wealthy, powerful families of the city.

Mary Beth's family were blue collar. Stephen's group had accepted her because she'd married him, but twenty years later she still didn't quite feel as if she belonged. Yet they were nice enough, especially after Aurora was born. She attended the same private school their children had, and her best friend was Kristi Whitaker, Pam and Kevin's daughter.

A hideous scandal from one of their own would rock their world in ways impossible to fathom. So far, their behavior had been as expected—warm calls of condolence and gifts of flowers and food.

No, they didn't know. Not yet.

The moment Mary Beth laid that worry to rest, another pushed forward. Without Stephen and given what he'd pulled, would they still accept her? She kneaded the knot at the back of her neck. "Do you think I'll lose their friendship?"

"If you mean Pam Whitaker, Marsha Jackson, or Susan Andrews, I don't know." Ellie shrugged. "Either they'll stick by you, or they won't." She snorted. "Though I don't know that it matters. None of those snobs are women I'd want as friends."

They didn't think much of Ellie either, probably because of her background. She was right, they were snobs.

Even so, Mary Beth valued their friendship. She enjoyed working with them on various committees and guilds, lunching and shopping together, and the tennis lessons and games. Surely that counted for something. Of course their relationships would survive.

Reassured, she pushed that worry aside and voiced another. "What about the ashes? We have only half the amount we should. Do you think anyone will notice?"

Before leaving Seattle a week ago, after a heated argument with That Woman, she'd agreed to split the remains.

"You're worried about somebody checking out the ashes? That's gross and morbid," Ellie said. "Not gonna happen."

"I know Aurora, and she will take a peek. Stephen was a big man. She'll wonder why there aren't more ashes."

Her friend's jaw dropped. "She's only fourteen, Mary Beth. She's never seen anyone's ashes before. Trust me, she'll never guess."

"But what if she figures it out? She's a smart girl."

"Then you'll explain the situation. You have to do it sometime."

"I know." Angry as Mary Beth was at Stephen, she dreaded sharing the truth with Aurora. The knowledge would *kill* her. She buried her face in her hands. "Oh God."

"You okay?"

"Would you be? I don't want to tell Aurora *anything*

'til after the funeral. She needs time to grieve for her dad without knowing what a bastard he is. Was." Screw the manicure. She bit down on a nail. It broke off with a satisfying snap. "Bad enough, telling my daughter. Heaven only knows what'll happen when everybody else finds out."

Her throat tightened, cutting off further conversation, and her stomach heaved. "I think I'm going to be sick."

"You're panicking. Take a deep breath, and let it out slowly."

Ellie pulled in a breath along with her, and they both exhaled loudly. "Better?"

Mary Beth nodded.

"Now I want you to listen carefully, because this is good advice. One step at a time. Nobody has to know anything yet. First we get through the funeral. After that, you meet with Kevin Whitaker to read the will and get that insurance payout."

"Do I tell him Stephen is a bigamist before or after he hands over the check?" Mary Beth asked, sounding bitter to her own ears.

"Maybe you won't have to tell him at all. Unless their names pop up in the will, which I strongly doubt, nobody'll find out about them."

Under different circumstances Mary Beth would have felt sorry for the woman and her child. Instead her emotions vacillated between hatred and rage.

She pushed her hair behind her ears. "But I've never been good at lying, and Kevin was Stephen's closest friend. He'll want to know why Stephen was in Seattle instead of Singapore." Another worry struck her. "What if That Woman contacts him or sues, or something?"

"I'm no lawyer, but working for one, I do know something about the law," Ellie said. "I researched 'bigamy' on Law.net, and from what I learned, Caroline Mason doesn't have a legal leg to stand on. In the eyes of the law, she's nothing but a mistress and mother of Stephen's illegitimate child. The estate owes her nothing." Ellie looked thoughtful. "Maybe you should find an attorney familiar with bigamy, someone who isn't part of the stuffy Jones, Westin and Hawkins firm. I could ask my boss for names."

Mary Beth shook her head. "Please don't. The fewer people involved in this mess, the better."

"If that's what you want." Ellie drained her glass. "Are you going to tell Kevin Whitaker, or not?"

"I don't know." Filled with indecision, Mary Beth bit her lip. "Maybe I won't."

"Whatever you decide, I'm happy to come along for moral support."

"Thanks, but I need to do this by myself. I'll call you after and fill you in."

"If you don't, I'll call you. It's late." Ellie scooted her chair back, stood, and carried her glass to the dishwasher. "We really should turn in."

They trudged up the stairs in silence. Ellie headed for a guest bedroom at one end of the hall. Mary Beth stopped outside Aurora's room. Her daughter had left the door cracked open and the reading lamp on. In the soft light her delicate features were relaxed. Her brown hair, which she kept short for swimming, stuck up in ragged spikes, the latest teen style at her elite, private high school. But clutched to her chest was a ratty old teddy bear

Stephen had bought her ages ago. Mary Beth hadn't seen the bear in a good three years, and the sight touched her. Her daughter thought she was grown up, but tonight she looked young and vulnerable.

Filled with tenderness and love, she smoothed the covers over the sleeping body. The girl's eyes opened.

"Mommy?"

She hadn't used the endearment in ages. Mary Beth's heart expanded further. "Just tucking you in, angel. Go back to sleep."

Aurora nodded and dutifully closed her eyes. "Love you," she mumbled.

"Love you back." Mary Beth kissed her forehead. She turned out the light, then tiptoed out.

Since Stephen's death Aurora had been as sweet and loving as she'd been before puberty had turned her into a moody, mouthy teen. She needed her mommy to comfort her in her grief.

Hold tight to your innocence for as long as you can.

All too soon the hideous truth would destroy Aurora's belief in her father. Stephen's betrayal would rob her of what was left of her childhood.

Anger burned away Mary Beth's weariness. How dare he do that to his own daughter! She stalked toward the second guest room with her hands clenched and her jaw set. She couldn't sleep in the bed once shared with Stephen.

Rage simmering, she scrubbed her face, used the toilet and changed into her flannel nightgown, all on automatic pilot.

Why, Stephen? In bed the question pounded in her mind, tormenting and relentless.

Was it her looks? Maybe she'd gained too much weight. Would he have taken up with That Woman if Mary Beth were slimmer and looked younger? She should have gone in for Botox like Marsha and Pam. Or a face lift, like Susan. But she'd always liked the tiny lines around her eyes. Smile lines, Stephen had called them. She'd believed him when he said he preferred her as she was.

The rotten sneak of a liar.

In a fruitless effort to fall asleep she tossed restlessly, turning from one side to the other. Heaven knew, she'd tried her best to make him happy. For twenty years her life had centered on pleasing him, loving him, making a comfortable, welcoming home for him. She'd cooked the rich foods he liked and had decorated their home in ecru and eggshell and the formal furnishings that suited his tastes rather then the bright colors and less formal furniture she preferred. She wore the clothes Stephen approved of, and belonged to San Francisco's best clubs and guilds. Except for Ellie, all her friends were the wives of men he worked and socialized with. Her life had revolved around him.

And he'd repaid her by taking another wife. Another *life.*

Her stomach churned bile and her nails dug painfully into her palms. She tossed onto her back, wondering whether she'd ever sleep again.

Chapter Three

On Bainbridge Island the sedate hands of the Bond Street clock pointed to midnight. Huddled in her favorite chair, an oversize, butter-yellow leather piece, freezing despite the fire crackling in the family room's handsome stone hearth, Caroline Mason hugged herself.

From a matching chair her father, himself a widower, eyed her with concern. "You cold, honey?" he asked in his gravelly voice.

The chill inside Caroline had nothing to do with the room temperature. She shook her head. Her usually energetic father looked as tired as she felt, his weathered face and keen, blue eyes sorrowful. After Stephen's death nine days ago, he'd flown up from Sarasota, where he co-owned and captained a marine tour boat. With the three-hour time difference it was half-way to morning for him.

"It's late," she said. "You ought to get to bed."

"Doubt I could sleep."

The faint strains of voices and the clink of silver and plates floated from the kitchen, where Becca and Hank, her sister and brother-in-law, were preparing for the after-funeral reception tomorrow and putting away the casseroles, cakes, and pies Caroline had amassed but couldn't eat. Becca and Hank ran a busy restaurant in Chicago, and though they'd arrived exhausted from a long week, they weren't sleeping much, either.

Only Jax and Meg and Molly, her young cousins, seemed able to rest. Thank heaven for that. Though Jax refused to sleep alone. Even with company, bad dreams shook her awake nightly. A seven-year-old child laid low by a loss and grief too vast to comprehend.

Stephen hadn't planned to die suddenly, and he'd certainly left a mess, with her, Mary Beth and their children unwitting victims. No wonder he'd traveled two out of every four weeks, sometimes leaving in the middle of a holiday. Business in Singapore, my foot.

Caroline shook her head at the blazing fire. Sitting in the hospital waiting room she'd liked Mary Beth. They were enemies now, yet also linked through Stephen and a whole tangle of emotions most people never experienced. Bigamy and betrayal. A wave of frustration, fury, and deep sorrow swept through her and her whole body trembled.

How could you do this to us? she silently screamed. Of course, there was no answer and never would be.

Without a word her father, who wasn't big on verbal expression, rose, plucked the jewel-tone afghan from the yellow and burgundy chintz sofa and wrapped it around her shoulders.

The kindness nearly did her in. For the jillionth time, her eyes filled. She pulled a fresh tissue from the half-empty box resting on the ottoman that matched the chairs.

Grim-faced, his own eyes glistening, the man she adored returned to his seat and stared into the fire.

Caroline hugged the soft afghan close. Her mother had crocheted it before she'd died four years ago, and she imagined the woman wrapping loving arms around her. Comforted, she nudged aside the tissue box, stretched out her legs on the ottoman and crossed her ankles. Her red and green striped socks with individual purple toes, a Christmas gift from Jax, cheered her. Stephen, whose tastes ran toward conservative, later had told her that he'd tried to steer their daughter toward a more sedate beige and cream striped set. But Princess Stubborn-Head, as he lovingly called Jax, had insisted on the colorful pair. They'd shared a carefree laugh over that, she and Stephen.

Barely a month had passed since then, but it seemed a lifetime. "Where did I go wrong, Daddy?" Caroline had asked herself this question over and over, but the answer remained elusive.

"Don't be so hard on yourself, Caro. Nobody saw this coming."

Her parents had adored Stephen. Six years ago, when her mother's on-again-off-again leukemia had flared up and taken a turn for the worse, and the insurance coverage ran out, her father had sold their Florida condo in a vain attempt to offset the staggering medical bills. Stephen had generously stepped in, and he and Caroline had refinanced their mortgage and borrowed more to help. Everyone had said her husband had a heart of gold. Fool's gold, as it turned out.

"We made coffee nudges," Becca announced in an overly cheerful voice, returning from the kitchen with a tray bearing four mugs heaped with whipped cream. Hank followed with a plate of cookies sent over by the ladies at the Unitarian Universalist Church, which Caroline and Stephen attended—or had, and where they'd married.

Caroline and her sister shared the same blond hair and blue eyes as their father, and were only eighteen months apart, but they never had been close. Still, Caroline was glad of her older sister's love and support. She liked her patient, teddy bear of a husband, too. She accepted a mug and a sugar cookie with a nod of thanks.

"I always said your life was too good to be true," Becca said as she and Hank sank onto the sofa. "To think I envied you for all your money and this beautiful house. I actually *liked* Stephen."

"Me, too." Again, Caroline's eyes filled.

Her father shifted uncomfortably. Becca pulled a tissue from her jeans pocket and blew her nose.

Sniffling suspiciously, Hank studied the whipped cream mounding his mug. "At least he left you a comfortable chunk of money."

"When are you seeing that lawyer? The one you picked from the yellow pages." Becca sneered. "Martin Cheesy."

Caroline prickled. "Cheswick, and what's wrong with using the yellow pages? I needed a lawyer." Stephen had handled their affairs, and he was gone.

"Since Stephen was a lawyer, surely you know more than a few capable attorneys. Why choose one you've never met?"

"I didn't want to use anyone we knew." She'd told Martin Cheswick, whom she'd hired over the phone, only that her husband had died. The rest of the despicable story she'd explain in person. She narrowed her eyes at her sister. "Would you?"

Becca, who never apologized for anything, shrugged and pressed forward. "When are you seeing Cheswick?"

"Early next week."

After the funeral, which was tomorrow at ten. No casket, just an urn of ashes. Half the remains of Stephen Mason, the man she'd thought was her husband. The bigamist.

Suddenly the thought of drinking anything, even Becca's delicious coffee, sickened Caroline. She set her mug and the cookie on the thick cream carpet.

"You need help getting the papers together?" Hank asked gently. His way of soothing over Becca's harshness.

All financial information was stored in Stephen's office which, as he worked from home, was downstairs. Caroline hadn't been able to force herself inside that room just yet, and for reasons unknown to her, hadn't allowed anyone else in there, either. She shook her head. "I'll do that tomorrow night."

Pulling the papers together and dealing with the attorney, the funeral service, the reception here, all the while holding herself together and keeping Stephen's sins a secret . . . it was too much. A groan of misery ripped from her chest. "Oh God, what a mess."

Her father sent her a helpless look. "We'll get through this, Caro. One day at a time."

Caroline grasped onto the sage advice. "I'm

awfully happy you're here, Dad." She aimed a grateful glance at Becca and Hank. "All of you. I just wish I knew what to tell Jax."

"That's easy," her sister said. "The truth—that her old man was a dirty, lying snake with two families."

True enough, but spoken by Becca, highly irritating. Caroline wondered how much more she could take. Thank God her sister and family were leaving Monday. Though poor Jax would be lost without her cousins.

The image of her daughter's freckled, grief-stricken face filled Caroline's head. Regret and sorrow flooded her heart. "I can't hurt her that way," she said, kneading the tense back of her neck. "She worshipped her father. I don't want anyone to know."

If only Stephen had honored that worship.

"I'd be happy to tell her for you," Becca offered.

Protective hackles up, Caroline leveled a warning look at her sister. "Don't you dare."

Becca said nothing, which was worrisome. Her silence could mean anything.

Hank shook his head, and Caroline's father shot his oldest daughter a flinty-eyed frown. "Whether or not you agree with Caroline's decision, you will abide by her wishes," he ordered in a low voice. "That means that aside from the people in this room and Caroline's attorney, no one is to know about Stephen." He leaned forward, toward Becca. "Is that clear?"

Caroline's sister had the good sense to offer a meek nod. "My lips are sealed," she conceded, to Caroline's relief. "But I think keeping this secret is a big mistake. Someday Jax will learn the truth and then . . ." She gave her hand an ominous shake.

"You're entitled to that opinion, and you may be right," Hank said, squeezing his wife's shoulder. "But this is Caroline's life. What she tells Jax and others is her business."

"Well said." Their father turned to Caroline. "You're a smart woman. You'll figure out what to say and when to say it."

She only hoped he was right.

One day at a time.

The organist played "Nearer, My God, to Thee" quite well, Mary Beth noted as she clutched Aurora's arm with one hand and Ellie's with the other and slowly headed for the front, middle pew of the Calvary Presbyterian Church sanctuary. The thick cotton had enveloped her once again, and she observed herself and her surroundings with detached interest.

Grief-stricken friends, clients, prominent attorneys and their families filled the room. *So many mourners for you, Stephen.*

Kristi Whitaker and her parents, Pam and Kevin, stood at the pew, waiting. Kevin had been Stephen's closest friend and with Stephen's brother too ill to travel, the Whitakers filled in as family.

His eyes bloodshot and watery, Kevin patted Mary Beth's shoulder. Pam teared up and murmured her sympathies. Kristi hugged Aurora while both cried openly. Even Ellie sniffled.

Mary Beth's chest felt full and tight. She longed for the release that would come from crying, but the frozen mass that once had been her heart refused to thaw. Still sandwiched between Ellie and Aurora, she sat stiffly on the hard seat. Kristi took the space next to Aurora, with Pam and Kevin beside their daughter.

Reverend Smigel, the regal but kindly minister, moved to the altar, his black robes swishing. He'd already conducted the Sunday morning services, so this made for a long day, Mary Beth thought. He cleared his throat, signaling the start of the service, and the music stopped.

Aurora reached for her. "Hold my hand, Mommy."

Mother-love penetrated the icy numbness. Aching for her daughter, Mary Beth laced her fingers tightly with Aurora's, their hands almost the same size. Her daughter was nearly full-grown, but still so much a child. As the minister praised Stephen's fine qualities, the girl bowed her head and sobbed quietly. Mary Beth sat wooden and numb and silent.

Why, Stephen? Why? The question ran through her head like a mantra without end.

Think about something else. She forced her attention to the flowers flanking the altar. Hot-house lilies, carnations, daisies, and gladiolas filled fat mourning vases. Stephen spurned daisies—had thought them common—but Mary Beth liked their warmth and cheerfulness. She never bought or used them, acceding to his wishes. Using them at his funeral was an act of defiance born out of anger.

Why, Stephen?

Reverend Smigel droned on.

Aside from minor derogatory remarks, not once in twenty years had her husband voiced any real displeasure with her or their marriage. If he had, they could have worked through any problems, gone for counseling, or ended up divorced. Instead, for the last decade he'd lived a dual life. Longer, if you counted dating Caroline.

Bad enough he'd slept with her. He'd also married her, made a home together, and given her a child. And claimed he was a widower.

Why?

She'd give up chocolate for the rest of her life to confront Stephen and learn the answer to that question. But he was dead, and his reasons had died with him.

A howl of frustration clogged Mary Beth's throat. Ellie squeezed her arm and warm hands behind her—Jim and Marsha Jackson and Peter and Susan Andrews—clasped her shoulders. They thought she was grieving.

Aurora shot her a funny, unreadable look. Her brow furrowed in confusion. Then her eyes narrowed, and she pulled her hand free.

Mary Beth's empty fingers curled into a fist. From beneath lowered lashes she glanced at the sober, pained faces of the men, women, and children to her right and left. Familiar faces and strangers, united in sorrow.

Stephen had helped, advised, and/or befriended nearly every person in the room, and even those he hadn't knew of his sterling reputation and high standing in the community. Not one of them appeared untouched. He was a good man. Or so they believed.

He'd betrayed them, too.

Fury straightened Mary Beth's spine and thinned

her lips. Ellie slanted her a wide-eyed look. She forced herself to relax.

The organist played the opening chord of "Amazing Grace." Everyone rose. While the mourners sang, Mary Beth stared unseeing at the prayer book clutched between her hands.

Her thoughts drifted. No doubt That Woman and her daughter were conducting their own version of a funeral on Bainbridge Island.

Horrible, horrible woman. Home wrecker.

"May I have a tissue, please?" Aurora whispered to Pam Whitaker.

Why not ask her own mother? What was that about? Mary Beth slanted her a puzzled look.

Sniffling, Pam opened her Dooney & Bourke purse and handed over a whole packet of tissues.

"Thanks." Aurora didn't so much as glance at Mary Beth, probably afraid she'd sob.

Mary Beth still didn't know when she'd share the awful truth about Stephen. Soon, she promised herself, anxious at the thought of causing her daughter fresh pain, and fearful of unlocking even more frustration and rage inside herself.

Was the other Mrs. Mason grappling with the same issues? Mary Beth hugged the prayer book close. She didn't want to know.

Chapter Four

"Let us know if there's anything we can do," the thirty-something male murmured to Mary Beth amid the noisy crush of mourners crowding the living room.

"Anything at all," echoed the lovely young woman clasping his arm.

They were a handsome couple. Mary Beth couldn't recall their names—with sixty attorneys working at Jones, Westin and Hawkins it was hard to keep everyone straight—but she recognized the faces.

"Thank you," she said, dipping her chin.

"Stephen was a wonderful man and a top-notch attorney," the man added. "He'll be sorely missed."

He wasn't wonderful, he was a liar and a cheat! Biting her lip, Mary Beth corralled her anger, which at this point would only hurt Aurora, and tried her best to appear the aggrieved widow.

"Yes, he will," she managed.

That was true. When she wasn't cursing him for living a double life, she already missed him terribly.

"We'd like to convey our condolences to your daughter," the man said, glancing around. "Do you know where she is?"

Mary Beth scanned the sea of people, but didn't see Aurora. Since the funeral her daughter had avoided her. She probably needed to deal with Stephen's death in her own way. Still, where had she gone? And where were her friends? She shook her head.

"I believe she's in the gazebo," Ellie said, suddenly materializing at her side. "Just walk through the french doors," she gestured toward the doors off the dining room, "cross the patio, and head into the backyard."

The couple nodded, offered twin smiles of sympathy, and moved purposefully away.

Mary Beth shot her friend a grateful look. It felt like decades since the funeral, and though night had fallen, mourners continued to pour into the house to pay their respects. The uniformed caterers Ellie had hired bustled back and forth, freshening drinks and replacing empty platters of prime rib, ham and roasted vegetables with steaming refills. Friends, acquaintances, and strangers clustered in the dining room, living room, and foyer, talking, eating, drinking, and occasionally laughing, as if this were a normal party, not an after-the-funeral reception.

"I haven't seen Aurora since the service," she told Ellie. "How's she holding up?"

"As well as you'd expect. Kristi and other girls from the swim team are out back with her. Some boys, too."

Mary Beth nodded, thankful for her daughter's friends and their support.

"Uh-oh." Ellie stiffened. "Don't look now, but here come the three rich bitches of Nob Hill."

Through the crowd Mary Beth glimpsed Pam, Marsha, and Susan. She'd spoken with each woman immediately following the funeral, and hadn't failed to note their mix of genuine sympathy and nosy curiosity over how she handled her loss. Which they'd no doubt analyze and discuss at length with other friends and acquaintances.

She didn't think she could bear more scrutiny. A groan slipped from her throat.

"You could plead fatigue and go to bed," Ellie suggested.

Mary Beth glanced at the powder room a few feet away. "Or I could duck into the bathroom, since that's closer."

"Do it. I'll hold them off."

She slipped into the room, locking the door. In here the sounds were muffled, and the light from the wall sconces was soft and pleasant. Bracing her arms on the tile counter she studied herself in the mirror. Not even the kind lighting hid her dull, limp hair, washed out coloring, or the twenty pounds she needed to lose. Grimacing, she turned away from her ugly reflection.

No wonder Stephen turned to Caroline.

The moment the traitorous thought formed, she angrily shook it off. "Damn you, Stephen," she swore, her throat thick with fury and grief. "I loved you. You had no excuse, and no right."

If she didn't hit something this minute, she'd explode. Her eyes narrowed at the antique Elmwood water pot filled with magazines and arranged just so near the commode. Stephen had purchased it after his last visit to Singapore. Or so he'd claimed.

"Lying rat," she seethed, kicking the thing so hard, it scraped a few inches across the floor. She didn't hurt it much. Not even the magazines shifted.

However the thin leather toe of her pump was dented and her toes throbbed painfully. Mary Beth almost smiled at that. Pretty tame for a temper tantrum. At least she'd released some of her pent-up rage. Feeling cleansed and ready to deal with her guests, she pulled in a breath and unlocked the door.

Ellie was nowhere in sight, but Pam, Marsha, and Susan stood waiting outside like blond, brunette, and red-headed vultures in designer suits.

Susan, whose flawless, surgically improved face knocked two decades off her sixty years, took a good look at Mary Beth. Her own face filled with sorrow, or would have. Given her inability to manipulate her features, most of the sadness was in her carefully made-up eyes.

"I've been watching you the past hour. Oh, sweetie." She opened her arms and pulled Mary Beth into a hug.

This close her expensive French perfume was overwhelming. Mary Beth started to pull away, but Pam and Marsha joined in the embrace, and she couldn't.

"You're doing fine," Marsha consoled.

"My God, if Kevin died I don't think I'd manage half as well," Pam added.

Their grief was real and they meant well. Maybe they were snobs and didn't like Ellie, but they were

Mary Beth's friends. Wrapped in their comforting warmth she longed to blurt out what Stephen had done. If it hadn't been for Aurora she would have. Her daughter deserved to know first.

"I think I need to lie down for a bit." She struggled away. "Tell Aurora and everyone else for me, will you?"

"Of course." Pam smoothed a hand over her page-boy, which thanks to its expensive cut had remained sleek and neat despite the embrace. "Tell Aurora I'll pick her up for school tomorrow at seven. If she's ready to go back, that is."

Mary Beth nodded. "I think she is, but if she changes her mind I'll let you know. Thanks."

"We'll call you," Susan promised.

"Good night." Marsha waved, her diamond-studded tennis bracelet sparkling.

Mary Beth plodded for the stairs in a fog. Thankfully the respectful visitors left her alone. She almost made it before Kevin Whitaker stopped her.

"There you are." He flashed his brilliant white teeth, which he'd paid a mint to brighten. "Can we go someplace private and chat?"

Something in his grief-stricken face, she couldn't figure out what, put her on alert. Dear God, did he know? She didn't think she could handle that, not here and not now.

"I'm really not up to it," she said. "Can't this wait until our meeting tomorrow?"

"Won't take long," he said as he grasped her elbow gently but firmly. "It's important or I wouldn't ask."

Determination glinted in his gray eyes and she

knew he wouldn't let her refuse. May as well get this over with.

She sighed. "All right, we'll use Stephen's study."

Neither she nor Aurora had ventured into the tasteful, sedate room Stephen had dubbed, "My office away from the office," since his death ten days earlier. Mary Beth had closed the door and not even the cleaning woman had entered.

Now as she flipped on the overhead light, an octagonal crystal affair that flooded the room in brightness, the air smelled stale. But the room was its usual orderly self, the large bamboo desk clean except for the framed photo of her and Aurora. The computer, printer, and fax were silent, and the mahogany bookshelves that lined a full wall were filled with neatly arranged law and reference books.

Which one dealt with bigamy?

Mary Beth fought the urge to laugh hysterically—nothing about this was the tiniest bit funny—and busied herself with pulling the heavy drapes over the dark picture window. When she turned toward Kevin, his expression was grave.

"What is it?" she asked, catching her breath.

Instead of answering, he gestured at the large tufted leather sofa and two raw-silk-covered armchairs. "Shall we sit?"

Given that her legs were suddenly unsteady, that was a good idea. "Why not?" She sank onto the rich leather of the sofa.

Kevin scooted a chair to face her. He sat down and leaned forward. "I wanted to alert you, there's a problem with the life insurance policy."

He doesn't know. Relief flooded her. Then she

realized what he'd said. Puzzled, she slanted her chin. "Oh?"

"The company claims Stephen borrowed against his policy." The attorney ran a hand through his silvery hair and his shrewd gray eyes studied her. "Do you know anything about that?"

"No." She shook her head. "I don't."

But then, she really didn't know much about what Stephen had done. What she did know was that she needed that money for Aurora and herself.

"You know as well as I do that Stephen makes—made—a very good living." She frowned. "With all our investments and no mortgage, why would he need to borrow at all, let alone against his life insurance policy?"

"I'm sure it's a mistake." Kevin offered a tight smile, no doubt meant to reassure. "At any rate, the insurers are researching the matter. It should be straightened out by the time we meet tomorrow morning."

As Caroline lay on her side of the king-size bed beside Jax, the tension holding her shoulders rigid and knotted eased for the first time all day. This morning's funeral and the endless reception that followed had passed in a blur of tears, grief, and anger, but she'd survived with Stephen's secret and her and Jax's dignity intact. Now, comforted by the sound of her daughter's rhythmic breathing and the faint clatter and conversation of her father, sister, and brother-in-law as they cleaned up downstairs, she thought she just might be able to sleep.

She snuggled closer to her daughter. The sweet

smell of Jax's coconut-scented shampoo and her warm little body further soothed Caroline's jagged nerves. Her eyes drifted closed. A mistake, for suddenly dozens of anxious thoughts crowded her mind. Today had been rough, and tomorrow would be, too. Becca, Hank, and their kids were leaving right after breakfast, and as badly as her sister grated on her nerves, Caroline would miss the support. Thankfully her father had decided to stay an extra week. Using Stephen's car he'd drive Becca and family onto the ferry to Seattle, then to the airport, while Caroline dropped Jax at school.

Continuing her child's familiar routine seemed important, and besides, she didn't want to bring Jax to Martin Cheswick's office. That, too, was in Seattle, and meant a ferry boat ride.

The instant the attorney's name popped into her head, she realized she'd forgotten to get the papers from Stephen's file cabinet. That and her dread of the legal meeting brought back the tension in spades. And the anger.

I hate you for doing this to us, Stephen!

Momentarily forgetting Jax, she bolted upright.

"Mommy?" Jax gave a drowsy frown.

Forcing calm, Caroline managed a reassuring smile. "How you doin', punkin?"

"I mith Daddy," she lisped, thanks to having lost her two front teeth.

Smiling sadly, Caroline soothed the strawberry-blond hair from Jax's forehead. "Me, too."

Even while she loathed him.

"Why are you sitting up?"

"I need to get some papers out of Daddy's office for the lawyer."

"Can't you do that in the morning?" One small hand reached up and touched her cheek tenderly. "Stay here with me. Pleathe?"

Caroline's heart melted. Jax needed her and *she* needed this precious time alone with her daughter. She stretched out again, pillow-to-pillow and face-to-face with Jax. "All right, but I'll have to get up extra early tomorrow. That means when you wake up I won't be here beside you."

"'Kay." Blue eyes so like Stephen's regarded her soberly. "Why doeth the lawyer need those papers?"

How to explain to a child? "To settle things and make sure we get the money we need to live." Her graphic design business brought in good money, but the two mortgage payments—one on the house and one on the vacation property—were steep. Add to that the gardener's and housekeeper's salaries, all the other expenses . . . Jax attended a quality public grade school, but there were four years of high-school tuition payments ahead, and then college. Thankfully the one thing Stephen had done was to take out a generous life insurance policy.

"Who'th Mary Beth?"

The question stunned Caroline. She couldn't stop a gasp. "What?"

"I heard Aunt Becca talking about her and Daddy."

"Oh?" Rage boiled up and Caroline tasted bile. She was going to wring her sister's neck. "Just when was that?" she asked more sharply than intended.

Taken aback, Jax popped her thumb in her mouth, a habit she'd kicked years ago. "Today. Is she Daddy'th friend?"

"You might say that," Caroline hedged, wondering

what Stephen's other wife had told her teenage daughter. Dealing with a moody adolescent had to be even harder than this. Her sympathetic grimace did not go unnoticed.

"You're mad that she didn't come to the funeral, aren't you? How come she didn't?"

The questions and the situation were crazy, and Caroline stifled an insane urge to laugh. "I'm not exactly mad at her, honey." No, most of her fury was directed at Stephen. "She lives in California and is . . . busy."

Mentally she crossed her fingers, hoping the vague reply would satisfy her inquisitive child.

"Mmm." For a few relief-filled seconds, Jax was quiet. Then she started in again. "You're mad at somebody, Mommy," she replied in a small, even voice. "Ith it Daddy?"

With those eyes seeming to stare straight into her soul, how could she lie? "Yes, it is."

Caroline was so angry she could barely stand it. Her hands fisted at her sides.

"Don't be," Jax said, sounding years older than Caroline. "He didn't mean to die. If you mith him, just clothe your eyes and say a little prayer. God will hear you, and so will Daddy."

Nonsense Irene Quackenbush, their minister, had no doubt filled her daughter's head with. But if the idea comforted Jax, Caroline wasn't about to quash it. "Is that so?"

"Uh-huh. I'm going to say a prayer right now. You should, too."

"Okay. Then let's go to sleep."

As Caroline pulled the thick eiderdown comforter

over them both, she caught a whiff of Stephen's cologne. "Old Spice for an older guy," he used to tease.

She'd liked the scent before. Now her stomach recoiled. Resisting the urge to fling the cover off the bed, she made a mental note to haul it to the cleaner's tomorrow. Another chore, but necessary if she expected to continue using the expensive, beautiful, and warm cover.

"Are your eyes clothed, Mommy?" Jax asked without opening hers.

"Yes," Caroline said, striving for calm.

"What are you telling Daddy?"

That she'd never forgive him. That she wanted to hurt him as much as he'd hurt her instead of feeling helpless and mute. "That I wish this was all just a bad dream."

Chapter Five

Thanks to her fluctuating emotions, which see-sawed between confusion, anger and grief, Mary Beth endured another bout of insomnia the night of the reception. Lonely and sick of her own thoughts, she longed to tiptoe down the hall to Ellie's room and talk. But her friend had returned to her own house in Oakland.

Around three A.M., seeking comfort, she padded silently across the lushly carpeted hallway to Aurora's room. Since the funeral they hadn't spoken more than a dozen words to each other, Aurora closeting herself in her room after her friends left.

No light peeked from the crack under the door, which for some reason was locked. Given her need for hugs and closeness the past few days, that was unexpected. But teenagers were unpredictable, and she *was* entitled to her privacy. Mary Beth hoped that come morning her daughter would again reach out to her.

The house was cold. Chafing her arms she returned to bed for more sleepless worrying. Kevin Whitaker had said the problem with the insurance was a mistake. She hoped he was right. By tomorrow afternoon she'd know.

But Stephen's bigamy was no mistake. Regardless of what Ellie had advised, Mary Beth knew she'd tell Kevin the truth. As Stephen's partner and best friend, he deserved to know. Mary Beth dreaded that part of tomorrow's meeting, and guessed that Stephen's betrayal would hurt Kevin as deeply as his death had.

Too upset to lie in bed one minute longer, she tossed aside the covers and rose. At five-thirty, showered and dressed, she went downstairs to make coffee. The caterers had cleaned up and put away the leftovers, and except for the flowers on every available surface, there was no evidence of the reception.

Anxious to keep busy Mary Beth carted half a dozen arrangements to the dining and living rooms. Then, set on breakfast with her daughter before school, she mixed a pitcher of orange juice before whipping up two of Aurora's favorite breakfast foods—a batch of homemade pancakes and crisp-fried bacon.

Bustling around the kitchen lifted her spirits a little, and mouth-watering aromas soon filled the air. Given that she'd eaten little over the past few days she should have been ravenous. But she'd lost her appetite along with her ability to sleep. The smells turned her stomach.

At six-thirty Aurora wandered into the kitchen, the same as every school morning. Unlike many private schools hers did not have a dress code, and she dressed in the fashion of the day—snug, hip-hugging jeans and a short, clingy T-shirt that exposed her navel.

Over the past few months her body had blossomed into womanhood. She was as tall as Mary Beth and just as busty. The provocative outfit was sure to attract attention from boys. Mary Beth considered ordering her to change, but that would lead to an argument she wasn't up to, not this morning.

She forced a pleasant face and drew Aurora into a quick hug. "Good morning, honey." Before she could kiss her daughter's cheek she ducked away.

"Morning."

Turning her back on her mother's gaze, she dropped her book bag by the back door. Eyes downcast she headed to the table, where she poured herself a glass of orange juice from the pitcher Mary Beth had filled. Then she flopped onto a chair.

The past few days she'd been sweet and loving. What had changed since the funeral? Mary Beth noted her daughter's pallid skin and the shadows under her eyes—not that different from her own. Grief, lack of sleep, no doubt, and the usual teenage mood swings.

"You're just in time for breakfast," she said, forcing a cheery voice. She piled a plate with pancakes and bacon.

Busy with her juice, Aurora failed to respond.

Determined to share a pleasant meal with her uncommunicative daughter, Mary Beth made a plate for herself and joined Aurora at the table. Her child flooded her pancakes and bacon with maple syrup, just as she always did.

Mindful of the calories Mary Beth trickled a thin line of syrup over her lone, extra small pancake. She speared a forkful. The cake was fluffy and steaming hot, the way Aurora liked. Her attention on her daughter, Mary Beth chewed without tasting.

Instead of digging in Aurora toyed with her breakfast, jabbing her fork into her food and pulling it out again. Not her normal inhale-the-food behavior.

Mary Beth frowned as she swallowed her food. "Why aren't you eating?"

"I'm not really hungry." Aurora stared at her plate.

"But honey, you love pancakes and bacon. And you have to eat."

One slender shoulder shrugged. "I'll buy something at school."

She sounded so low. Mary Beth ached to comfort her, but clearly her daughter was in no mood for a mother's embrace. She bit her lip. "Are you sure you want to go back today? You could stay home. I know your teachers would understand. I have an appointment with Mr. Whitaker at two, but we could spend the rest of the day together."

"Stay here with you?" At last Aurora met Mary Beth's gaze, her eyes hot and narrowed in disapproval. "You haven't even cried for Daddy."

So this was the reason for the bad mood. She hadn't realized her self-absorbed daughter had noticed. "We all grieve in different ways," she said.

The teenager shot her a challenging look. "Bullshit. I've seen you cry over Hallmark commercials."

Now she'd gone too far. Mary Beth pointed her fork at the girl. "There'll be no swearing in this house, young lady."

Her stern rebuke earned her a raised chin and

tightened mouth that was so much like Stephen, Mary Beth winced.

"I know why you haven't cried. You don't love Daddy!"

Stunned at the accusation, Mary Beth gaped at her stricken child. "Of course I do! Did."

Aurora's hostile expression demanded an explanation. Mary Beth sighed and decided to tell the truth—some of it. "I want to cry more than anything," she admitted, silently imploring her daughter to understand. "But I can't," she finished in a low, pain-filled voice.

She had Aurora's full attention now. The girl leaned toward her, riveted on Mary Beth's face. "Why not?"

Because your father is a cheat and a liar, and I despise him. Oh, how she wanted to say the words aloud. But this was the wrong time. So she crumpled her napkin in her fist and swallowed back the words. "There are things you don't know," she said, sounding remarkably calm.

"Like what?"

"It's complicated."

Her expression thoughtful, Aurora pushed a strip of bacon around her plate. "This has something to do with why Daddy was in Seattle instead of Singapore, doesn't it?"

"I can't talk about this, Aurora." *Please, not yet.*

A exasperated breath huffed from her daughter's young lips. "I'm not a baby, Mother. In five months I'll be fifteen. That's practically grown-up. You can tell me." She widened her eyes and cocked her head a fraction, the way she did when she wanted something.

Not right before school. The mere thought of how Stephen's betrayal would upset her daughter made Mary Beth ill. She nudged her plate aside and shook her head. "I promise I will, but this isn't the right time."

Aurora rolled her eyes. "That's just an excuse. If Daddy were here, *he'd* talk to me right now. He liked sharing his thoughts and feelings with me. He said so. You want to know why?" Her head lifted defiantly. "Because he knew *I* loved him."

"I loved him, too, angel." Which was no lie. How Mary Beth could love and hate Stephen at the same time was beyond her, but she did.

"Don't call me angel! That's Daddy's name for me."

Mary Beth slanted her angry daughter a puzzled look. "What's this *really* about?"

"If you cared at all about Daddy, he wouldn't have been gone so much." Her eyes filled.

"You think your father traveled two weeks every month because of me?" How dare Stephen use her as his excuse to leave town! The thought of him complaining to Aurora, the two of them commiserating over Mary Beth's shortcomings, was so painful she gasped. "Did he actually tell you that?"

Aurora stared at her as if she'd grown six arms. "Of course not, Mother. But I'm not blind. I saw how strained things were between you two."

They *had* argued a lot, mostly over Stephen's being gone so much. "I missed him, honey, and wanted him home more. That's mostly what we fought about."

The teen's mouth pursed stubbornly. "I'll bet

he'd have stayed home a whole lot more if you'd been nicer. Then he might be alive instead of dead."

Mary Beth's heart was no longer numb and frozen. That Aurora blamed her for Stephen's absences, and ultimately for his death, hurt unbearably. Her very soul seemed to break in half. She hugged her waist. "That was mean."

"Well, it's the truth," her daughter said, but she hung her head.

Heaven above, was she right? Had the fighting driven Stephen into Caroline's arms?

Outside a car honked.

"There's Kristi's mom." Aurora jumped up.

Mary Beth rose, too, following her daughter as she grabbed her coat from the rack by the back door and slipped into it. She scooped up her school bag and slung it over her shoulder.

"Wait just a minute."

The young spine went rigid. "What is it *now*, Mother?"

Mary Beth resisted the urge to cup Aurora's shoulders and pull her into a hug. There was enough tension without adding fuel to the fire. She shoved her hands into the pockets of her cardigan. "Are you going to swim practice after school? What time will you be home?"

"I don't know and I don't care. Good-bye."

Aurora spun away and marched toward the door in loud, angry strides. Without a glance in Mary Beth's direction she jerked open the door, then slammed it shut behind her.

Mary Beth's knees shook so badly she couldn't stand. She sank onto the floor. Sick at heart, she listened to her daughter's rapid footsteps across the pavement. She heard a car door close and the engine rev as the vehicle drove off.

So much for a pleasant breakfast.

In the sudden silence she shuddered and covered her face in her hands. At long last, the tears came.

The soft beep of the Bose alarm clock woke Caroline from a dreamless sleep. For one instant blessed oblivion clung to her and she reached out drowsily for Stephen.

Instead of connecting with his morning beard her fingers grazed Jax's smooth cheek. Memory and pain flooded back with brutal intensity. As Caroline's eyes shot open her daughter murmured and rolled over. Thank heaven for small favors. School didn't start for hours, and Jax needed her rest. Besides Caroline wasn't up to facing those sad eyes and the possibility of more hard questions. She slipped silently from her bed and tiptoed into the master bathroom for her robe and slippers.

Her feet were icy and the warmth from the heated marble floor tiles felt good. Two weeks ago she'd have stood still, soaking up the luxurious warmth. Today she wasn't capable of absorbing even this simple pleasure.

The house was quiet—at this hour everyone was asleep—as she stole down wide stairs that spiraled gracefully between the wall-to-ceiling glass windows flanking the front and back of the house. Outside all was dark, but come daylight, the back-of-the-house view of Lake Washington was spectacular and unobstructed. The half acre of woods between the house and street also was lovely.

The two-hundred-foot lakefront lot had cost Stephen a bundle. Add to that their custom-designed home and top-of-the-line furnishings and they'd spent close to one and a half million dollars. Stephen had used a million dollars of his own money, and they'd borrowed the rest to finish the job. Their home had been a source of pride for him, a symbol of his success in the business world. Caroline loved it, too, and never failed to thank her lucky stars for her fairytale life.

But fairytales were fiction, just like her marriage to Stephen. Anger and pain crowded out everything else, and every step down the thick carpeting jarred.

Some thoughtful soul had set the automatic coffee maker, and freshly brewed coffee awaited her. She filled a mug, added milk, and carried the steaming drink through the dark living room and down another flight of steps, where both her and Stephen's offices were. Bypassing hers, which was cluttered with work, she headed for his. The door was closed, exactly as it had been eleven days ago, the day Stephen died. Dread filled her. She didn't want to go in, not by herself. Standing before that door, heart thudding, she fought the urge to flee.

"Nothing to be afraid of, silly," she murmured. "Just go in there, grab the will, life insurance policy, and financial folder, and leave."

She opened the door, which automatically turned on the chandelier and desk light. As always the masculine room was neat and orderly—pristine teakwood desk and matching two-drawer file cabinet, state-of-the-art computer, fax and printer, books aligned on the shelves, dove-gray pillows plumped against the tucked navy leather sofa, matching drapes drawn. The stale air smelled faintly of Old Spice.

Nausea roiled in Caroline's stomach. She set her coffee beside a framed photo of her and Jax, then opened the drapes. She unlocked and opened the windows. Fresh, frigid air rushed in. Instantly she felt better. Better to be cold than physically ill.

She sat down in the desk chair, a comfortable leather swivel affair on wheels. From here she could easily reach the file cabinet where Stephen kept everything.

The bottom drawer, where he stored their personal documents, whispered open. She extracted a fat file labeled "Investments" and set it on the desk. Then she pawed through the cabinet in search of the will and life insurance policy.

No sign of either in the bottom drawer. She checked the top, which was filled with client folders, and then each desk drawer. One drawer held six booklets of ferry tickets, which she needed for trips off the island. She stuffed those into her robe pocket and returned to her search. *Where did you put those things, Stephen?* The way things were going, who knew whether there even *was* a will or life insurance? The sick feeling returned to her stomach and spread a chill of fear through the rest of her body. Until she remembered the safe deposit box.

Yes, he must've stored the most important documents there. She decided also to search the client folders in case the documents were misfiled. There were dozens to look through. Someone had to inform each client of Stephen's death. Caroline didn't think she could bear to make those calls.

She slid out a file, opened it, and leafed through the contents. What she saw shocked her. Instead of the Stephen Mason, Principal, letterhead Stephen used, every document bore the dignified stamp of Jones, Westin and Hawkins, the San Francisco firm Mary Beth had mentioned. Caroline checked every file. All were from the San Francisco firm. Meaning that Stephen never had been in business for himself. A bitter smile curled Caroline's lips. How was it she hadn't known?

Another betrayal. Tears filled her eyes, which she angrily swiped away. Hadn't she cried enough? "Focus on the insurance and the will," she ordered herself.

She booted up the computer and scanned every file. Finding nothing she shuffled through the rolodex. The activity soothed her frazzled nerves, and she soon found the name of the insurance company and agent handling their homeowner insurance. Nothing else, though. Maybe the same person took care of all the insurance. She slipped the business card into the already bulging pocket of her robe.

Why hadn't she paid attention to these things? Because this was Stephen's realm, and because she foolishly hadn't wanted to think about death.

"Fool" hardly described her self-contempt. She was thirty years old, a modern woman running her own small business. Yet she'd slipped into the role of docile homemaker no different from her mother's generation.

Upstairs she heard her father's gravelly voice followed by Becca's feminine murmur. No other voices, making this a good time to deal with Becca.

Despite pledging silence, her traitor of a sister had mentioned Mary Beth Mason within earshot of Jax.

The anger that moments ago had given way to hurt flared again, ugly and hot. Livid, Caroline snatched up the file, stood, and marched upstairs.

Chapter Six

Late Monday morning, Mary Beth sat in an armchair across Kevin Whitaker's massive cherry wood desk. Thanks to this morning's long, hard cry, her throat felt raw, her nose was stuffed up, and her eyes were puffy and burning. Instead of the release she'd expected she felt drained and vulnerable.

Possibly hard-of-hearing, too. Surely she'd misunderstood. Arms close to her body, hands locked together, she frowned. "You're telling me the house I've lived in for close to twenty years, the house we paid off twelve years ago, is mortgaged for two and a half million dollars? That's absurd."

"Not according to the bank." Kevin gestured at the sheaf of papers in front of him. "You and Stephen borrowed against the equity."

"How can that be, when I knew nothing about it?" Bewildered, she shook her head. "There must be some mistake."

"Your signature is all over these documents, Mary Beth. At least, I believe these signatures are yours." He slid the papers toward her. "Check the tabbed pages."

She leafed through the thick document, scrutinizing each place she and Stephen had signed. Unfortunately every signature was genuine.

Good God in heaven. She studied the date on one page. May second, eleven years ago. What had she signed so long ago? At last she remembered.

"I recall signing these forms, but Stephen never mentioned mortgaging the house. He said we were purchasing investments for Aurora's college fund."

"You didn't read the documents?"

The question sounded like a rebuke. Mary Beth raised her chin. "Why should I? I've never been good at deciphering financial terminology." Hadn't Stephen told her that often enough? "Besides, I trusted him."

And once again, he'd betrayed her. How many more deceptions would there be?

"So now I'm strapped with a huge mortgage." She plowed her hand under her hair and massaged the back of her head, which felt tight. "Paying it off will take a hefty chunk out the life insurance money."

Kevin's already sober face lengthened. "About that . . ."

Her stomach knotted in apprehension. "More bad news?"

"I'm afraid so. Just before you arrived I spoke with the insurance company. Unfortunately Stephen did borrow against the policy." Kevin's eyes were dark with sympathy. "There's nothing left for you and Aurora."

Mary Beth had gone numb and icy again. So

where did the tears come from? Like a stranger standing at a distance she watched numbly and impassively as they rolled down her cheeks while her body shivered and her arms hugged her middle. Unable to think or speak, she stared out the huge picture window behind Kevin's desk. From her vantage point she could see nothing but the gray January sky. Her life was as empty and cold.

"Mary Beth?" Kevin said with alarm. "Are you all right?" He pushed a box of tissues at her.

"I don't know." She dabbed her eyes and willed herself to think. "This means I'll have to cash in some of the stocks and bonds."

The attorney's concerned expression told her what she already suspected.

She watched as she pulled into herself, shaking her head in disbelief. "Don't tell me Stephen already cashed them?"

"I'm afraid so."

"There's always the savings account." Stephen had insisted on keeping fifty thousand dollars there, in case of emergency.

"Yes, but three thousand dollars and eighty cents won't last long." Kevin showed her the statement the bank had faxed over.

"Oh, Stephen." At least Aurora's tuition was paid through June. A horrible thought pierced the shock. Mary Beth placed her palms on the desk and leaned forward. "Don't tell me he stole from Aurora's college fund."

"There is no college fund."

Shock and distress rendered her speechless. Kevin reached across his expansive desk and touched her hand, the pristine white Egyptian cotton cuffs crisp and handsome against his hand-tailored navy suit.

How dare Stephen hurt their daughter this way! Furious, she snatched back her hand. "That bastard," she spit, with such venom that Kevin's eyes widened in shock.

"I'm truly sorry, Mary Beth." Looking on the verge of tears himself, he swallowed. "Stephen was a close friend, but I had no idea . . . I wish I knew what he did with the money. If he had drug or gambling problems . . . I never guessed. No one did."

"Did he leave us *anything* of value?"

"Personal property—cars, jewelry, silver, and furniture. And the real estate itself. There is some equity left. You could borrow against it."

"And just where am I supposed to get the money to make the monthly payments?"

For once the attorney had nothing to say.

She'd have to sell the house. *No!* It was the only home Aurora had known, and Mary Beth refused to uproot her. Hadn't she been through enough?

She eyed Kevin, who was suddenly busy straightening the sheaf of papers on his desk. "Is there anything else I should know?"

"Well, yes." He cleared his throat and shifted in his chair. "Stephen is listed on two joint deeds of trust in Washington State, one a residence on Bainbridge Island, and the other a cabin and fifty-acre wooded parcel near the Canadian border. The other name on the property is," he thumbed through papers until he found the document, "Caroline Mason."

"Why am I not surprised," Mary Beth muttered. Her chest was tight again and she wanted to cry. But she was too upset for tears.

Furrows appeared on Kevin's brow. "Do you know her? Because I don't recognize the name."

Time to push Stephen off what was left of his pedestal. "Well, hear this." She squared her shoulders and looked Kevin in the eye. "Caroline Mason is Stephen's *other* wife. My dear departed husband was a bigamist."

There, it was out.

In the beat of silence that followed, Kevin's jaw sagged and he seemed to age a decade.

"Good Christ almighty." He slumped in his chair and scrubbed his hand over his face. "I don't believe it."

"Believe it. I met Caroline at the ICU. Stephen 'married' her ten years ago. They even have a seven-year-old daughter. That's why he was in Seattle. I'll bet my BMW he spent every penny of our money on *them*."

Hurt showed plainly on Kevin's face. "Stephen never said a word." His hair stood up in spots, evidence of his bewildered state of mind. "He was my closest friend and a trusted partner in the law firm our fathers helped found, yet I never even suspected." He aimed an accusing look at Mary Beth. "Why didn't you tell me sooner? I had the right to know."

"If this happened to you, would you tell people?" She didn't wait for a reply. "What are *my* rights?"

Her question jerked Kevin back into lawyer mode. "I'm not well-versed on bigamy, but if what you're saying is true, Stephen committed a criminal act. In the eyes of the law both you and the other woman are victims. If Stephen were alive we could prosecute, but given the situation . . ." he pulled in, then blew out a weary breath. "You and Aurora are both eligible for social security benefits, so we'll start that ball rolling."

"Oh, *that*'s a relief." Her sarcastic tone surprised her and again shocked Kevin, who knew her as an even-tempered, unflappable woman. "Anything else?"

"I really can't answer that without contacting Caroline Mas—the other woman's—attorney."

"What will she get out of this?"

"Other than social security benefits for her daughter? At this point I don't know."

"Is she eligible for social security, too?"

Kevin shook his head. "Only her daughter."

Mary Beth felt absurdly pleased that That Woman would be denied this small benefit. Even though the bigamy wasn't her fault, Mary Beth despised her.

"Do you have her attorney's name?" Kevin asked.

Since that night at the hospital Mary Beth and Caroline had had no contact. As far as she was concerned, they never would. She shook her head. "You have her street address on that deed of trust. Go from there."

"Good idea," Kevin said, eyeing her with respect.

"How much will we get from Social Security, and when will we get it?"

"Benefits are paid monthly and should kick in within a few months. But the payments won't be nearly enough to cover your expenses."

"Oh, great. What are Aurora and I supposed to live on, credit cards?"

"I have a settlement check from our law partnership that will see you through the immediate future. Unfortunately it won't last long. I suggest you find a job."

The whole situation was too much. Mary Beth laughed, the sound more like a strangled cry. "Since I haven't worked since college, and all I did there was write out lecture notes for disabled students, that'll be real easy."

She dug the toe of one pump into the lush ecru carpet. "I don't even have a college degree. Stephen promised he'd take care of me forever." She'd been thinking about finishing her schooling, taking her time, and then finding work. But now? She forced a smile. "Looks like the joke's on me. Only it's not funny."

"Not funny at all." Kevin steepled his hands beneath his solemn chin and studied her. "Stephen was like a brother to me," he muttered. "Why did he do this, and why didn't he tell me?"

"If and when you figure that out, would you please let me know? Because I'm just as clueless." She glanced at her watch, surprised to see how late it was. "Aurora will be home soon, and I should go. If we're through here."

"We are, except for the settlement check." He handed her a check for twenty thousand dollars.

With the hefty mortgage payments and other bills, it was enough to carry her through six weeks at most. Kevin was right, she needed to find a source of income.

"Thanks." She tucked the check into her purse. "There is one more thing."

Kevin, who had slid back his chair, stilled. "Yes?"

"I want your word you won't tell anyone about Stephen just yet. Not even Pam." The woman loved to gossip. In no time she'd spread the scandal all over town. " I don't want Aurora learning that her father was a bigamist from somebody else. Let me have tonight to break the news to her."

Kevin released a gasp of outrage. "I would never breach our attorney-client privilege. As Stephen's executor I—"

Mary Beth interrupted with a gesture. "Give me a break. I'm not stupid. Stephen was a partner here. The rest of the firm *should* know. And I'm sure you'll want to discuss how to deal with the reporters who are bound to come snooping." A scandal created by a well-respected attorney in the prestigious firm was sure to draw plenty of unpleasant media attention.

"All right." He looked sheepish. "I'll give you twenty-four hours."

They both stood. Kevin escorted her through the plush reception area. Mary Beth wasn't up to facing anyone from the firm, but damned if she'd let people see her despair. She held her head high. To her relief, the receptionist had left for the evening and any attorneys still working were closeted in their offices.

"You'll call me after you talk with Caroline's lawyer?" she asked at the elevator.

He nodded. "You'll be hearing from me soon."

Knowing she should hurry home but dreading the evening to come she walked slowly through the near-empty garage under the building. Maybe she'd call Ellie from the car before driving home. She needed to rant about Stephen's unbelievable thoughtlessness with her best friend. She also needed to shore up her courage for what lay ahead.

Because ready or not, want to or not, it was time to tell Aurora the whole truth about her father.

* * *

As Caroline sat across Martin Cheswick's mahogany desk Monday afternoon she was still fuming from her fight with Becca. Her sister and family had left in a rush for the airport, Becca in huffy silence, their father jangling the car keys and shaking his head. Feeling vindicated but wretched, Caroline had dropped Jax at school. Then she'd headed for the bank, where the safe deposit box had yielded two car titles and the mortgage documents for the house and cabin, but no insurance policy and no will. Her selfish liar of a husband had betrayed her yet again.

Now this?! "You mean to tell me, Mary Beth Mason's lawyer contacted you this morning, before you and I even met?"

"Certainly caught me by surprise." The attorney drew his large hand through his hair, which was dark and wavy and needed a trim. Vertical lines slashed the space between his bushy eyebrows. "If I'd known Stephen was a bigamist I'd have been better prepared."

Feeling as if she'd been reprimanded, Caroline stiffened. "Excuse me, but I didn't want to tell you until we met face-to-face."

Martin—he'd asked her to use his first name, and she'd done the same—spread his hands, palms out, in a take-it-easy gesture. "Hey, I'm on your side." Looking straight at her, he seemed sincere. "I understand why you waited. This is a delicate matter."

"To say the least. How on earth did her lawyer find you?"

"Apparently he called your house. Somebody there gave him my number."

The only person home was her father. Caroline made a mental note to talk to him about sharing personal information with strangers.

"And now she's suing me." Things just kept getting worse. Acid burned painfully in her stomach and she tasted bile. Back in college, thanks to an overdose of stress, she'd developed an ulcer and had experienced the same symptoms. It wouldn't be much of a surprise if she'd worried herself another. "I married Stephen in good faith. He said his former wife had died. Why should I be penalized for his lies?"

"I agree, what happened to you is despicable and unethical. But, while I appreciate your argument, according to the dictates of the law, you and Stephen Mason never were married because he already had a wife." Kind brown eyes met hers, the best part of his long, large-featured face. "I'm sorry, Caroline."

She was thirty and he wasn't but five years or so older, but he seemed sharp and experienced. She liked and trusted him. Which, given the recent developments in her life, probably wasn't wise. Her trust antenna was obviously warped. But he was her attorney, and she needed him.

"'Sorry' won't pay the bills," she said. "What happens now?"

"You're certain there's no will?"

"Nothing so far. I'll keep looking, but I don't hold much hope."

"Then in the most likely case, Mary Beth Mason

sues for at least half the assets you hold jointly with Stephen, claiming his share as her own."

"Everything is held jointly with Stephen," Caroline said. Their house, the cabin and acreage, the cars and the investments.

The implications spun dizzily through her brain. She remembered Mary Beth's face, the haunted and frigid glint in her eyes as they stood over Stephen's body, and shuddered. "She can do that?"

The corner of Martin's mouth quirked—whether in wry humor or grimace, Caroline wasn't sure. "She can try."

She'd never thought of herself as tenacious, but the fierce need to hold onto the assets she and Stephen had purchased and grown made her exactly that. "I don't care about the cabin or Stephen's things, but I won't give up Jax's and my house. Not to her or anyone else."

The imperturbable attorney took in her angry tone without reacting. "How did you pay for your home?"

"The same way everyone else does—with money."

"Whose funds?"

"Stephen paid cash for the lake-front lot, the architect, and the builder, his wedding gifts to me. We took out a loan for the rest, and later refinanced for more to pay my mother's health costs and make the down payment on the cabin and land."

Martin jotted down notes on a yellow legal pad, his large hand dwarfing the silver fountain pen. "What about the monthly payments? Were they made with money Stephen earned?"

"Mostly, but we used part of my earnings, too."

Stephen had pitched a fit about that. He was old-fashioned and thought he should pay for everything.

But Caroline earned a good living and had stood firm about contributing, and he'd grudgingly given in.

"If the funds Stephen used for your home came out of his and Mary Beth Mason's assets, she can claim you owe her that money and any equity from funds Stephen used to pay down the mortgage."

"But that's over a million dollars! I don't have that kind of money."

Martin nodded at the papers. "Actually, one point three million. Mary Beth Mason could force you to sell everything."

"The hell she will. Not the house."

"Well, then." Looking thoughtful, her attorney rubbed his chin. "We'll counter claim that your assets were acquired under the doctrine of meretricious relationship."

"What does that mean?"

"That you and Stephen had a quasi-marital relationship with joint tenancy. In plain English, you lived as man and wife without the benefit of matrimony, with shared assets that now belong to you."

Caroline frowned. "That sounds so cold and cheap." The love between her and Stephen had been warm and beautiful. Or so she'd believed. Absently she rubbed the burning pit of her stomach.

"Regardless how it sounds, the goal is for you to hold on to your assets. There is another possible option. You could refinance the house and cash out Mary Beth Mason's interest. But that won't work unless you net the amount she wants. And of course you'd have to qualify for the new monthly payment."

Which already was astronomical. "I earn a nice living from my work but not enough to cover the existing monthly payment. I'd never qualify for an even bigger mortgage." She exhaled a heavy breath. "What should I do? And don't tell me to sell. Even if I considered that option, and I won't, I'd never net one point three million dollars. We, that is, I, owe too much. I'll find some other way." If only she could find the insurance policy. "You'll call and check on the life insurance?"

He nodded. "Right away, but you stand to lose those funds, too."

Caroline's stomach felt as if someone had set a match to it. She gritted her teeth. "Not if I can help it. I will fight this with everything I have."

"Okay by me, but be aware, this could drag on for years and end up costing you a fortune. All told, Kevin Whitaker, who is the other attorney, and I stand to make money from our fees, if and when we earn them. But there's no guarantee either you or Mary Beth Mason will. Are you sure you want the legal headache?"

At least he was honest. And she was mad and scared and not about to give up. "I gave Stephen over ten years of my life. I deserve something for that. So does Jax." A new worry bubbled up, and she locked her hands at her waist. "How will I pay you? I don't exactly have the money."

"I'll take my fee out of your settlement."

"Even if it takes years?"

Martin nodded. "That's the way I work."

"And if there is no settlement?"

"Luck of the draw. But I intend to fight for you, Caroline, and I intend to win." The intercom buzzed. "That's my two o'clock." Martin Cheswick stood, signaling the end of the meeting.

Caroline, too, rose. Lanky and at least six-feet-five,

his frame reminding her of Abraham Lincoln, her lawyer towered over her as he escorted her to his door.

"Over the next few days I'll take a closer look at the assets and do what I can to find that insurance policy," he said.

"Thank you."

His hand engulfed hers in a firm shake. "I'll be in touch."

Chapter Seven

Sitting beside Mary Beth on the den sofa and facing the dark thirty-six-inch flat-screen TV, Aurora covered her mouth with her fingers and shook her head over and over. "I don't believe you, Mother. Daddy did not have another family."

The look of horror on her daughter's face ripped what was left of Mary Beth's battered heart to shreds. She wanted to lean close and pull Aurora into a comforting hug, but the don't-touch-me expression warned her away.

Aurora stood up and backed away from the tan, suede-covered sofa, as if movement would erase the truth. The wall stopped her. "You're lying."

"I only wish I were," Mary Beth replied in a drained voice she barely recognized.

A heavy silence filled the room, broken only by the ticking of the Howard Miller decorative clock.

Wrapping are arms around her stomach, Aurora eyed Mary Beth and at last spoke. "Is that why you didn't cry at the funeral?"

"Mostly." She was crying now. Since this morning, she couldn't seem to stop.

More silence as her daughter stared at her, the look on her face impossible to read. Mary Beth could only imagine what she must be feeling. The moment the thought formed, anger flushed Aurora's face.

"Why didn't you tell me sooner? I had the right to know!"

Hadn't Ellie advised her to tell Aurora right away? Mary Beth hadn't listened. Now she wished she had. "I didn't know how." She blew her nose. "It came as such a surprise, and I was in shock. I still am." She couldn't get over how Stephen had left her and their daughter virtually penniless—a heartless, selfish deed she wasn't ready to share just yet. One upset at a time.

The tears vanished under her own anger. "We will get through this."

Somehow.

"Does anybody else know?" Aurora asked.

"Ellie. And Kevin Whitaker. He's our lawyer now, so he had to know. I told him today. He agreed to keep the information to himself for twenty-four hours. After that . . ." She gave a helpless shrug.

Aurora stared numbly at her. "So by tomorrow afternoon, everybody will know that Daddy was a . . . a . . ."

"Bigamist."

The ugly word hung between them, a burden of shame.

"I can't go back to school. Ever." Aurora stopped hugging herself to bury her face in her hands. "My life is over."

Mary Beth sympathized, but tuition had been paid, there were no refunds, and money was tight.

"If your friends judge you for your father's sins, they're not real friends," she said. "But if you want to stay home the rest of the week, you may."

If her daughter heard, she gave no indication. "Did you meet her? Daddy's other wife?"

Mary Beth nodded. "At the hospital in Seattle."

"Does she—did they—have kids?"

"A seven-year-old daughter."

The hurt on Aurora's face was unbearable. Mary Beth stood and started toward her. Abruptly her daughter's expression changed. She glared at Mary Beth with contempt and loathing.

"Don't you come near me. It's all your fault Daddy did this!"

She'd unknowingly hit on Mary Beth's deepest insecurities. Flinching, she sank onto a chair. "That's cruel and unfair. If Daddy had said he was unhappy, we could have gone to counseling, or divorced. But he never told me." She met her daughter's dark, confused gaze. "Instead he broke the law and hurt a lot of innocent people."

Aurora plugged her ears and shook her head. "Daddy wouldn't have needed another family if you'd been nicer to him. I hate you!"

Ashen and hollow-eyed, she spun toward the door and fled. Rapid footsteps pattered down the hall, through the living room, and up the stairs.

Mary Beth shivered. She'd thought Stephen's death and learning of his bigamy were bad. This was far, far worse. Beyond even tears.

If only she could feel numb again. But the cottony, distant feeling had given way to agony. She couldn't deal with this alone. She did the only thing she could think of—called Ellie.

* * *

Three weeks after the funeral, determined to pull her life together and move forward despite her financial woes, Mary Beth sat down on a bar stool—the kitchen had an eating bar as well as a regular kitchen table—and called Susan Andrews, whom she'd only heard from once since the funeral.

Mary Beth guessed that she felt uncomfortable. The death of a long-time friend was hard enough to take. When he turned out to be a bigamist to boot . . .

"How are you?" Susan gushed with syrupy concern.

"As well as can be expected, thanks, but I need something to keep me busy." Aside from combing the want ads every morning. "Before Stephen died I was about to start soliciting donations for the silent auction. I'd like to go ahead and—"

"That's very sweet of you, but we won't be needing your help. You should be focusing your energy on yourself and Aurora."

"I appreciate the concern, but what I want and need is to—"

"Oops, there's my other line. Take care."

Click.

Mary Beth frowned as she hung up. This wasn't the first time she'd been rudely cut off. Hadn't Marsha Jackson behaved virtually the same way regarding the garden club? And Pam Whitaker was almost as bad. Yes, she still drove Aurora and Kristi to swim-team, but she refused to let Mary Beth reciprocate. Whenever Mary Beth invited her in for coffee, she always had a ready excuse as to why that wasn't possible. As for the PTA which Pam chaired, no one had told Mary Beth about the last meeting. They'd cut her from their email list and phone tree, acts Pam no doubt was behind.

None of her "friends" would admit to the *real* reason they'd dropped her. It wasn't just that without Stephen, she didn't truly belong. No, this was something else. It was almost as if . . . as if Stephen's bigamy had tainted her.

Almost? Mary Beth snickered. Every time she walked through the hallowed doors of Jones, Westin and Hawkins, she felt as if she had a contagious disease. Nothing people actually said, but the knowing looks and whispers were impossible to miss.

She'd been wronged, yet somehow everyone—including her own daughter—faulted her.

Aurora avoided her whenever possible. She'd dyed her hair black and had taken to wearing heavy eye make-up and tight, black clothes in clear defiance of Mary Beth. The days she didn't have a ride to school, she caught a city bus so, as she'd so sweetly phrased it earlier this morning, she "wouldn't be stuck in the car with *you*." She ate dinner in her room, and only spoke to Mary Beth when forced.

That hurt terribly. And also infuriated her.

The anger that simmered constantly under the surface flared. Mary Beth exploded. Her gaze lit upon Stephen's sterling silver baby spoon, which he'd insisted she display beside his silver baby cup and bronzed baby shoes on a shelf in the kitchen. She rose from the stool, moved to the shelf and snatched up the spoon. Holding it by its little silver handle, she dropped it into the disposal and turned on the switch.

The clashing, grinding sound was most satisfying.

Why hadn't she thought of this sooner? Raising her fists to the ceiling, she screamed bloody murder. After a few moments, drained, throat sore, but feeling better, she shut off the disposal.

Suddenly Ellie popped through the back door.

"I heard you screaming clear around the front of the house. What in the world?"

Feeling too good for shame, Mary Beth extracted the mangled silver and held it up like a trophy. "Stephen's baby spoon."

She tossed it into the garbage can under the sink.

Her friend—her only friend—broke into a sly smile. "You she-devil. I haven't seen that much pepper from you since college."

"I had to do something, but I really didn't plan on having an audience." Shock at her behavior finally hit, and Mary Beth sank meekly into a kitchen chair. "I can't believe what I just did. How childish."

"You've suffered a lot. Childish is okay."

"I suppose. But that spoon was sterling silver. I should've ruined something less valuable."

"I think you chose the perfect item." Ellie dropped a bakery sack on the table and helped herself to coffee. "The man born with the proverbial silver spoon in his mouth went bad, and now, so did his spoon."

"When you put it that way . . ." Mary Beth, who'd lost weight but ironically no longer cared, pulled out a sticky bun and bit into it. "Aren't you supposed to be at work right now? It is Wednesday morning."

Ellie sat down opposite Mary Beth. "I worked twelve long hours yesterday, and this is comp time.

I thought I mentioned that on the phone last night."

They talked daily, for which Mary Beth was eternally grateful. "If you did, I don't remember." She licked cinnamon from her thumb. "Even though you just saw me at my worst, I'm glad you stopped by. Any particular reason why?"

"As you pointed out, it *is* Wednesday. Weren't you supposed to hear from Kevin Whitaker around now? I'm here for moral support, and from what I just saw and heard, either you're doing okay or there's been another setback." About to sip her coffee she paused and fixed Mary Beth with friendly concern. "Which is it?"

Mouth full, Mary Beth didn't reply. There had been a few snags. Caroline Mason had hired a sharp attorney, and Kevin warned that untangling the financial mess could take months, possibly years. Despite the law, which stated that Caroline Mason deserved nothing. If only she'd accept that gracefully and pay Mary Beth what she deserved. But the stubborn woman refused, which would cost Mary Beth a fortune in legal fees she could no longer afford. Kevin was, after all, an attorney. He'd only work *gratis* for so long. Of course, Caroline didn't care about that. The dirty blond bimbo didn't care about Mary Beth and Aurora, period.

Hatred washed through Mary Beth, and she pushed the rest of her sticky bun away. Though she itched to let out an enraged howl or destroy something else, instead she pulled her thoughts from the horrid woman who had ruined her life and shook her head.

"Kevin hasn't called yet. This morning's bad

mood comes courtesy of Susan Andrews. She just cut me loose from the ballet guild fundraiser."

"And this comes as a surprise?" Ellie's expression soured. "I hate to say this, but I told you."

"I know, but it still hurts. Those women cut me out of their lives so fast. . . . Nobody's said it, but I think they blame me for what Stephen did. That's what pushed me over the edge this morning."

Ellie's mouth hardened and her eyes narrowed and blazed. "Those cold-hearted bitches. They should be ashamed," she said with indignation enough for both her and Mary Beth. "Well, their loss. You always were too good for them. Good riddance." She brushed her hands together. "Don't worry, they'll get theirs. It's called 'karma.'"

Even though the concept of "karma" had been around for millennia, Mary Beth associated it with New Age philosophy, something she never had embraced. But now . . . "What about *my* karma?" she asked, shooting a look upward. "I must've done something really bad to deserve this."

"I don't know about that. All I know is, the best revenge is to react to their appalling behavior with love and grace."

"Love?" Mary Beth snickered. "I'm too angry and hurt for that."

"Experience that anger and that hurt, then release them. That's how you rise above the crap, and the only way to 'win.'"

"Easy for you to say. You're not an outcast."

"This is a big city. You'll make new friends."

Mary Beth wanted the old ones back. She wanted to reclaim her place among the women who socialized, volunteered, shopped, and played tennis together. She started to sigh and ended up yawning.

Ellie squinted at her. "Another bad night, huh?"

"Money worries." She'd let the housekeeper and lawn service go and had stopped the manicures and hair appointments, but thanks to staggering mortgage payments, credit card debt, household bills, and Aurora's lessons, her cash reserve was dwindling fast. A few more weeks and . . . completing that thought scared her so badly, she felt sick to her stomach. "Thank God for social security payments," she said. "No matter what, we'll be able to eat and buy gas."

"I have a couple thousand saved up if you want it," Ellie offered for the dozenth time. "You can pay me back when you're on your feet again."

"I couldn't do that, but I appreciate the offer more than I can say. I appreciate everything you've done, Ellie."

"Then appreciate this. Your money troubles aren't about to disappear, at least not in the near future. Aurora should know. When are you planning to enlighten her?"

"Well . . ." Mary Beth rubbed the space between her eyebrows, which felt tight and on the verge of growing into a headache. "At the moment things are horribly strained between us. When she learns that we're teetering into poverty . . ." She shivered with dread. "It won't be pleasant."

"Regardless, you must tell her," Ellie said. "Buried under all that teenage drama queen stuff is a girl with a good heart. She might handle the news better than you think."

"One can hope," Mary Beth said, but she was skeptical.

"If it was up to me I'd make that conversation happen now. Don't put it off even one more day."

"I suppose you're right." She glanced at the silent phone. "Maybe Kevin will call with good news. If he untangles this mess soon and gets our money back . . ."

"And if he can't? Thought any more about a job?"

"Constantly, but the ads in the paper want people with college degrees and work experience. That leaves me out." Mary Beth grimaced. "I'll be lucky to make minimum wage. Which won't even make a dent in the monthly mortgage payment. I wonder whether I should even bother."

Ellie looked glum. "You really are in a bind."

"Don't you go getting depressed on me. I need a pep talk."

"Okay. You're a resourceful woman. I know you'll figure out something."

"That's what I need to hear." An idea sparked, nothing long-term, but a short-term fix. Mary Beth waved her hand in the direction of the dining room. "Know anyone in the market for high-quality furniture?"

Chapter Eight

Several hours after Aurora took a dinner plate to her room in her usual brooding silence, Mary Beth stood before her closed door with a mug of cocoa—the only goodwill offering she could think of. Despite expensive sound-proofing throughout the house she could hear the loud rock music. The barrier between her and her daughter was as harsh as the music and as thick as the eggshell-color door, but Mary Beth was determined to break it down. Especially now, after a disappointing call from Kevin.

"These things take time. Be patient," he'd counseled.

With her bank account nearly empty she couldn't afford patience. She would sell Stephen's car, his computer, and office equipment, and a good deal of the furniture. That should help. First though, she intended to follow Ellie's advice and tell Aurora the truth about their dwindling bank account.

The music stopped. Feeling as if she was about to face a firing squad she held tightly to the mug with one hand and knocked on the door with the other. "I brought you some cocoa. May I come in?"

A new song started and abruptly stopped. "If you must," came the muffled but surly reply.

The usually messy room, which an interior designer had decorated with input from Aurora and Stephen and at considerable expense, was as spotless as a vacant hotel room. The stuffed animals sat neatly on the custom-made shelves Stephen had insisted on, and the books and CDs were lined up without one spine out of place. Even the canopy bed was made, the ivory and rose satin and velvet throw pillows arranged just so. The only human touches were Aurora's cell phone and iPod on the bedside table.

Stephen would've approved, but Mary Beth frowned. What was going on? "I'm not sure I'm in the right place," she teased. "This used to be my daughter's room. But it's so neat and clean . . ."

Sitting at her desk, facing the computer and hunched over an open history book, Aurora tensed without raising her gaze from the text. "You like it this way, and so did Daddy."

Not for the first time, Mary Beth wondered whether Stephen's need for order had come from living a dual, chaotic life. She kept the thought to herself. "True, we expected you to be neat and tidy. But you *are* human, and humans make messes."

No reaction or comment.

"Here's that cocoa." She set the giant-size blue mug in front of the computer, which flashed a provocative picture of Mandy Moore as its screen saver. "I added marshmallows, whipped cream, and chocolate sprinkles, the way you like it. How's the homework coming along?"

"I was trying to get it done, until *you* showed up." At last Aurora raised her head. "I still have to finish this chapter, work on my math, and start a rough draft of my English paper, and it's getting late. So make this fast, Mother."

With that snippy tone and belligerent expression she was itching for a fight. But tonight required maturity and calm, and Mary Beth refused to take the bait. She perched on the immaculate, padded window seat, which was as big as a three-quarter-length sofa. Aurora had left the drapes open. Even though it was black outside, Mary Beth thought she could make out the gazebo and trees. "I was hoping we could talk."

Aurora turned in her seat to face her. "Don't tell me there's more bad news."

Mary Beth flinched at the burdened expression darkening her daughter's face, and almost changed her mind about saying anything. But no, Aurora had the right to know. "I don't like the tension between us," she said. "I'd like to work things out."

The half-hearted, one-shoulder shrug and lowered eyes were better than nothing.

Pulling in a breath, Mary Beth pressed her point. "We're the only family each other has. We need each other, Aurora, especially now."

"You're not my only family," her daughter sneered, pain burning in her eyes. "I have a dumb little half-sister, don't I?"

Mary Beth ached for her daughter. "I suppose you do. I'd give anything to change what your father did, but I can't."

Aurora caught hold of a spike of hair and pulled it between her fingers. "If only I'd made better grades or acted nicer or kept my room this clean. Maybe then . . ." Her fingers worried another spike, and another.

"Oh, honey. Is that what's been bothering you?" Mary Beth bit her lip. "Nothing your father did was your fault. Or mine," she added, willing herself to believe that. She held her daughter's gaze.

Aurora's eyes filled. "I'm sorry for what I said before. I don't blame you and I don't hate you."

Sweet balm to Mary Beth's heart. "You were hurt and upset," she said. Acting on instinct she stood and opened her arms.

Aurora hesitated a scant moment before hurling herself into the embrace, both of them crying. It felt so good to hold onto her daughter. "I've missed you," she said, sniffling as she pulled back.

"Me, too."

Mary Beth went into Aurora's bathroom and got them both tissues, and Aurora retrieved her cocoa. They sat down on the window seat and blew their noses. Aurora's heavy mascara had run, and she dabbed beneath her eyes with a clean tissue. Without the makeup, she looked younger and more vulnerable.

"How are things at school?"

"Hard." Cradling her mug, she carefully scooted to the end of the window seat, resting her back against the side. She pulled her legs up and balanced the mug on her knees.

Mary Beth kicked off her beige slippers, then mimicked her daughter's posture at the opposite end of the window seat. Their toes—hers painted, though badly chipped, in the same color as the long-gone polish from her last manicure/pedicure five weeks ago, Aurora's masked by black socks—were less than an inch apart. Two pairs of adult-size feet.

"My friends want to pretend nothing has changed," Aurora said. "If I mention Daddy, they get quiet and won't look at me. I'm not even sure they *are* my friends anymore," she murmured softly.

Teenagers could be so cruel. "You've known most of those kids your whole life. I'm sure they're still your friends."

"I don't want to talk about it." Shifting nervously, Aurora shot her a sideways, guilt-ridden look. "Did Miss Carey call you?"

The swim-team coach. "No," Mary Beth said, wary. "Why would she?"

"I sort of stopped going to practice."

"Oh?" Mary Beth said, her goal of staying calm slipping. "Why?"

Her daughter stared at her knees. "Because I quit the team."

"You did *what*?!" Aurora never accepted change well and rarely initiated it herself. That she'd done this was a testament to her bad state of mind. "But all your friends are on the team."

"Stop calling them my friends." She moved her mug to the window ledge.

No one had contacted Mary Beth—not Pam or the coach. Didn't they care at all about Aurora? Anger burned hot in her belly. Bettina Carey would hear from her later tonight. "What happened?"

"I just don't like swimming anymore."

"I wish you'd discussed this with me," Mary

Beth said, thinking she might have changed her daughter's mind.

Emotions twisted the beautiful young face into a mask of hurt. "After you kept all those secrets from me, why should I share anything with you?"

"I was trying to protect you," Mary Beth said in a defensive voice as loud as her daughter's.

"I don't need protecting!" Aurora shot from her seat. "And I don't want you in my room, Mother. So get out."

Mary Beth's spirits plummeted, and suddenly she felt bone-weary. "I should have been more honest from the start. I'm sorry." She caught her daughter's gaze. "I want to talk, not fight. Please let me stay."

For a long moment she wasn't sure whether Aurora would. At last she nodded and returned to the window seat. This time, facing forward with her back straight.

Better than nothing. Mary Beth let out a breath. "If you haven't been at practice, what have you been doing every afternoon?" Her daughter's fearful expression—she'd scared her with her anger—hurt. Mary Beth made a silent vow that she would not let her negative emotions ruin their first real conversation in weeks. "I truly want to know."

"Promise you won't get mad?"

"No more bawling you out." She held up her fingers, Girl-Scout style. "I'm available and willing to talk about anything, any time—and I promise not to lose my temper." She saw by Aurora's face that she believed her.

"I've been hanging out with some kids."

"New friends?" That was a good sign, wasn't it? "I'm pleased to hear that. Tell me about them."

"Why?" her daughter asked, again suspicious.

"Because I'm interested," Mary Beth replied, pleading with her eyes. "What are their names?"

"There's Sasha and Kelly, and Mike. They don't care about who my dad was or what he did. They just take me for who I am."

Mary Beth liked the sound of that. "Do I know their parents?"

"I don't think so." Aurora ducked her head, avoiding her gaze. Apparently finished sharing information, she plucked her mug from the ledge and indulged in a long, slow drink.

Mary Beth wanted to know more about the new friends but didn't dare ruin the shaky truce between her and Aurora. "I'd love to meet them." She smiled. "Why don't you invite them over sometime?"

"Maybe I will." Aurora angled her head. "Just don't keep secrets from me ever again. Not telling me about Daddy really sucked."

The perfect segué for the next blow. Mary Beth cleared her throat. "There is one last secret—that I know of, anyway."

Her daughter fixed her with a somber stare, so heavy and adult-like that *she* felt like the child. Bracing for the emotional pain she was about to inflict, rage at Stephen rising like acid in her throat, Mary Beth blurted out the truth. "Your father mortgaged the house and spent all our money. We're broke."

To her surprise, Aurora gave a blasé nod. "I wondered when you'd finally tell me."

"You knew? How?"

"Right before I quit the swim team, I heard Mrs.

Whitaker talking about us on her cell. You know how loud she is." Aurora's cheeks flushed. "She said we were about to become charity cases."

"Charity cases?" The nerve! "That filthy gossip. Who was she talking to?"

"Um . . . Mrs. Jackson, I think."

Was that why Aurora had quit the team? Mary Beth wanted to shake Pam. "Our problems are nobody's damn business." She was so mad she didn't even care that she'd uttered a cuss word in front of her child. Exactly how much had Kevin shared with his blabbermouth wife, anyway? God knew how many people she'd told. Fury shook her, and she made a silent vow to tell the miserable woman and her husband off as soon as she left this room. After a call to the swim coach. Maybe she'd fire Kevin, too . . . No. Unfortunately she needed him.

"I know you hate her, but she's Kristi's mom," Aurora said. Her eyes held a silent, but difficult-to-ignore appeal.

Gratified that Aurora and Kristi were still friends, Mary Beth nodded. "I understand. You don't want me to do anything to jeopardize your friendship. So I shouldn't yell at Pam?"

So much for chewing out the horrible woman. She *would* resign from the PTA though, so she wouldn't be forced to speak to Pam.

"Please don't. Not Mr. Whitaker, either."

"He deserves it even more for violating attorney-client confidentiality," she said. One look at Aurora's worried face and she backed down. "All right, I won't yell. But I will tell him I'm not pleased that he shared our private business with his blabber-mouth wife."

Having grown up around Stephen, Aurora understood confidentiality. She nodded. "Will I be switching to public school?"

"Not until you start high school in the fall. But we do have to cut the extras. Our cell phones, the private clarinet lessons, your swing dance class, Saturday art school—all have to go. I'm sorry."

"No more text messaging?" Mary Beth nodded, and Aurora grimaced. "Okay. Should I find work? I'm too young for a real job, but I can babysit after school."

The spoiled teenager suddenly had morphed into a lovely young woman. Mary Beth's heart swelled. "That certainly will help, but I expect you to put school first. We're both eligible to collect social security benefits, which will help some. And Mr. Whitaker is suing for the money Daddy gave Caroline. The law says it belongs to us, but she's fighting back." Mary Beth didn't hide her expression of disgust. God, how she detested the woman. "It could be years before we see a penny of that."

"That's awful! I hate her!"

"Me too."

"We have to do something to her!"

"Believe me, I would if I could. But unlike your father I'm a law-abiding citizen." A silly thought struck her, and she raised and lowered her eyebrows. "We can always hope aliens from outer space grab her and take her to a galaxy far, far away."

Aurora did not smile. "This is no time for jokes, Mom. What are we gonna do?"

"I wasn't kidding. I wish she'd disappear from the

face of the earth. But since that's not likely to happen, I've decided to sell your father's Mercedes, his office equipment, and all the furniture in his study. Lots of the other furniture, too. If the buyers are willing to pay what I ask, we'll end up with a decent chunk of cash, enough to tide us over for a month."

"Only a month?"

"You wouldn't believe the bills we owe." Mary Beth couldn't stem a heart-felt moan. "I worked up a résumé and I've been looking for a job that pays more than minimum wage. But I don't have any skills or education, so finding something may take awhile."

Aurora set her mug beside her. "What happens when the money runs out?"

No sense sugarcoating the truth. "We'll probably have to sell the house."

"We can't. I love this place! I was born here!"

"I love it, too, but your father strapped us with a huge mortgage and no way to make the payments." She didn't want to worry Aurora more than necessary, but their no-more-secrets deal forced her to. "We'll probably end up renting."

"Renting!" Aurora gasped. "We can't buy a smaller house?"

"For that we'd need a loan, and I doubt any bank will take a chance on us."

Her daughter set her jaw. "So that's why Mrs. W. called us charity cases." A moment later her eyes filled. "This is so embarrassing! Hasn't Daddy done enough without this, too?"

Feeling helpless, Mary Beth could only shrug.

Suddenly Aurora pummeled the padded seat

with her fists. The mug fell sideways, spilling what was left of her cocoa onto the expensive chintz. She didn't seem to notice. "Why did he do this to us?"

The stain, a "disaster" that would have sent Stephen into apoplexy, cheered Mary Beth, but not enough to mute her own fury. What was left of her nails bit into her palms as she curled her hands into fists and let her anger color her voice. "Unfortunately, we'll never know."

"You're certain I can't sell *any*thing?" Caroline asked two weeks after that first meeting with Martin Cheswick. They were sitting in the back corner of the Starbucks beneath the building where he worked. They'd set up a weekly Wednesday meeting that began after she dropped Jax at school. In the two meetings so far, Martin had picked up the tab.

An introvert by nature, she had no close friends. Acquaintances, yes—clients or the mothers of Jax's friends—but no one she could *talk* to. Certainly no one who knew what Stephen had pulled, except Martin, and she'd come to look forward to seeing him.

"Anything at all?" she pleaded.

"We've been over this before, Caroline." He shook his head, his hair brushing the collar of his blue oxford shirt. Not the crisply-pressed Egyptian cotton Stephen had worn to impress clients, but neat and clean. "You can't—"

"Sell off a single item of what you call my 'comingled properties' until the lawsuit is settled," she finished. In other words, she was stuck holding on to everything.

Two weeks ago she'd learned that the investments listed in Stephen's files had been liquidated. Equally horrendous, hours of fruitless searching had failed to produce either the will or the life insurance policy. This last "surprise" hurt more than everything else. Leaving Jax basically penniless and unprotected was the worst possible offense. How could he have done that?

For ten years Caroline had lived with and loved Stephen, had thought she knew him. But he wasn't that protective, caring man at all, and she now questioned her judgment and decisions with doubt and skepticism. Stephen had been dead exactly thirty-one days, but Caroline felt as though she'd aged a hundred years. She marveled at the happy, carefree person she once had been.

Even if there had been insurance or a will, everything was tied up in the lawsuit. She needed money now.

"I wish to God that I had investments of my own," she said for the twentieth time.

Thankfully, despite a few weeks off, her loyal group of clients had stuck with her. But the money earned from them didn't nearly cover the mortgage payment and other bills. The continual worry and anxiety were eating her alive. She couldn't sleep and had lost her appetite.

Her ulcer—diagnosed and medicated, but not yet healed—burned in her stomach. Caroline winced.

Noting her grimace, Martin shook his head. "I warned you this would take a long time. You may end up with nothing."

"I realize that, but I have to try." After three weeks she was comfortable enough for honesty. "An old college ulcer flared up. I shouldn't be drinking coffee."

He eyed her large, three-quarters-full cup. "Not without a lot more milk." He opened his palm. "Hand it over."

"I don't use sugar," she reminded him.

"I know." He carried her drink to the milk bar, his long legs eating up the few yards.

Was he a real friend, Caroline wondered, or simply her attorney? A month ago she'd have replied without a thought that he was a friend. But now, uncertain of herself, she wasn't sure.

When he returned and set the cup in front of her the dark liquid had changed to light-brown. "This is the last time I spring for coffee," he said. "Next week it's cocoa or hot milk."

"Yes, sir," she said, and his wide mouth quirked.

Everything he did and said showed that he was a nice, decent man. She knew that his wife had died of cancer shortly after their first wedding anniversary and that he'd never remarried. For eleven years he'd stayed true to her memory.

Why couldn't she have chosen a man like Martin? She'd thought she had.

Had she been stupid, or blinded by material things? Neither choice left her feeling good about herself.

"I'm doing everything I can to untangle this mess and get you what I think you deserve," Martin said, resuming the conversation. "But Mary Beth Mason has a cracker-jack attorney and he's working just as hard for her."

Mary Beth owned her house and everything in it. She probably had life insurance and tons of money. Resentment boiled through Caroline. She wished the greedy witch would back off, if only for Jax's sake.

Her daughter seemed to be coping well, except at night. The nightmares had stopped, but she still demanded to sleep in Caroline's bed. Caroline knew that was wrong but couldn't banish her little girl to her own room. Not yet.

"The mortgage payment is due March first, less than two weeks from now." No need to mention the mortgage payment for the cabin, the utility bills, funeral expenses, credit card debts, or medical costs incurred around her ulcer. "The social security check Jax received last week was pathetically small. Is there nothing we can do to speed things along?"

"I know you don't want to ask your family," Martin said as he leaned his forearms on the table. "But now is no time for foolish pride. Could your father loan you some money?"

He'd offered, but as it was he barely squeaked by. Since Caroline and Jax didn't have the funds to fly down and visit him over spring break, as they usually did, he was coming again to the island. That was all the expense he could afford. She shook her head.

"What about Becca and Hank?"

Caroline still wasn't speaking to her sister, and besides, she could never ask Becca. "That's not possible."

The big, brown eyes she'd come to know and trust whether she should or not, met hers. "I could arrange a loan."

Desperate as she was, she still had some self-respect. She wasn't about to lose that, too. "Absolutely not," she said. "I don't want a loan. What I want is to be free to sell off my assets."

"Unless you want even more trouble from Mary Beth Mason, you can't."

The vindictive hag was probably laughing herself silly over this whole mess. At the very thought, Caroline's temper exploded. "I hate Mary Beth Mason! Damn her to hell!" she seethed, beyond caring that her voice had risen.

Several patrons in the noisy, crowded coffee bar turned to stare, but the unflappable Martin remained calm and seemingly unaffected by her outburst. "Getting mad won't help."

"Maybe not, but with my life in limbo and sliding toward the garbage heap, anger's about the only thing I can do without getting arrested."

The words earned her a wry smile. "At least your sense of humor's intact. Did I mention I'm looking for a graphic designer to revamp my website and keep it updated?"

"No, you didn't." Caroline eyed him skeptically. "Do you really need help, or is this a pity offer?"

"What does it matter, as long as I'm willing to pay? By the way, how much do you charge?"

"Not enough to cover my expenses."

"You may as well take the job," Martin said. "Some money is better than none. I'm tied up with clients in the morning, but why don't you stop by with a contract after lunch tomorrow. I'll explain what I want, and we'll go from there."

Money was money, and he was right, she desperately needed the work. Whether she paid every bill or not, she and Jax still needed to eat. She swallowed her pride and nodded.

PART TWO

Contact

Chapter Nine

Aurora stole guiltily toward her mom's dresser. Actually the guest-room dresser, since what had been her mom and dad's bedroom set was at the consignment shop.

Her mom had trucked furniture from every room except the den, kitchen, guest room, and Aurora's bedroom to the shop, along with some of the silver and china and paintings. The store owner claimed everything would sell soon, but soon wasn't good enough. They needed money now. Her mom was doing her best to juggle the bills, but things kept getting worse. Her friends had turned their backs on her. Except for Ellie, who was funny, nice, and a good person.

Not good enough to help with the money problems, though. Aurora hated the circles under her mom's eyes and how skinny she'd gotten. Her clothes had looked old and frumpy before. Now they hung on her like hand-me-downs from a person two sizes too big. You'd have to be nuts to hire a woman looking that bad. Plus she kept trying for jobs she wasn't qualified for. She hadn't worked before, and the positions she applied for were for people with education and experience.

Aurora felt sorry for her, but her mom would die of embarrassment if she knew. So Aurora kept that to herself, along with lots of other stuff.

Like those new friends. They didn't go to her school. They were older and out of high school. She'd met them at the mall. Aurora thought they were cool, especially Mike, who had a wolf tattoo on his bicep. Afraid he wouldn't like her if he knew she was fourteen, she'd told him she was sixteen. He took her for rides on his motorcycle, and had kissed her lots of times. If her mom knew she'd probably flip out. Luckily she was too wrapped up in their financial troubles to notice any love bites, which Aurora hid with turtleneck sweaters and her mom's concealer.

She wasn't supposed to use her mom's stuff without asking and shouldn't snoop around her private papers, either, but this was an emergency. The card she wanted lay under the stack of legal documents on top of the dresser. Conscience pricking, Aurora grabbed it. She hurried from the room, then headed downstairs for the kitchen phone. If her mom came home early from job interview number ten thousand, Aurora would hang up to avoid any questions.

As she reached the main level she caught sight of the living room. The furniture had been gone for weeks, but every time she came downstairs the emptiness caught her by surprise, like a fist slugging her chest. For that reason she avoided it and the dining room as much as possible. Both always had been reserved for company, anyway.

The closer she got to the kitchen, the more scared she felt. "Think about what happened this afternoon," she said, her voice loud in the quiet.

When she'd walked in from school, her mom had been on the phone. Nothing strange about that, except that the man talking to her was from a collections company. Aurora knew this from the way her mom squeezed the receiver and worked her jaw. People from those companies were nasty. This guy was so mean, her mom had turned white and blinked a lot. Then she'd slammed down the phone. Her mom!

She wouldn't talk about the call, but Aurora knew she was upset. That probably hadn't helped with the job interview which she was late for. With all the stress on her shoulders, who could blame her for not landing a job?

At least the ad her mom had put in the paper had worked. Right off, the Mercedes her dad drove and everything in his office had sold. But it wasn't enough money to pay all the bills.

The way things were headed, they were going to lose their house. Stupid old Mr. Whitaker hadn't done anything but tell them to be patient. Well, patience wasn't working.

The realtor was coming by this weekend to get the papers signed and put up the For Sale sign.

Somebody had to do something!

Aurora knew it was up to her. Time to let Caroline Mason know just how much damage her lawsuit had caused.

Eyes on the carpet in order to avoid the stark

barrenness of the dining room, she strode into the kitchen.

Throat tight and mouth dry, she sat on a stool at the bar. Her fingers shook as she studied the card she'd brought downstairs, but she wouldn't let a bad case of the heebie-jeebies stop her.

She picked up the phone.

As Caroline and Jax walked through the kitchen door after school, the phone rang.

"Telephone!" Jax raced to answer it.

Too soon for potential renters to call. Caroline had placed an ad, offering the basement as an apartment, but it wouldn't run until tomorrow. Could be the jeweler. This morning she'd dropped off her wedding ring for an appraisal. Regardless of what Martin had advised about selling assets she was beyond desperate for money and beyond caring about the fit Mary Beth Mason and her lawyer might throw.

Breathless, stretching on her toes, Jax reached for the wall phone. "Mathon rethidence, Jax speaking."

Caroline glanced at the caller ID box. *Unavailable,* it read. Which meant it wasn't the jeweler. More likely a collection agency. If only they'd leave her alone. Lord help Jax if one of the nasty people who'd been nagging lately yelled at her.

Fearing for her daughter she snarled, "Give me the phone," and snatched the receiver from her astonished child's hand.

Jax shot her a terrified look. Then her face crumpled and she began to cry. Contrite and shocked at this ugly side of herself she'd never realized she had, Caroline stooped down to hug and comfort her, while she frowned into the phone. "Hello?"

At the other end, someone let out a small but audible breath.

Impatient to get off the phone, she never gave the collections man a chance. "How many times must I explain," she seethed in a barely civilized tone. "I recently lost my husband. I'm doing the best I can to pay my bills."

To her surprise and relief the caller hung up. Caroline patted herself on the back. If she'd realized rudeness worked, she'd have used it earlier.

She turned her full attention to her daughter, whose sobs had dwindled to sniffles. "I'm sorry, punkin. I didn't mean to frighten you. That was a terrible way to behave."

"'Th okay, Mama. You were scared it was another mean man, huh?"

Sometimes her daughter's perception amazed her. "Yes, I was. I didn't want him to say bad things to you."

Jax nodded her understanding, which only fueled Caroline's guilt. Two months ago she'd been an even-tempered, easy-going woman. Now her emotions were sharper and stronger and bigger than they should be, and she cried often and lost her temper over little things. Regardless, she'd always shielded Jax. Until now.

Cringing at the monster she'd turned into, she forced a loving smile and cheerful tone. "How about I make your favorite—cocoa with mini-marshmallows?"

"Could you?" Jax clapped her hands, then fixed

her with an adult-like sober face. "But aren't you afraid I'll spoil my pappite for dinner?"

"Appetite." Another change was that Caroline no longer enforced many of the strict rules she and Stephen had set for Jax, which now seemed overbearing and unnecessary. Regular meals? Sometimes. Too many sweets? No such thing. "Dinner's going to be late tonight," she said. "You need something to tide you over. Why don't you pull your step stool over to the stove and help me mix the cocoa? Then you can do your homework while I make dinner."

They mixed enough for two cups, one for her and one for Jax. Sitting at the kitchen table, adding marshmallows as needed, they shared the treat while Jax prattled happily about her day. Stephen's death hadn't affected her enthusiasm for school. She loved everything about first grade—her teacher, her friends, and even the homework. Caroline wished she could muster up even a thimbleful of that fervor, but the weight of her emotional and financial burdens had all but smothered her zest for life.

"When are we gonna call Aunt Becca? I mith Meg and Molly."

Caroline was still steamed at her sister and wasn't about to contact her. But how to explain? "They're very busy, but I know they love and miss you. Soon," she hedged. Maybe Jax would forget. She smiled. "Did Miss English read from *The Secret Garden* today?"

"Uh-huh, and I got to sit with Jenny and Ramona." Jax launched into a long monologue of what happened in the story. Half an hour later, after seconds on cocoa and plenty of more excited chatter, Caroline closed the marshmallow bag.

"I could sit and listen to you forever, but if I don't start dinner we'll never eat." She tweaked her daughter's nose. "And you, missy, had best do your homework." She nodded at the table where they sat. "Want to do it here?"

Without a moment's hesitation Jax shook her head. "At my desk." She loved using the pint-size "homework" desk Stephen had bought for her room when she started school last fall.

"Holler if you need help," Caroline said. She got busy, putting together her daughter's favorite meal—home-made macaroni and cheese and hot dogs, with peas on the side.

As she sprinkled the grated cheese into the steaming pasta, the phone rang. Wiping her hands on her jeans she moved to answer it. *Unavailable*, the LED said.

Not again. For the second time that afternoon she tensed. Anger flooded back as she grabbed the receiver. "Hello."

After exhaling a breath, the caller again hung up. Caroline frowned. Was this some pervert's weird version of a dirty phone call? Whatever, it was beyond irritating.

When the same thing happened five minutes later, she left the receiver on the counter. After about two minutes the annoying off-the-hook beeps stopped. She would've left it that way, but clients sometimes called in the evening. So shortly after kissing Jax good night and tucking her into bed—Caroline's bed—she replaced the receiver.

She now had sixteen long-term clients, Martin included, and despite working for hours today, there still was plenty to do. Not that she minded. She was earning good money, more than she ever had before. Not enough to cover the expenses, though. Renting out the basement would take care of the shortage. Once she rented it she'd move her office upstairs, and she ought to box up some of her things tonight, too. For now, work called. She was deep in the process of updating the website for a local retail store when the phone rang.

Engrossed in her work, she answered. "Caroline Mason."

A soft breath preceded the click and dial tone. Caroline narrowed her eyes. No caller ID on this phone, but she'd bet her left arm the one in the kitchen said, *Unavailable.*

Silent harasser, intimidator, sexual pervert—whoever it was, it had to stop. Enough was enough. Jaw set, she punched in star, followed by six nine. The phone rang.

Seconds later the person who was harassing her picked up. "Hello?"

The voice was female, possibly a teen. Caroline was both surprised and infuriated. The silly, thoughtless girl needed to be taught a lesson. "Who is this?" she demanded. She heard the same breathy sound that had preceded each hang-up, and quickly warned, "Don't you dare hang up. If you do, I'll call the police." A lie, but the girl didn't know that.

"I won't." She sounded scared, defeated and very young.

Caroline almost felt sorry for her, but she was angry. "If this is some kind of prank you and your friends are playing, please stop. You're scaring my daughter and me." She sensed the girl listening, and went on. "We're . . . we're alone now, and we've been through a lot."

She heard a sob. That touched her, and she softened. "Listen, I wasn't really going to contact the police. I just want you to *think* before you use the phone. Don't call strangers and hang up on them. You never know what they're dealing with."

Now the crying was louder.

Alarmed, Caroline sought to ease the girl's guilt. "There's no need to get upset. It's okay, honey. Let's both just put this behind us and forget it."

"I c-can't forget," the girl blubbered, "not ever. I h-hate you."

The weak tone hardly matched the ugly statement. Unable to fathom why this teenager hated her, Caroline frowned. Last time she'd attended church weeks ago, she'd caught a fourteen-year-old with her mother's car keys, about to back the minivan into the street. "Is this MacKenzie Sandoval? Because if it is, you got yourself into trouble for driving your mom's car without a license."

"I'd never do anything that dumb."

At least the crying had stopped. More confused than ever, Caroline pressed for information. "If you're not MacKenzie, who are you?"

"Someone you'll never meet. Just please, leave my mom and me alone."

"I don't understand. Who is this? What's your name?"

"I have to go now. Good-bye."

Caroline listened absently to the dial tone while she silently listed all the mothers with teenaged daughters she knew who had reason to hate her. Her mind came up blank.

The upstairs phone with the caller ID panel would give her the number. Setting aside her work, she climbed the basement stairs.

Two minutes later, having scrawled the number on a piece of paper, she returned to her computer and called up the online reverse directory.

"Is this some kind of sick joke?" Sweaty and tired from hours spent packing twenty years' worth of books, videos, CDs, and DVDs into moving boxes, Mary Beth sank onto the family room coffee table.

"I'm afraid not. Your daughter called and hung up three times yesterday."

Astounded, Mary Beth gaped into the phone. "What makes you think Aurora would call *you*? She doesn't have your number."

"Apparently she does. We have caller ID, that's how I know. It certainly wasn't your voice. She was a teenage girl."

"She wouldn't do that." But maybe those calls explained her daughter's sullen mood, the circles under her eyes, and her haunted expression this morning. Mary Beth had assumed she was upset about putting the house up for sale next week. Why hadn't she asked?

Because Aurora wasn't saying much these days. After that talk in her room a month ago things between them had improved, but only for a short while. She vacillated between warmth and resentment, leaving Mary Beth hurt and confused. She didn't know what to do, and every day her daughter slipped farther away from her. She'd failed as a wife and continued to fail as a mother.

Stop it. Lips compressed, she shoved away the despicable self-derision. Now was no time to stress about that, and she was not about to waste her precious time and energy talking to a horrible woman who happened also to be a lunatic. Tired, grumpy, and mad, Mary Beth scowled at the large box she'd just filled. "If you have concerns, have your lawyer contact mine."

"This isn't about you and me, it's about your daughter. She needs help."

Maybe so. That she couldn't supply whatever it was Aurora needed, stung. She let out her frustration and pain on Caroline. "Which is your fault, you filthy home-wrecker. I'd like to slap your face!"

She heard a gasp. "I'm no home-wrecker. Stephen cheated on me and Jax, too. It's hard enough dealing with the hurt and pain and struggling to put food on the table without your daughter harassing us."

Mary Beth set aside the harassment issue, which she didn't for one moment believe. "Food on the table?" She laughed without one scintilla of humor. "Oh, that's funny. Thanks to you, Stephen bled us dry. He spent our money on you and left us nothing. Do you hear me? *Nothing.* At least you have a job."

"Which doesn't begin to cover the bills. I'd sell off our assets, only thanks to you and your lawyer, everything is tangled up in the lawsuit."

Mary Beth opened her mouth, but Caroline cut her off.

"And don't you dare lie to me about your financial situation, Mary Beth Mason. Not while you sit in your big, expensive Nob Hill house, drive your expensive foreign car, and spend your fat insurance proceeds. What's the matter, did you have to lay off the chauffeur? Gee, that's a shame."

"I—"

"How much money can one woman and child spend?" Caroline pressed in a voice growing more shrill by the moment. "I can't believe your greed."

The audacity! "And I can't believe this phone call! Don't you ever call here again." Mary Beth clicked off, but that wasn't satisfying. She hurled the receiver at the opposite wall. It hit the polished wood wainscoting with a dull thud. Her hands shook, and then her entire body trembled.

Remorse quickly followed. She had to stop these childish outbursts. What if she'd broken the cordless phone? Money was tight and she wouldn't be able to replace it.

Mentally crossing her fingers she retrieved the poor receiver and tested it. The dial tone was fine, and the buttons worked. Thank heavens.

As for the small dent in the wainscoting . . . let the buyers, whoever they might be, deal with that.

Her mind spinning, she replaced the receiver in its cradle. The more she thought about what Caroline had said, the more the words made sense. Aurora probably *had* called her. Mary Beth kept the phone number, which she'd never intended to use, with a stack of legal papers.

But why call Caroline Mason? In order to contact the enemy, and Caroline *was* their enemy, she must've felt desperate. Mary Beth groaned. "What have you done, Aurora? Why didn't you come to me?"

Was talking to the person you were suing some kind of violation? It was in some legal cases. In this one, though? She didn't even consider contacting

Kevin about this. They hadn't met in person in weeks, and every time she called he seemed pressed for time and anxious to get off the phone—if he took her calls at all.

Resentment washed over her. Either Kevin Whitaker was a coward afraid to face her, or a traitor no longer interested in helping her. Or both. She loathed the man and wondered how she'd ever stood socializing with him or his revolting wife.

The things she'd put up with for Stephen. . . . And for what?

Her anger spiraled and she wanted to hurl something else at the wall. But she was through destroying their possessions. The best revenge was to make a new life, even if it meant moving to a two-bedroom apartment in a seedy neighborhood. Which, given that she had yet to find a decent job, might be where she and Aurora would end up.

She would channel her energy into packing and figuring out what to say when Aurora walked through the door after school.

It was time for another talk.

Chapter Ten

When the kitchen door opened at four-twenty, Mary Beth was waiting with her hands on her hips. "About time you walked in."

Aurora started, clearly not expecting her mother to be waiting at the door. "I stopped at Mrs. Perkins' house to interview for another after-school babysitting job. She says I can watch Chloe Saturday afternoon. If that works out, I'm hired." She dropped her backpack on the floor, then slipped out of her coat. When Mary Beth failed to greet the news with enthusiasm, she added, "I told you about that, Mother. Did you forget?"

"Must have."

Her daughter eyed her warily. Then sighed. "You're going to yell at me, aren't you? Can it at least wait 'til I get a snack? I'm starved."

Her upbeat mood and strong appetite were a nice change, but Mary Beth refused to let those positives side-track her. However, Aurora might be more willing to talk with a full stomach. Arms crossed, she nodded at the refrigerator. "Get something and sit down."

"Okay."

Aurora grabbed the cheese and sliced several thick slabs, which she set on a plate from the Mikasa Italian Countryside dinner set. Stephen had insisted on the plain, off-white dishes, which Mary Beth never had liked. Maybe she'd sell all twelve place settings and the serving pieces and buy something colorful—and cheap—with the proceeds, she thought while she pulled the crackers from the cabinet and Aurora poured herself a glass of milk.

They sat down at the table, Mary Beth with a mug of coffee left over from breakfast and reheated in the microwave. She would've preferred fresh, but her budget no longer allowed the waste. Her eyes on her plate and her mouth busy, Aurora ate as if she were alone.

Fine with Mary Beth, who after checking the time every five minutes in anticipation of Aurora's coming home, now needed a few extra minutes to compose herself. Why the upcoming conversation scared her, she couldn't say. But scared she was. She waited until her daughter's plate was nearly empty and the milk gone before she spoke.

"Anything you want to tell me?"

Color faded from Aurora's face. "Did Mrs. Jeffries call you?" The school principal. Her eyes widened. "She said she wouldn't. I didn't start that fight in homeroom, I swear. Kristi did."

"What fight?" Mary Beth asked, curiosity forcing a detour off the subject she intended to pursue—the phone calls to Caroline.

"You mean the principal didn't call?" Aurora looked as if she wished she could take back her words.

"What fight?" Mary Beth repeated.

Her daughter hung her head. "Kristi and some of her friends were saying mean stuff about us."

"Were they now?" Mary Beth wanted to strangle those former friends for making Aurora's life so miserable. She looked forward to transferring her daughter to a new school in the fall, where she hoped kids weren't so cruel. "What kind of stuff?"

Her daughter's face reddened. "I-I can't remember exactly, but I told her to be quiet. She laughed and stuck out her tongue. I *had* to slap her."

"I'd have to agree," Mary Beth said, amazed that her daughter's behavior didn't upset her. Two months ago it would have, but her perspective on life had changed. She wondered whether Aurora's new friends had stuck up for her, but that could wait. "This is about something else. The phone calls."

"What phone calls?" Aurora stalled, but her guilty look spoke volumes.

Mary Beth scrutinized her until she squirmed, all of two seconds.

Her daughter worked her napkin—they'd taken to using cloth because that was cheaper—between fidgety fingers. "How'd you find out?"

"Caroline called here today."

"She did?" Aurora shot her a horrified look. "God, Mom, I am so sorry." Her eyes filled. "I can't do anything right."

"You do lots of things right," Mary Beth soothed. "But why did you call her?"

"Because she's ruining our lives and I'm sick of her! I told her to leave us alone."

That seemed like normal enough behavior. Relieved that her daughter didn't need emergency counseling, which cost money they didn't have, Mary Beth let out a breath. "I've often thought about doing the same thing myself."

"You have?"

"Oh, yes, but I'm not as brave as you."

It was the right thing to say, for Aurora's shoulders straightened and she opened up. "I was really scared. The first time I called, her little girl answered. Then Caroline came on the line and I hung up." For a moment she was silent, then she added with a troubled frown, "I hate them, Mom, but they sounded really nice."

A thought struck Mary Beth, and she fiddled with her coffee mug while she figured out how to voice it without sounding as if she'd gone soft. She hadn't, and she still disliked Caroline Mason. "No need to feel guilty about your feelings, honey. They're suffering, too."

"Here's a key to the basement door," Caroline told Delia, a twenty-one-year-old computer geek with purple-tipped hair, with a mixture of relief and trepidation. Aside from her college dorm she'd never lived with strangers before, let alone a woman who wore a dog collar for jewelry. But she needed the money, and Delia wanted to move in right away.

"And here's my check for the first month's rent, right on time."

Which would go into the bank right away, before the mortgage payment, due today, April first, bounced. Thanks to Delia's rent check and the money the jeweler had offered for the wedding ring—not as much as Stephen had paid, but better than nothing—Caroline had mailed the payment knowing it wouldn't bounce. She still was one payment behind, but meant to catch up soon. Somehow.

"I cleared the top shelf in the refrigerator for you," she told Delia.

"Thanks, Mrs. M., but I don't have any groceries today."

"Let's try your key, then, and make sure it works."

They went through the backyard to the door on the side of the house. Caroline had traded her website skills for moving help and had transferred her office to a small room off the den, and relocated a bedroom set from one of the upstairs guest rooms into her old office. She also had shuffled Stephen's office furniture and equipment into the storage area of the garage, giving Delia an extra, unfurnished room.

"Sure is a beautiful house," Delia said as she inserted the key.

Caroline glanced at her muddy combat boots and wondered how long the off-white carpet would stay clean. "Would you mind wiping your feet?" she asked as Delia opened the door.

"Oh. Right." Delia scraped her shoes on the welcome mat. "With the rain and all . . ." She shrugged.

"No problem," Caroline said. "Now that we know the key works, I'll leave you to unpack and get settled. I'll be out running errands. Do you need anything from me before I go?"

"Nope. I gotta leave for work at two-thirty. Will you be back by then?"

"I doubt it," Caroline said. It was a busy day. She planned to stop at the jeweler's to pick up the check, then make a deposit at the bank. After that, catch the ferry and meet Martin for lunch. They'd missed their usual coffee date, as Delia was moving in and Martin had a meeting with clients. "I'll be gone until I bring Jax home from school. What time will you be home tonight?"

Her tenant shot her a surly look that reminded her of a defiant teenager. "Why do you want to know?"

Only nine years older, Caroline felt eons more mature. She didn't want to start off on bad footing, and she made a mental note to give this woman plenty of space. "Because late-night noises scare me."

Even when Stephen had been alive, when he traveled, she'd worried. And that was with an expensive security system, something she no longer could afford. "I don't want to mistake you for a prowler."

Delia nodded her understanding. "My shift ends at eleven, and I'll probably go clubbing after, so it'll be late."

Allowing Caroline and Jax to spend their evening alone. This was going to work out fine. She smiled. "All right then, see you tomorrow."

An hour later Caroline and Martin sat across from each other at a bustling café near the ferry terminal. It was pathetic how much she'd looked forward to this. But when your only social life was with your lawyer, who had become a friend . . .

"How's the new tenant?" he asked after they ordered.

Caroline didn't care much for Delia, but at least she could cover the gap between what Caroline could afford and the mortgage payment. "She's not exactly what I had in mind when I placed the ad, but I'm relieved to have her," she said over the noise. "She works swing shift, which means Jax and I have the house to ourselves every night and at breakfast."

"Sounds ideal."

She nodded. "The best thing about renting the basement is the monthly check and making the mortgage payment on time." Fearing a stern lecture, she didn't mention that she'd sold her wedding ring.

"How was Jax's field trip to the Children's Museum?"

The school outing had cost Caroline precious earnings, but she couldn't begrudge her daughter this small pleasure. "We both had fun."

"You needed that. Has she moved back into her own bed yet?"

He asked the same question every week. Caroline didn't mind. She looked forward to reclaiming the bedroom she was slowly redecorating to suit her tastes. "Not yet, but we're talking about it. I may resort to offering her candy or a toy if she sleeps in her own bed."

"Bribery, eh?" His eyes twinkled. "Will that work?"

"I'll let you know."

A harried, middle-aged waitress delivered their sandwiches and they dug in.

"Your dad still planning to visit during Jax's spring break?" Martin asked a moment later.

Caroline nodded. "The week after next. Since the Florida tourist season has started he won't stay long, but a short visit is better than none." She fiddled with the toothpick that held her club sandwich together. "Before this mess, we vacationed in Florida every spring, along with Becca and her family. Dad worked during the day and spent the evenings with us."

His coming here meant time away from earning his livelihood. She felt bad about that, but couldn't wait to see him. "What about your parents?" she asked. "Where do they live?"

If the personal question bothered Martin he didn't let on. "My father is a foreign diplomat. At the moment my parents live in Kenya. My brother and his family are in Tokyo."

"Wow. And I thought Florida and Chicago were far away." She liked knowing this little bit about his family. "How often do you see them?"

"Not often enough."

Caroline wondered what he did on holidays—did he spend them alone, and was he lonely? But she'd pried enough.

They finished eating in companionable silence. At last Martin wiped his mouth and set his napkin next to his plate. He waited for Caroline to finish before pushing his plate aside. The man looked gangly and less than refined, but he had impeccable manners as well as a sharp mind.

"I expect you want to know what I learned about Mary Beth Mason's financial status." Reaching into the briefcase he'd set on the floor, he slid out the now-thick file and set it in front of him.

Caroline had told him about Aurora's phone call last week and the subsequent unpleasant conversation with Mary Beth. "This should be interesting," she said.

"And illuminating." Martin opened the file. "Credit reports show that she owes two point five million on the house. She's two months behind on the payments. Credit card debt is high and also unpaid, as are some of the utilities." He glanced at Caroline. "Mary Beth Mason is in serious financial trouble."

"Same as me," Caroline said, while the other woman's words, which she couldn't seem to forget even after a week, rang fresh in her mind. *Thanks to you, Stephen bled us dry. He spent our money on you and left us nothing. Do you hear me? Nothing.* She hadn't been lying. "I suppose that should make me feel better, but it doesn't. I can't believe I'm saying this, but I actually feel sorry for the woman. And now I know she's suing me out of more than a need for revenge."

The attorney's expressive eyes narrowed. "Make no mistake, revenge is a big part of this. Speaking not as a lawyer but as a human being, I certainly understand her need to hurt you, and yours to do the same to her."

"I'm not trying to hurt Mary Beth. I just want what's mine."

"Sure about that?" Martin's slightly raised eyebrows made Caroline think.

"Maybe I *do* want to hurt her," she admitted. "That makes me a bad person, huh?"

"It makes you human."

His gentle smile absolved her and brightened her spirits. "You really seem to understand people."

"All part of good lawyering."

He was a good man, too. "Why haven't you remarried?" she asked, horrified at her audacity.

"Haven't met the right woman."

"If you don't date, you never will."

"What makes you think I don't date?"

The thought of him taking some woman out bothered Caroline, but she didn't know why. The man deserved happiness. "Is she nice? Because you should be with someone wonderful."

"Thanks, and back at you."

Caroline shook her head. "It's way too early for me. I'm still mourning, while hating the very man I mourn." There was nothing funny about that, but she laughed. "If that makes sense."

"It does. But someday you'll be ready to move on."

"I don't know. I don't think I'll ever be able to trust a male again. Aside from my father, and maybe Hank. And you."

He smiled. "I appreciate that and promise not to abuse your trust. How's the ulcer?"

Caroline touched her stomach, which was blissfully pain-free. "Almost healed. Physically, I feel better every day."

"You certainly look healthy. You've gained weight and there are roses in your cheeks."

As compliments went, it wasn't much. But Caroline hadn't heard anything close to flattery in ages. She flushed. "Having the money to make the mortgage payment will do that to a woman."

Chapter Eleven

As Jax skipped toward the gorilla habitat at the Woodland Park Zoo in Seattle, Caroline hooked her arm through her father's. After days of nonstop rain, the sky had cleared. This was a beautiful April Sunday, sunny and unseasonably warm, perfect for the last day of spring break and his last day in town.

"I'm so glad you came, Dad. But four days is such a short visit, and you traveled such a long way. I wish you'd stay longer."

"You know I can't, not with tourist season heating up. Sam's a competent partner, but he can only handle so much by himself."

Her father hadn't meant to stir up guilt, Caroline knew, but she felt it just the same. "I wish we could have come to Florida instead, the way we used to . . ."

"No worries," he said, giving her arm an affectionate squeeze. "I like the Northwest." His paternal gaze lit on her face. "You look good—much better than last time I saw you."

"Thanks, Dad."

Two sets of parents and their excited children

passed by. Jax, who was a few yards ahead, turned to stare at them. Caroline smiled. "The past few months have been awful, but I think I'll survive. Especially now that I have a tenant to help with expenses."

Her father had met Delia, and his pained expression said he didn't much like her. Caroline understood. But . . . "Don't tell me you disapprove of what I've done," she said. "Because without her rent check, I can't make ends meet."

"I think turning the basement into an apartment is a fine idea. But Delia seems . . ." he shook his head as if searching for words, "young to be out on her own. And that awful music she plays so loudly . . ."

She liked rap and heavy metal, and she liked them loud. "I'm planning to talk to her about that," Caroline said. "Believe it or not, she's twenty-one. At that age I was married."

And what a mistake that had turned out to be. Neither Caroline nor her father said so, but the sentiment hung in the air. They both were silent, their footsteps thudding dully over the packed dirt path.

Suddenly Jax spun around and raced toward them, pigtails flying. "Hurry up, Mommy and Grandpa." She pointed at the gorillas sunning themselves in the savannah habitat that mirrored their native home, then grabbed Caroline's free hand and tugged her and her grandfather forward. "Look, a mommy and baby!" she shouted, so excited she jumped up and down.

Her enthusiasm was contagious. Caroline and her father grinned as they stood beside her, catching whiffs of the pungent animal scents that mark all zoos, and watching the great apes' human-like activities.

"Are they a family?" Jax asked, pointing at two gorillas, one grooming the other.

Caroline hadn't a clue. "I think they must be," she replied. "They certainly seem close."

Jax was silent a moment. Then, her small forehead furrowed, she glanced at Caroline. "Are you still mad at Aunt Becca?" she asked, all traces of her lisp gone.

Eyes on her daughter, Caroline felt rather than saw her father's speculative gaze. He wanted to know, too. This was the second time Jax had asked about Becca, and Caroline still didn't know what to say. "You asked me that before, remember?" she said, dodging the question.

"Well, they didn't come with Grandpa to visit." The stubborn set of Jax's jaw reminded Caroline of Stephen. "I want to play with my cousins."

Now Caroline looked at her father, his stricken expression letting her know the standoff between his daughters was painful to him.

"I know you do, honey," Caroline soothed.

"You could call them," her father said.

Jax stared at Caroline, her eyes hopeful. "Could we?"

Despite that longing look and the responding ache in her own heart, Caroline refused to make the first move. "I wouldn't want to bother them right now," she said, shooting her father a don't-you-dare-butt-in look. "April is a busy time at their restaurant."

Which was partly true, but Becca always had made time for spring vacation in Florida, even if Hank stayed behind to run the restaurant. Often Stephen had done the same, joining the family for a day or two before leaving to work with one client or another. Or so he claimed. The weasel probably had spent the time with Mary Beth and Aurora instead.

The thought put a sour taste in Caroline's mouth and darkened her mood. Refusing to go there on such a perfect spring day, she turned her thoughts to Florida and Becca. Spending a week in the hot, humid climate relaxed them both, and they managed to get along, their kids splashing in the sometimes-chilly ocean waves while they lazed under big umbrellas and sipped margaritas.

Those days were over.

"Look, a caterpillar!" Delighted, Jax squatted down to study the fuzzy creature inching over the grass.

Thanking her lucky stars for the distraction, Caroline moved a few feet away with her father, where they could see Jax but talk out of earshot.

"Other than Becca and Hank, we don't have any family, Caro," he advised. "For Jax's sake, you ought to mend the fences."

Her jaw dropped. "Have you forgotten what my interfering sister did? And after she gave her word to keep her mouth shut." Caroline still couldn't believe Becca had gone against her wishes. "God knows what she'll say next."

Jax shot her a puzzled look and she realized she'd raised her voice. She forced a reassuring smile before turning back to her father.

"Becca learned her lesson," he said in a low voice. "She won't say another word on the subject."

Not believing that for one minute, Caroline eyed her father. "What makes you think so?"

"She promised me."

"Last time she promised *me*, she broke her word. I'm skeptical. Besides, she hasn't even bothered to apologize."

"You've always been the mature one," he pointed out. "You could take the first step."

Caroline shook her head. "Becca was in the wrong, and *she* should contact *me*. Now could we please drop the subject? This is your last day here, and I'd like to enjoy what's left of it."

Sitting on the back patio of what was soon to be someone else's home, Mary Beth filled her and Ellie's highball glasses with Glenfiddich, the last bottle of the expensive scotch in the house. She didn't drink often, and never before dinner, but this afternoon called for alcohol—and plenty of it. She set the bottle and Ellie's glass on the glass-top, wrought-iron side table between them, then settled herself on the padded wrought-iron chair and waited for her friend's toast.

Squinting against the lovely late-afternoon sun, Ellie raised her glass. "Here's to the sale of your house. Congratulations, and may this be the start of a new and better life."

Mary Beth copied the gesture, but couldn't summon much enthusiasm. The offer had come early this afternoon and hadn't quite sunk in. She'd listed the house on March thirty-first, a mere twenty days ago. Things were happening too fast!

She shot a wistful look at the gazebo Stephen had insisted they build, then beyond to the hills and graceful maple, Spanish fir and acadia trees and the homes nestled among them. A view she wasn't likely to have in any two-bedroom apartment she could afford. She took a healthy swig of her drink. The burning sensation that warmed her throat and belly felt good. "I don't know about better, but it sure will be different," she said, smacking her lips. "I just wish Aurora were here." She sipped again.

"You have the number of the hotel. Why don't you leave a message for her at the front desk?" Ellie suggested.

"Because I don't want to ruin her trip."

It was spring break and her daughter had left this morning for Hawaii, a vacation nanny for Chloe, the five-year-old she babysat. Nice that her daughter got to travel, even if it was as menial labor. So different from last year when they'd traveled to Cabo for break, Stephen taking a rare full week off for the trip. What had he told Caroline, and how had he explained his tan?

Why am I thinking about her? Mary Beth frowned. Lately she often wondered how the other woman was doing and feeling, and how her little girl was getting along, but just now she was sick to death of Caroline and the mess she'd caused. She solemnly drained the glass.

"Hey, this is supposed to be a celebration," Ellie reminded her. "How much will you net on the sale?"

"I don't exactly know, but after I pay the realtor commission and pay off the credit cards and other bills I'll be lucky to end up with a few thousand dollars." Glum, Mary Beth refilled her glass and drank. "Not much to show for twenty years of my life."

"Putting this in a positive light, let's count your blessings," Ellie said, but she, too, looked somber.

"At least the collectors will stop harassing you. And you'll finally be out from under the mortgage. You don't need a foreclosure blackening your credit."

"It's already black enough," Mary Beth commented. "But those are things to be grateful for." Her brain felt pleasantly fuzzy. Her wayward thoughts turned again to Caroline, who was also burdened with too many bills. She glanced at Ellie. "Because of the lawsuit, Caroline can't sell her house."

"Did you ever stop to think that if she files for bankruptcy, you're, pardon my clichéd tongue, up shit creek without a paddle?"

"Nope, never did." Mary Beth gulped more scotch, which she no longer could taste. "Kevin hasn't mentioned that, either." She started to shake her head, but that made things spin. "Funny how you're a better lawyer than he is and you don't even have a law degree." So funny, she giggled. "Maybe I'll fire him and hire you."

"Much as I hate to say this, Kevin Whitaker is your best hope. He knows your case in and out. You're meeting with him tomorrow, to review the sale agreement, right? Ask what happens if Caroline files for bankruptcy."

The realtor had delivered copies of everything to the attorney, and Mary Beth had requested a face-to-face conference. "Okay. Did I tell you we're meeting at the Nob Hill Café on Taylor Street instead of his office? Guess I no longer fit with the client image preferred in the hallowed firm of Jones, Westin and Hawkins." Not that she wanted inside those pretentious doors. But it would have been nice if she'd been the one to suggest a different meeting place. "I'm making him pay for lunch.

Judgmental old poop." Liking the sound of that, she repeated it. "Old poop, old poop."

Ellie slanted her a warning look. "If you don't slow down on that stuff, I'll be scraping you off these terra-cotta bricks."

"I don't care." Mary Beth propped her legs on the matching ottoman and waved her glass airily, spilling what was left of the contents on her blouse. "Oops," she said, reaching for the scotch.

"You're sloshed." Ellie snatched the bottle from her hands. "How about we put away this stuff and eat dinner? I'll order a pizza. My treat."

"Not hungry, and I *want* to get drunk."

"You'll be sorry in the morning."

"I don't care."

"Well, I still have to pack tonight for my trip to Montana *and* get up for work tomorrow. I'm staying sober, and I need food." Ellie returned the bottle to the table, then pulled her cell phone from her purse. "What do you want on your pizza?"

"Glenfiddich." Now that was hilarious. Mary Beth broke into laughter.

Ellie frowned as she made the call. "It'll be an hour if we wait for delivery and twenty minutes if I pick up," she said. "I'll go get it. You sit tight."

"I'm not goin' anyplace. Except the little girls' room." Mary Beth grabbed the bottle, pushed out of her chair and followed her friend inside.

When she finished in the bathroom, Ellie was gone.

The sun was about to set. No longer in the mood to sit outside, especially alone in the dark, she sank onto a bar stool and poured another drink. As she sipped, her attention roved over the state-of-the-art kitchen where she'd lovingly prepared meals for Stephen and Aurora. So many gadgets, pots and pans, and dishes, so many spices and cookbooks. She hadn't started packing up this room, and that would take time. "Weeks," she muttered, her voice loud in the stillness.

It was too quiet in here. Loneliness settled heavily in her chest. Why hadn't Ellie taken her along? She wasn't *that* drunk. Not yet.

As she nursed her drink, her gaze settled on the phone. Suddenly she wanted to talk to someone. Caroline Mason's number was in her purse, which just happened to be sitting on the other stool. She reached for it, almost losing her balance.

"I have nothing to say to That Woman," she argued as she pawed through the contents, tossing them aside. She pulled out the card with Caroline's number on it. "This is crazy."

And for some reason, terribly important.

She reached for the phone.

Chapter Twelve

It had been a rotten day, and Caroline felt raw and too distracted to sit at the computer. Cleaning always made her feel better, and since she'd let the housekeeper go . . . She grabbed a sponge, rags, and cleanser and headed for the main floor powder room. There was something soothing in the routine, physical effort, not to mention the immediate, positive results.

And Lord knew, she needed something positive. She scattered cleanser over the light green ceramic sink. Poor Jax was sick. Wouldn't you know she'd catch something the day spring vacation ended. Within hours of putting her grandpa on the plane, she'd complained of a sore throat. Strep, the doctor said at their Monday afternoon appointment. In order to pay for the unexpected expense of her child's prescription—Caroline no longer carried medical insurance—she'd scaled back on groceries. They'd arrived home from the pharmacy just before dinner, Jax cranky and miserable, and Caroline frazzled.

In no mood to cook dinner, thankful she'd planned for last night's casserole to last two nights, she'd grabbed the container of leftovers to microwave. To her shock there was barely any casserole left, not even enough for Jax. A dirty spoon lay in the dish.

Only one person could've done that. Delia.

Caroline attacked the sink with her sponge. This wasn't the first time Delia had eaten their food, but the behavior had stopped during her father's visit. She'd lived here nineteen days now, and enough was enough. First thing tomorrow Caroline meant to have a serious chat with her—if she could catch her. Delia's hours made that tough. But with Jax home sick, Caroline would be here whenever her tenant wandered into the kitchen. She turned on the water, rinsed away the soap, and wrung out the sponge.

And the music! Caroline had tacked messages on the door, asking her to please lower the volume. So far the decibel level hadn't changed, and she was tired of the middle-of-the-night, loud music that sometimes woke her and Jax. It was lucky they were on a large lot with plenty of trees buffering both sides of the house, or the neighbors would be having fits.

The music had better not wake Jax tonight. It had taken Caroline forever to get her to sleep. As always when she was sick, she wanted her daddy. Her heartbroken sobs for Stephen had chafed Caroline's still-raw wounds. Hostility, anger, and grief had bubbled up as they hadn't for weeks, until she'd cried right along with Jax.

She polished the mirror next, glancing at her reflection. She wasn't crying now, but she looked and felt as if she'd been through a tornado. Dark circles under her eyes, hair limp and dull. She'd always admired her complexion, which was smooth and porcelain-like. Now it was blotchy and ugly.

God, she was a mess. Thank heavens no one would see her tonight. Still, it was enough to drive a woman to drink—if only she could afford a bottle of wine. She gave herself a rueful smile. Unfortunately there wasn't a bottle to be had. No longer in a cleaning mood, she gave the toilet a lackluster swipe.

Wait. . . . Delia had wine.

Payback time. Feeling guilty for what she was about to do, but also in the right, Caroline marched angrily toward the kitchen, detouring first at the laundry room, where she dropped off the cleaning supplies. In the kitchen she opened the fridge. Delia's shelf held nothing but a half-empty bottle of wine cooler, three beers, several half-eaten tubs of chip dip, and a jar of processed cheese spread. No wonder she stole Caroline's food.

Wine cooler ranked at the bottom of her list of preferred wines, but she was desperate enough to drink anything. Maybe if she used one of the good wine goblets it'd taste better. Inside the sparkling crystal the pale red liquid certainly looked better. As Caroline started for the family room to prop up her feet and relax, the phone rang. She glanced at the ID pad. *Unavailable.* Good, a collections person. Itching to tell somebody off, she snatched up the phone—this one was cordless—and continued to the den.

"So pleased you called," she said, chuckling gleefully to herself.

"Caroline? I's Mary Beth Mason. How're you?"

Caroline was more than surprised, but the slurred voice tipped her off. "You're drunk," she said. She flipped on a lamp and settled into a chair.

"That I am. I sold the house this afternoon. Couldn't make the payments."

Something Caroline easily identified with. "Oh. I'm sorry."

"Not as sorry as I am. Aurora's gonna be so mad when I tell her. But then, she's always mad."

"She doesn't know?"

"It's spring break. She's in Hawaii."

"Hawaii, huh?" Caroline sipped her wine, which tasted like cherry Kool Aid. Wrinkling her nose, she set the glass on the side table, slipped off her sneakers, and tucked her feet under her. "You can't be that bad off."

"She's working as a nanny." Mary Beth laughed. "Can you b'lieve it? My daughter, who never wanted for anything."

"Nothing wrong with working," Caroline said. "Why don't you call her?" *And leave me alone.* Man, she wished that wine tasted better. She thought about hanging up, but for some reason didn't.

"Tha's what Ellie said—call her. But I don' wanna ruin her fun."

"Who's Ellie?"

"My bes' friend. She's leavin' after work tomorrow to visit her sister in Montana. No Ellie, no Aurora—'s gonna be a rough week."

"I know about lonesome. My father just left after a short visit, and I don't have any close girlfriends." For some reason Caroline thought of Becca. As a pre-teen her sister had been her friend, but once puberty had hit. . . . She sighed. "You're lucky."

"Not really. Ellie's the only one who hasn't ditched me. Everybody else treats me like dirt. But I don' wanna cry in my scotch. How's your kid—what was her name—doing?"

"Jax. She was okay until today. She has strep and when she's sick, she wants her father."

"Aurora was like that, too. Now she doesn't need anybody. Certainly not me. She'll hate moving into a two-bedroom apartment. But then, so will I. God, it'll be so small."

Caroline genuinely felt for her. She shook her head. "I'm sorry, Mary Beth."

"Tha's the second time you apologized. Forget sorry. Why don't you just pay me what you owe me?"

She didn't sound angry, simply hurt and confused.

"I don't have any money. The house and vacation property are heavily mortgaged. There isn't much else."

"Oh well, thought I'd check."

She went silent. Caroline wondered if she were taking a drink. "But hey," she said, "if you dropped your lawsuit I could sell the vacation property, Stephen's car, and his office things. I'd split the net amount with you." Selling that stuff wouldn't bring in much, but might get rid of Mary Beth and this mess.

"Nice try, but nope. Hol' on while I freshen my drink."

Caroline heard the liquid slosh noisily into Mary Beth's glass. She decided to give the wine cooler another chance. Still awful, but she needed it.

"I'm back," Mary Beth said. "Why d'you s'pose Stephen did this to us?"

"I've asked myself that a million times. I don't know, except that he was a jerk." Even so, Caroline still loved him. Not that she'd take him back if he were alive. She'd probably shoot him. Yet she couldn't force her heart to hate the man.

"There's something we agree on. I like you, Caroline. I'm also jealous of you."

"Why? We're broke, too."

"Because you still have your house."

"Barely. I'm a month behind with the mortgage, and I took in a tenant I can't stand."

"A tenant, eh? Thas' a clever idea."

"You wouldn't say so if you met Delia. She's a twenty- year-old punk rocker who steals our food and plays loud music in the middle of the night."

"Sometimes Aurora does that. She doesn't steal food, though. You shoulda rented to somebody older."

"I was in a hurry."

"I'll bet Aurora'd like Delia," Mary Beth said, sounding mournful.

Caroline had often thought of the teenage girl. "I've been wondering about her. She doing okay?"

"We've had a few good conversations, but mostly she ignores me." She sniffled. "I miss her."

Great, now Mary Beth was crying. There was nothing worse than a drunk who felt sorry for herself. Caroline glanced at the empty fireplace and shook her head. "She'll come around."

"You think?"

"Sure I do." Caroline hesitated. That wasn't quite true. She cleared her throat. "Counseling might help, though, talking to a neutral person who'll listen without judging her."

"Can't afford that. I do know that she's sorry about those calls to you. And she's made a new group of friends, which tells me she's okay mentally."

"That sounds positive."

"Uh-oh, there's my door. Probably Ellie with the pizza. Le's talk again sometime."

"I'm not sure that's a good idea," Caroline said. "But this has been . . . interesting."

"Sure has. 'Bye."

She hung up wondering what Mary Beth would think about the conversation once she sobered up. She'd probably kick herself. Caroline smiled as she rose from her chair. Odd, but she wasn't as angry as she'd been before the call.

She emptied her glass in the kitchen sink, stuck it in the dishwasher, and headed upstairs.

Mary Beth hadn't been out to eat in months. Too bad she had to waste the momentous occasion with the despicable Kevin Whitaker, but thank God he'd wanted a lunch meeting instead of breakfast. She'd been too hung over this morning for breakfast.

Now the pounding in her head had dulled somewhat and her stomach had settled enough to eat. She'd always liked Italian food, and the Nob Hill Café specialized in that very thing. Kevin had reserved a table in the Vicino Room which, with its dark green walls and subdued atmosphere, was a good place to talk.

He was already seated at the table, sipping coffee,

eyes on the documents before him. He didn't see her yet.

For some reason nervous, she walked toward him with her head high, trying to look as if she still belonged in her St. John suit and tan Cole Haan pumps and matching bag. Never mind that she'd pulled her hair into a twist because it needed cutting or that the suit was last year's and two sizes too big. It was a classy outfit, and anybody with a shred of taste knew it.

She was nearly at the table when Kevin at last looked up and saw her. His eyes widened with surprise, and she knew the outfit and her demeanor had indeed impressed him. Satisfaction rolled through her.

Gentleman that he was, he stood to greet her. "Good to see you," he said, shooting a perfunctory smile at her shoulder instead of her face. "It's been awhile."

For over two months the man had all but brushed her aside as if they'd never met or socialized. "Your choice, not mine," she managed sweetly, while anger seethed through her.

Now he looked directly at her, his expression hurt. "That's not fair, Mary Beth. I'm doing everything possible to help you, but you know I'm a very busy man." He leaned toward her as if about to share a confidence. "I'm not charging you one penny, either."

She waved her hand dismissively. "I know all that, and I appreciate your not charging me." She also knew that if Stephen were alive Kevin would have accommodated her every need and whim without a moment's hesitation.

He sniffed. "Do I smell scotch?"

Horrified, Mary Beth shook her head. "New mouth wash," she fabricated, wishing she had a breath mint. She also wished she could go back and undo some of last night—getting drunk was the least of it. She'd called Caroline Mason. Good God. Cringing, she sat down. "Could I get some coffee?"

After the server filled her cup and took their lunch orders, Kevin started the meeting.

"The real estate agreement looks fine, but I wish you'd let me look at it before you signed."

That scared her. "My realtor and I read through it. We thought it looked okay. Did I make a mistake?"

"Nothing that can't be fixed. I've made a few changes for you to initial. I'll make sure the amended documents are delivered to the realtor this afternoon." He slipped an expensive gold pen from the inside pocket of his custom-tailored suit. "If you'll just initial, then sign where indicated—"

"After what Stephen pulled, I'm through blindly signing documents," Mary Beth said. "I want to review and discuss each of your changes." She shot Kevin a level look. "And I want your word that what we discuss here will not be shared with anyone, including your wife."

Now he looked as if she'd stabbed him through the heart. The man should have been an actor. "You know I don't talk to Pam about my clients' business."

"Well she certainly knows a lot about my finances. Or so I've heard through the grapevine. She hasn't said a word to my face about that, but then lately, she hasn't talked to me about anything, period. Guess she's as busy as you."

Mary Beth couldn't believe her mouth. Where had this new bold person come from?

Kevin flushed. "Oh, she is."

Making the man squirm was new to her and surprisingly gratifying, but not the purpose of this meeting. "Never mind." She nodded at the papers. "I'm sure you want to get back to the office as soon as possible. Let's get on with this."

Forty-five minutes later, after she understood the changes Kevin wanted, which included the closing date and a clause regarding the appliances and deck furniture, and after she'd finished her pumpkin ravioli in cream sauce, she initialed the changes and added her signature where Kevin wanted it.

"That concludes that," he said, slipping the documents into his briefcase.

"Dessert?" asked the waiter, a thirty-something male who'd kept a careful eye on them since pouring Mary Beth's coffee.

Kevin patted his round stomach. "None for me, thanks."

Mary Beth was full, but a free meal was a rare treat. Besides she really could stand to gain back a few pounds. "I'd like a tiramisu," she said.

Kevin nodded politely, his face pained. Clearly he wanted to get back to the office.

"There is one more thing I want to discuss," she said after the waiter left. "What if Caroline Mason declares bankruptcy? She can't sell anything for cash and she's as broke as me, so isn't that a possibility?"

"What are you getting at?"

"If that happens I won't collect any of the money she owes me."

"Depends on what the bank nets after the foreclosure sale. You could end up with something, but not what you deserve."

Mary Beth squinted, trying her best to recall last night's rather fuzzy conversation. "I think she'd prefer to sell off some of her assets and split the proceeds with me."

Kevin looked down his nose at her, as if she were a child. "Have you forgotten that this woman is as upset with you as you are with her? From what her attorney says, she'd rather lose everything than pay you a dime."

"People change their minds, you know. She offered to split what she nets from the vacation property, Stephen's car, and his office stuff." Mary Beth winked, something she never did. "But I think she's desperate enough that some good lawyerly persuasion from you might convince her to give up two-thirds."

"You heard from her lawyer?" His shock was almost comical.

Mary Beth stifled a grin. "Not him. Caroline. We had a phone conversation."

"She *called* you, and you didn't tell me?"

"I'm telling you now. It only happened last night." Mary Beth was tempted to lie, but lies only caused pain. "I called her." No need to mention the motivating role scotch had played.

"You actually had a civilized conversation?"

"That surprised me, too, but we did." Mary Beth had enjoyed talking with her nemesis, mainly because Caroline was the only one who truly understood what she was going through. That didn't mean she liked the woman. She didn't, and never could. "She's taken in a renter to help with the mortgage payments, but like me she's behind on everything." She glanced at Kevin. "What do you think?"

He pursed his lips thoughtfully. "You never know, and since you did talk rationally to each other . . ." He shrugged. "I'll contact Martin Cheswick right away. But Caroline Mason is your enemy. I wouldn't get your hopes up."

"I won't," Mary Beth said. But she couldn't help feeling optimistic.

Chapter Thirteen

Early in the afternoon following the strange but pleasant phone call from Mary Beth, Caroline tiptoed downstairs after checking on Jax. They'd had a rough night, but now her young daughter lay peacefully asleep. For once in her own bed. She seemed to find comfort in the familiar wallpaper, stuffed animals, and her desk—something that would interest Martin next time he asked. Not their usual Wednesday, which was tomorrow, because Jax would still be home from school. Caroline hated to miss their get-together, but she didn't have much choice.

The real test for Jax would come tonight, when the medicine kicked in and she started to feel better. Then who knew whether she'd stay in her bed or migrate back to Caroline's.

Caroline didn't care as along as Jax let her sleep. She was exhausted, and now her throat was scratchy. She hoped to God she didn't have strep.

As she reached the main floor she heard noises in the kitchen, meaning Delia was up. Now was the perfect time to confront her. As Caroline strode across the foyer male laughter rang out. Surprised and shocked, she clipped toward the kitchen. She stopped in the threshold and took in the scene.

Wearing a T-shirt that barely covered her pink panties, her tenant was straddling a shirtless, shoeless male and kissing him passionately. Two dirty bowls and a box of Caroline's cornflakes and milk sat on the kitchen table, together with a lighter and an open pack of cigarettes.

Caroline did not allow cigarettes in her house, and Delia knew it. Off all the. . . . Incensed, she marched into the room. "Excuse me."

Wide-eyed, Delia hopped off the man's lap. "What are *you* doing here?" she asked as she tugged at the hem of her T-shirt. She wasn't wearing a bra.

"This is my house," Caroline snapped. "I live here." She glared at the sleep-rumpled man. "Who're you?"

"This is Bender. Meet my landlady, Caroline Mason."

"Howdy." Bender shot Caroline a blatantly sexy look—ugh—then reached for the cigarettes. She snatched up the pack before he could. "I don't allow smoking in my home." She shot a chilly frown at her tight-lipped tenant. "Delia knows that."

She waited for an apology but received a dirty look instead.

Looking remorseful, Bender scratched the back of his neck. "Sorry. I'm trying to quit." He shoved the matches into his jeans pocket, then stretched out his hand. Caroline dropped the cigarettes into his open palm. "I'll have a smoke outside," he told Delia. He made a fast exit out the back door.

"I'll come with you—" Delia started.

Caroline stepped between her and the door. "Not until we have a little chat."

The tenant narrowed her eyes and crossed her arms, reminding Caroline that she didn't respond well to authority. She sucked in a calming breath, but she was tired and grouchy and beneath her tenuous composure her anger smoldered.

"I don't want strange men traipsing through the kitchen," she said in what seemed to her a reasonable tone. "I have a seven-year-old daughter."

"I paid my rent, so it's my kitchen, too." Delia leaned her narrow hip against the stove. "Jeez, he wasn't naked or anything."

Just about. "Well, I don't want him up here. That isn't part of our rental agreement. You invite him over, he stays in the basement." The girl opened her mouth to argue but Caroline didn't give her the chance. Her gaze homed in on the milk and cereal. "And another thing. You've been sneaking our food since you moved in."

"Sooorry." Delia rolled her eyes and gestured at the table. "Does this look like sneaking? I'm out of breakfast stuff, so I borrowed yours. Big deal."

The snappish attitude begged for a fight, but Caroline was determined to talk this out. "It *is* a big deal," she said. "This isn't the first time, or even the second. I gave you a shelf in the refrigerator and cabinet space for your supplies. So please stay away from ours."

Delia remained silent, her expression hostile.

Caroline forged on. "Next point, your music. You play it so loud, we can hear it all the way upstairs. It wakes up both Jax and me in the middle of the night. You're able to sleep in, but we have to get up early. So keep it turned down."

"No way!" Delia said, sounding like a disagreeable teen. "Those tunes are meant to be played loud."

"Then wear headphones."

"I don't like to."

This conversation was going nowhere. If this was what Mary Beth dealt with, she felt for her. "Do you ever back down on anything?"

"Not stupid rules I don't believe in."

Fed up, Caroline made a snap decision. "I don't think this is working out. I want you to leave."

"You're kicking me out?" The girl's jaw dropped. "You bitch!"

"Don't call me what you are," Caroline rebutted. "I'm a reasonable woman with reasonable expectations. You're not. I want you out."

Delia's hands fisted. "Too bad. I'm paid up 'til the end of the month."

Which was true. If Caroline had had the means she'd have refunded some of the rent, but she didn't. "All right," she conceded. "The way I figure it, you've eaten at least one day's worth of rent in my food." Guilt pricked her about the wine cooler, but she'd only taken one glass. "That leaves nine days."

"But what if I can't find a place by then?" Delia whined.

"Move in with Bender," Caroline quipped, marveling at how smooth she sounded. Inside she was a ball of nerves.

"Fuck you." Wheeling around, Delia stalked off.

Instantly Caroline regretted her actions. What if

Delia caused trouble, somehow destroyed the basement or stole something more valuable than food? Shaken, she sank onto Jax's step stool.

Not only that. Now she had no extra source of income to help with the mortgage. She meant to catch up, not fall further behind. Groaning, she buried her face in her hands. Wait 'til Martin heard about this.

Time for a new ad in the paper. With any luck, this round she'd find someone mature and reliable, a grandmotherly-type woman who didn't resort to screaming vile things and calling her names.

Bitch indeed.

By Thursday, Jax was well and ready to head back to school. Even better, she'd slept all night in her own bed. Cause for celebration, except that Caroline awoke feeling terrible. Her sore, blistered throat could only mean one thing—strep. Thank God for Dr. Azose, Jax's pediatrician. He'd warned that she was likely to catch the infection, and after she put in a call to him, kindly phoned in a prescription, saving her the expense and bother of seeing her own doctor.

She managed to drop Jax at school and pick up the antibiotics. In twenty-four hours she'd feel better, but at the moment she was feverish and miserable. She kicked off her shoes and collapsed on the tone-on-tone, beige damask living room sofa, which faced the floor-to-ceiling windows.

The spectacular view drew Caroline's attention but did nothing for her flagging spirits. She never had been good at being sick. It depressed her, and this morning she felt as gray as the rainy April sky. In the distance the drab ocean waves, dulled by the dark clouds, gently lapped the shore. A green and white ferry glided toward the Bainbridge Ferry dock.

Yet despite the dreary weather there were patches of color to brighten the morning. Pink cherry blossoms, fiery red azaleas and purple-flowered rhododendron bushes dotted the yard leading down to the water. Everything needed pruning but Caroline couldn't afford the time to tackle the job herself. Truth was, she didn't enjoy gardening, only the results. This was nesting season, and the birds were busy, too. She watched a pair of robins carry twigs in their beaks to a tall evergreen.

She just hoped Mr. Robin didn't take on a second Mrs. while still married to his first wife, because that would end very badly.

The thought left her even more depressed and put a bitter taste in her mouth, but swallowing hurt. She'd make tea with honey, she decided, and then head upstairs to bed and do her best to push the negativity from her thoughts.

As she padded toward the kitchen the doorbell rang. In no mood for company she frowned. Who could that be? Bypassing the kitchen, she headed for the front door. Through the glass windows on either side of the door she saw Martin juggling two coffees and a small white sack. With Jax home sick yesterday, they'd had talked on the phone. She'd told him about kicking out Delia and he'd updated her on Mary Beth. They'd rescheduled a face-to-face for today, canceled this morning via voicemail, Caroline letting him know she was sick.

Forgetting how low and awful she felt, and wishing she'd put on makeup, she fluffed her hair and opened the door. "What a surprise," she said. "What are you doing here?"

Rain had spattered the shoulders of his black trench coat and raindrops glistened in his hair. He smiled. "You can't come to me, so here I am."

Caroline shook her head. "You're a busy man, and this is way beyond the call of duty. Besides, you updated me yesterday about the Mary Beth situation."

She still couldn't believe the woman had agreed to let her unload some of her assets. So what if Mary Beth got two-thirds of the proceeds? That wouldn't amount to much anyway, and all Caroline cared about now was the house. When she felt better she'd call and thank Mary Beth.

"You really didn't need to come," she said.

"Deprive you of your weekly cappuccino and blueberry scone?" Martin's mouth quirked. "As your lawyer and in good conscience, I couldn't do that. I'd already cleared my calendar for our meeting, and there are a few items I want to discuss." He handed her a coffee and the sack, picked up the briefcase at his feet, and started to move inside.

"Wait," Caroline said, stopping him. "I should warn you, I took my first dose of meds only an hour ago. I'm contagious for the next twenty-three hours. If you come in, you might get sick."

"If you're up for a visitor, I'll take my chances." He shot her a concerned look. "I won't stay long."

Any other visitors, no. But this was Martin. Funny how the sight of the man lifted her spirits. The sky didn't seem quite so dark, and she thought the sun might break through. "In that case, please come in. May I take your coat?"

"No, thanks." He wiped his feet carefully on the throw inside the door. "Just show me where the closet is."

While he hung up his coat she slipped into the kitchen for two plates, then walked him through the foyer and into the living room.

"Nice place," he said as he took in the view, lofty natural wood-beamed ceilings and expensive decor.

"The bland color scheme is Stephen's, but I do love the light and space."

"No wonder you refuse to part with it."

"Not ever," Caroline stated fervently. "This is Jax's and my home, and always will be."

"If you win the lawsuit," Martin reminded her. He sat down on a raw silk cream-and-beige-striped Queen Anne chair, his long thighs extending beyond the seat. "Mary Beth wants her million point three settlement. She won't back down on that."

After setting the plates on the white marble-top coffee table, Caroline returned to the sofa. "Since I'm not selling and don't have that much equity in the place, she'll be waiting forever."

She made a mental note that when she did phone Mary Beth, she'd make sure the woman understood that the house was not included in the disposal of assets. Martin already had informed the other attorney, but Caroline wasn't taking any chances.

She would not, could not lose the house. Which meant she badly needed to catch up on the mortgage. Which meant . . . "I need a new tenant, and fast," she said as Martin pulled the treats from the sack. "You wouldn't know of any little old ladies looking for a place to live?"

He shook his head and bit into to his muffin. "You put an ad in the paper, right?" he asked after swallowing a mouthful.

"Two days ago." She looked longingly at her scone, but her throat felt too sore to eat. "It ran yesterday, but I haven't had a single call yet." She chafed her arms. "I'm worried."

"You'll find someone," he said, the certainty in his soulful eyes reassuring. "Do people at your church know you need a tenant?"

"I haven't been there in a good long while," Caroline said. Several weeks after the funeral service she'd sought out Ilene Quackenbush, the minister, but had found no comfort in their conversations. Mainly because her need to protect Jax had kept her from disclosing Stephen's bigamy. Ilene was unlikely to betray any confidences, but Caroline wasn't about to test that.

Martin shrugged. "Doesn't mean you can't ask them to spread the word."

"I suppose not," Caroline mused. "I'll call the secretary later today."

"Good."

He finished the last of his muffin. She'd only seen him take one bite, but then he usually ate quietly and rapidly, finishing in record time, yet somehow genteel and refined. That fascinated her.

"What's going on with Delia?" he asked, setting down his plate.

"I haven't seen her since I asked her to leave yesterday morning." Caroline hadn't heard her, either—not one loud note of rap or rock. "I'm not sure she even came home last night. I hope she finds a new place soon." She glanced at Martin. "Cross your fingers she doesn't destroy the basement." The very thought gave her heart palpitations.

"If she damages *any*thing, your trusty lawyer will do what he can to collect damages." He sent her the straight-on look he used when doling out advice. "Next time, you'll get and check references, and collect a damage deposit up front. You'll also sign a rental agreement, which I picked up for you." He dug into his briefcase for the legal-size document, then set it on the table.

"Understood. Thank you." She gave a meek nod.

"Don't sign anything that lasts more than six months," he advised. "In case things go wrong."

That made good, common sense. "I never even thought about any of this stuff." A sip of coffee hurt terribly, and Caroline set down her cup. "I wish I'd talked to you before I let her move in."

"You're talking to me now, and I know you won't make the same mistakes twice."

She let out a humorless laugh. "I won't." Then shot Martin a hesitant glance.

"But?"

"The ad in the paper doesn't mention the damage deposit," she confessed, feeling stupid.

Stephen would have reinforced her negative feelings, but Martin didn't. "Nothing to worry about," he said in his non-judgmental, reassuring tone. "You'll explain about that when potential renters call, and it'll be written into the agreement."

"Okay. Thanks." She managed a smile. "I don't know what I'd do without you."

"All part of the job. If you want, we can go over the blank form now."

"With this strep bug, I'm not thinking clearly," Caroline said. "Can it wait until tomorrow? I know I'll feel better then. Will you have time to go over it on the phone?"

"I'll make time. I should go, but there is one more thing. Did you list the vacation property?"

"Right after we talked yesterday. I'm using the same realtor who sold it to us. She stopped over last night for a key and I signed the listing agreement. I also called the dealer where Stephen bought his car and asked him to sell it. Oh, and there's an ad in the paper for Stephen's entire office, furniture included."

"Strep hasn't kept you down," Martin said. "You've been busy."

Caroline nodded. "I can't wait to get out from under some of this debt."

"Keep me informed. Now, you need rest."

Since Caroline longed to climb into bed, pull up the covers, and sleep, she didn't argue.

Martin stood. "I'll let myself out. Get well soon."

Chapter Fourteen

Saturday night, slumped in a chair borrowed from the kitchen, Mary Beth sat in the dark of the empty den. Thank heavens Aurora came home tomorrow. Even her moodiness would be better than this oppressive silence. She raked her fingers through her unwashed hair and grimaced that she'd let herself go like this. But things had gone downhill after Tuesday's lunch with Kevin, and the rest of week had been sheer hell. Tonight she felt wounded and vulnerable and very sorry for herself.

Moving after twenty years was no easy task. Wanting to do as much as possible while Aurora was gone, she'd spent every day since that lunch in a packing frenzy of sorting and tossing and packing.

The plan was to look for apartments and a job, too. But memories and doubts had held her prisoner in her own home. She hadn't anticipated that.

If only she hadn't stopped to look through the photo albums stored on the shelves of this very room. Photographs of her wedding day, when she was young, pretty and crazy in love. Stephen had looked equally smitten. He had been.

When had that changed?

As she leafed through the pictures, bits and pieces of her life floated back. The first time they'd taken Aurora with them on vacation, she'd been four and they were all joyously happy.

Later albums revealed a different story. By the time Aurora was eight, Mary Beth had sensed changes in her husband. Often he seemed distant and preoccupied. Even the photos captured this, showing perfunctory rather than genuine smiles from them both. Oblivious, Aurora continued to beam like a ray of sunlight between them. Despite Mary Beth's growing sense that something was wrong, that she and Stephen were growing apart, she'd convinced herself that she was imagining things, that they were as happy as they once had been.

Why hadn't she paid attention to what her intuition told her? If only she'd pushed Stephen to open up. They might be divorced, but at least she wouldn't be the widow of a bigamist.

She'd been sitting so long, her behind ached. Exhausted, miserable, filled with self-loathing for the passive, weak woman she'd been, she returned the chair to the kitchen, then plodded upstairs to run a bath. Soaking in the tub, she cried. Then sick of feeling sorry for herself, she slipped into an old, flannel nightgown and padded downstairs to heat up a can of soup and pour herself a glass of . . . nothing alcoholic.

After Monday night and the hangover Tuesday, she was through with hard liquor. A glass of wine now and then, period. But tonight she wanted milk.

As she sat on the barstool eating her soup, she stared at the half-full boxes everywhere and felt lonely and sad all over again. *Quit feeling sorry for yourself!*

What she needed was to stop reminiscing and stop stewing. The way to do that was to reach out to someone else, the one woman who understood and shared her pain.

As she touched the phone it rang. The only people who'd call at this hour were Aurora or Ellie. Mary Beth loved both dearly but at the moment she wasn't up to talking to either one. She willed the phone to silence but it ignored her. On the seventh ring she picked up. "Hello?"

"Mary Beth?"

"Caroline." Her relief colored her voice. "You must have ESP I was just about to call *you*."

"You don't sound good," Caroline said in a toneless, unenergetic voice that matched Mary Beth's mood.

"You don't, either."

"Just getting over strep throat. Jax had it first and gave it to me."

"I remember those days. That's no fun."

"Nope, but I think I'll live. Are you sick, too?"

"Not physically." Eager to talk, Mary Beth did not hold back. "I've been packing, and got stuck looking through old photo albums. My wedding day, Aurora's birth, family vacations." Tears gathered behind her eyes, and she pressed the space between her brows, hoping to push away the pain. "At the moment I feel as bad as I did right after Stephen died."

"I know what you mean. Every time I think I've moved forward, I seem to slip back."

Caroline had just expressed Mary Beth's very feelings, which was incredibly comforting. "Exactly." This time nothing stemmed the tears. Mary Beth swiped her eyes and swallowed thickly. "How are we going to survive this?"

"As my wise father suggested, one day at a time. We will survive, if for no other reason than to prove to ourselves and the world that we're strong, resilient women. We are, you know."

Precisely what Mary Beth needed to hear. As quickly as the tears had come, they dried up. She sniffled and lifted her shoulders. "This is going to sound crazy, but I'm glad I know you."

"Me, too."

In the moment of comfortable silence between them, Mary Beth almost smiled. The swift change in mood didn't surprise her. All week her feelings had yo-yo'd every which way.

"When does Aurora get back?" Caroline asked.

"Late tomorrow afternoon. I took your and Ellie's advice, by the way, and let her know the house sold."

"And?"

"She handled the news better than I expected. She actually thanked me for telling her." Which had surprised Mary Beth no end. "I'd planned to go apartment hunting this past week, but that didn't happen. I think I'll take her with me so she can help choose a place."

"Sounds like a wise decision."

Mary Beth snickered. "I never felt less wise in my life."

"I'm with you there, too," Caroline said. "Wait 'til you hear the latest about Delia."

As Caroline described the confrontation with her tenant and Bender and the woman's choice vocabulary, Mary Beth's jaw dropped. "That sounds like a nightmare."

"It has been. We've managed to avoid each other until today. She said she found a new place. Thank goodness."

"I'll drink to that, but it's only milk. Now what?"

"Find a new tenant. Martin—my lawyer—gave me a blank rental agreement. We went over it paragraph by paragraph. I'll be checking references and asking for a damage deposit. Which reminds me, when you find an apartment, don't sign a lease for longer than six months. Martin says that way you don't end up stuck in a possibly bad situation."

"Thanks for the tip. Kevin never bothered to mention that. Martin sounds like a good attorney."

"He's the best."

At the extra warmth in Caroline's voice, Mary Beth smiled. "You really like him, don't you?"

"I do. We've become good friends."

"Or possibly more?"

"Please, Mary Beth! It's way too soon."

"I suppose," Mary Beth conceded. If Caroline felt as raw as she did, it probably *was* too soon. But the way she talked about Martin certainly sounded like more than friendship. Seeds definitely had been planted for a romantic relationship in the future. She kept that to herself. "My attorney, Kevin, isn't much of a friend. Did I mention he and Stephen were partners and very close? They knew each other forever, yet Kevin never even guessed what Stephen was up to. He seems to hold that against me."

"That's so unfair. I'd be hurt and offended."

"I am, but since he's not charging me . . . I'm relieved you're looking for a new tenant," she said. "I certainly don't want you to declare bankruptcy."

"Believe me, I don't want that, either. Is that why you agreed to let me sell off some of the assets?"

She nodded, but Caroline couldn't see that. "Yes. By the way, I appreciate your giving me two-thirds of the proceeds."

"Much as I hate to admit this, I'd rather give most of the money to you than end up with nothing in bankruptcy."

"I'd appreciate a check as soon as possible."

"After selling your beautiful home?" Caroline scoffed. "I doubt you even need it."

"I wish," Mary Beth said. "I had to sell fast, so I priced it on the low side. There are two big mortgages, plus the real estate commission and a stack of bills to get rid of. I'll be lucky to wind up with enough to pay for the moving expenses. And since I can't seem to find a job . . ."

"I'm not sure when you'll get a check," Caroline said. "The vacation property may take awhile to sell, and won't net much. The other stuff should move faster, but who knows for how much. So don't get your hopes up."

Resting her cheek on her fist, Mary Beth almost laughed. Here she was, boldly talking money with the woman who sat on a pile of equity that belonged to her. "I'll take whatever I can get," she said, sounding stiff to her own ears. Fighting over money wasn't exactly conducive to the warm fuzzies.

Caroline cleared her throat. "There is one thing I want to make clear. I won't sell my house."

"That's what Kevin tells me. Just remember, one

point three million dollars of that house is mine. My lawsuit isn't going away."

"Do what you must, but don't think for one moment that I won't fight your every move. I aim to live in this house 'til the day I die, and no lawsuit will change that."

Fighting words if ever Mary Beth had heard them. Anger tightened her mouth. "I loved my house, too, but circumstances forced me to give it up."

"Nothing will force me," Caroline stated with fervor. "And for your information, my home isn't worth more than a million and a half. Deduct the mortgage and real estate commission and there isn't even five hundred thousand in equity."

Stubborn witch. "That's not my concern." Mary Beth sniffed. "Just remember, I will get mine. I'll ride you until you build up the equity and cash me out—even if I'm dead. Then the money goes to Aurora." She narrowed her eyes as she spoke. "I want what is mine, Caroline, and make no mistake. I will get it."

"I don't see one penny of that money as yours," Caroline returned in a loud, angry voice. "It belongs to Jax and me."

Mary Beth's face felt hot. Her neck was tight and stiff and her stomach clenched in fury, but at least she no longer felt sorry for herself. She gripped the phone in her shaking fist. "I think we'd best hang up now, before we both say things we can't take back."

Despite her anger and hatred, she didn't want to jeopardize the relationship she had with Caroline, tenuous and bizarre as it was.

"That's the first sensible thing you've said in a good while," Caroline said coolly. "Good night."

The phone clicked and she was gone.

The Monday after spring break, after school, Aurora took the bus to the Perkins' house. She'd just spent a week with them in Hawaii, but they still wanted her to watch Chloe every afternoon. Fine with Aurora. She hated being in her stripped-down house with her mom packing more and more into boxes for the move. She didn't want to move, period, but the house was sold. Even though her mom had to sell, Aurora hated her for it. She preferred spending time with the Perkins family, who loved each other and had plenty of money.

But today she wished she could go to the mall and meet Mike instead. They hadn't seen each other in over a week, which worried her. If she didn't see him soon, she feared he might stop liking her. Sasha and Kelly already had. They no longer hung out with her.

Since Chloe and a friend were upstairs, playing, she decided to call Mike. But no one answered at his house. Dejected, she hung up. Someone knocked at the door. Aurora peered through the peephole. Mike! Her heart lifted. Quickly she unbolted and opened the door.

Bringing a rush of cool, damp air with him he strutted inside, black leather bomber jacket whispering as he moved. His gaze traveled over her body, making her glad she'd worn her black belly shirt and hip-hugger jeans.

She laughed. "What are you doing here?"

"It's been a whole week. I couldn't stay away another second. I missed you, babe."

She liked when he called her that. "Missed you, too."

"Nice tan," he said, looking at her stomach. "Are we just gonna stand here with the door open?"

Aurora hesitated. "I don't know. I'm not supposed to have company . . ."

"Who's gonna know?" Mike winked, then ran his finger down her cheek. "Come on, Aurora."

Nobody ever had liked or wanted her like this and she loved that Mike did. Unable to resist him, she gave in. "Okay, but Mrs. Perkins will be home in half an hour. You have to be gone before that. And if Chloe or her friend comes downstairs, you're out of here."

The second she closed the front door Mike pulled her close and kissed her. She hooked her arms around his neck and forgot about her problems. He was the only boy she'd ever kissed. He tasted like cigarettes, which was gross. She didn't like his big tongue, either, but admitting that meant you were a lesbian, and she wasn't. He nibbled her neck just below her ear, and she went soft and warm inside.

She nestled closer. He was breathing harder now, and so was she. She was so involved in the kiss, she hardly noticed when he sneaked his hand under the hem of her shirt.

As his hand slid across her skin Aurora stopped him. "Don't."

"Please, babe, let me." His fingers fanned out, stroking her ribs and grazing the sides of her breasts. "You'll like it, I promise."

The last thing she wanted was to push Mike away. She needed him and thought she might love him. But she felt uncomfortable and all mixed up, not ready for this. Breaking a searing kiss, she tried to explain. "I don't—"

"Aurora," Chloe called from upstairs, "Come up and play with Jordan and me."

The voice was dangerously loud. Jerking away and grateful for the interruption, Aurora tugged down her shirt. "In a minute," she called. "You have to leave," she whispered to Mike.

"But things were just warming up." He shot a hot look at her mouth and her breasts. "When can I see you again?"

"I'm staying here all weekend. You can come back then. Now go."

"I'll call you," he said as he slipped through the door.

Not five minutes later Mrs. Perkins pulled into the garage. Aurora gave her brow a mental swipe. What a close call that had been. This weekend she'd be a whole lot more careful.

Chapter Fifteen

Wednesday morning, standing beside Martin in the apartment Delia had vacated the night before, Caroline covered her mouth in disgust. "Didn't I tell you?" She'd walked through the place last night, horrified by the destruction, and had asked Martin to ferry over and meet her here instead of Starbucks. "Just look at this place."

Cigarette butts and smashed cornflakes littered the floor, the empty box—the same brand Caroline used and had accused Delia of stealing—tossed carelessly into the corner. Burn holes ruined what had been a beautiful, cream-color rug. An overflowing ashtray had been emptied onto the tan chenille sofa and rubbed into the cushions. Dozens of nail holes pockmarked every wall, and deep, eye-level gouges scarred every one of the enamel-painted wood doors.

Martin muttered and shook his head. "Bad as it is, I don't think the damage is substantial enough to go after her. You probably wouldn't recover any money."

"That's disappointing," Caroline said. "At least she's gone. I suppose I should be thankful for that."

"Evicting her wouldn't have been pretty," Martin agreed. "Did you order new locks?"

Caroline nodded. One more expense she couldn't afford, but a definite necessity. Delia had left the keys on the coffee table, but she could have made copies. "The locksmith will be here this afternoon."

Martin poked his head into the bathroom, which thankfully looked fine—or would, once she scrubbed it. From the look of the filthy sink, toothpaste and water-spattered mirror, and grimy tub and toilet, Delia hadn't bothered to clean while she lived here.

Caroline grimaced, and Martin headed for the empty room that had been Stephen's office. For some lucky reason Delia had ignored this room. But the bedroom. . . . Condom wrappers and used condoms lay scattered around the bed, and the expensive mattress was stained—with what she didn't want to know.

Viewing the evidence of her former tenant's sex life with Martin was both repulsive and embarrassing. Caroline's face warmed, and she averted her head.

"At least we know she practices safe sex," Martin quipped.

They returned to the living room. Caroline wanted everything perfect for Faye Roberts, her sixty-something, never-married new tenant. Faye neither smoked nor drank, and regularly attended a small, independent church—exactly the grandmotherly type Caroline had hoped for. Each of her three references had sung her praises. Best of all, she'd signed a six-months' lease and had handed over a check covering the rent, which was earmarked for the May mortgage payment, and the damage deposit. The apartment had looked messy when Caroline showed it last week. Thank God it hadn't looked—or smelled—like this.

She wrinkled her nose. "You wouldn't happen to know how to get rid of the stale cigarette smell, would you?"

"Soap, water, and a good airing out should help."

Frowning, she scrutinized the burn marks in the middle of the expensive carpet. "I don't think those burn marks will wash out." A fact that sickened her. "And I can't afford new carpeting."

"Hide them under an area rug," Martin suggested.

Caroline liked that idea. "There's a beautiful Persian rug in one of the upstairs guest bedrooms."

"Genuine Persian?" Martin asked. When she nodded, the creases between his brows deepened. "I wouldn't take any chances with that."

There was a limit to caution. Caroline pooh-poohed the advice with an airy wave. "Faye doesn't smoke or drink, and her three references all mentioned how neat and clean she is. She'll take good care of everything."

"If this were my place, I'd hedge my bets, leave the Persian rug safely upstairs, and buy something inexpensive for this room."

"You would?" He hadn't steered her wrong yet. She gave in with a reluctant nod. "All right, but I hate to spend Faye's damage deposit so soon. I'll find something at Home Depot."

They headed upstairs to the kitchen, where coffee and treats, this time made by Caroline's own hand, awaited them. "While you're at Home Depot, get a couple boxes of spackle and wood filler, and some wall paint." Martin washed his hands in the sink, so tall he stooped over to turn the faucet. "You supply those, and I'll bring the brushes and tarp." He dried his hands and sat down at the table.

With so much to do in a short time, his offer to help was tempting. But he was a busy man, and she already owed him so much. . . . Caroline shook her head as she washed her hands. "That's very sweet, but you really don't have the time."

"My nights are free," he said as she poured coffee and took a seat across from him. "Tell you what, I'll trade doing repairs for dinner."

She liked Martin sitting at her table, and the thought of him eating with her and Jax pleased her more than it should have. The other night Mary Beth had asked whether she liked him as more than a friend. Did she? No, Caroline decided, it really was too soon. Besides, it was obvious he didn't feel more than friendship for her.

A friendship that lit up her life. Caroline smiled at him. "That's an offer I can't turn down. Let me clean up the debris first. Why don't you come tomorrow night, say sixish?"

"I'll be here." As he helped himself to a slice of coffee cake his lips curled into a rare, full-beam grin.

Basking in the warmth, Caroline cut herself a piece. "You have a nice smile. You should use it more often."

"I would, if I ate like this." He speared a huge bite and chewed with relish. "Best coffee cake I ever tasted," he said with such enthusiasm, she laughed.

"You're easy. You're doing all that work for one measly dinner seems lopsided in my favor."

"I haven't had a good, home-cooked meal in longer than I can remember. That's worth a fortune. Just ask my belly."

He *was* on the thin side. Caroline made up her mind to cook something highly caloric. "Food aside, you haven't met Jax. She might talk your ears off."

"I don't mind talkative females." His eyes twinkled.

"Speaking of talkative," she said, "did I mention that Mary Beth and I spoke a few nights ago?"

"Again?" Eying her with surprise, Martin waited silently for her to continue.

Caroline nodded. "She finally called Aurora and told her the house sold. She took it pretty well. They'll be apartment-hunting next week, so I told her your rule about the six months' rental agreement."

"You did, huh?"

Though his face conveyed nothing, his voice held a shred of something—either disbelief or disapproval.

"There's nothing wrong with us talking, is there?"

"Not if you're both okay with it."

"Mostly, we are. But sometimes . . ." Recalling the unpleasant end to that last conversation, Caroline frowned. "Even though I explained that there isn't enough equity she insists that her share in this house is one point three million dollars. She says if I don't pay her, she'll collect the money when I die. Or rather, Aurora will." Caroline's voice had risen along with her exasperation. "Mary Beth Mason is the most hard-headed person I've ever known."

Martin's brows arched. "I know someone just as stubborn."

She shot him a furious look, but with the humorous

glint in his eyes and angelic expression, she couldn't stay mad. She gave a grudging smile. "You're damn right, I am."

"You don't have to talk to her, you know."

"The funny thing is, when we're not yelling at each other I enjoy our conversations. She's the only person who truly understands what I've been through. What I'm still going through." Caroline laughed at herself and rolled her eyes. "There's one for the analysts, huh?"

Martin rubbed his chin speculatively. "Maybe you *should* talk to a professional."

"Tell some stranger my husband was a bigamist?" Caroline shook her head. "No thank you."

"It's not your fault."

She thought about her young, sweet daughter. "I realize that, but I don't want Jax to find out what Stephen did. The fewer people who know, the better."

"Therapists don't share what they learn in counseling, but I suspect you're aware of that." Martin's eyes were shrewd and knowing. "What you're really saying is, you don't want help. Or maybe," he tapped one finger against his lips, "you want to protect Stephen's reputation."

At the very idea, Caroline bridled. "I certainly do not. My only goal is to protect Jax. She wouldn't understand everything, but all the same her world would tilt. She's suffered enough. But you're right about one thing—I don't want emotional 'help.'" She had Mary Beth for that.

"Okay, okay." Martin raised his hands, palms out. "But someday, no matter how careful you are, the truth will come out. Jax will discover that you've lied to her. What'll you do then?"

"She'll never find out," Caroline stated with certainty. "The only people who know are you, your paralegal, my family, and Mary Beth. Mary Beth and Jax will never meet, and my family . . . they've given their word." True, Becca had reneged, but Caroline intended to keep her daughter away from her sister. She eyed Martin. "Unless you betray my confidence, the secret is safe."

"You know I won't," he assured her with a level look. "Nothing that happens in my office goes beyond those walls."

Hands on her ample waist, the blond apartment manager—Sarah Bates, her card read—peered at Mary Beth over her black-rimmed glasses. "What do you think?"

Working to muster enthusiasm, Mary Beth gestured at the small living room of the vacant twelve-hundred-square-foot apartment. "It's not bad."

Not wonderful, either. Mary Beth noted Aurora's unhappy expression. "Could I have a moment alone with my daughter?"

"Certainly. Just remember, there are other people in line for this unit. It'll go fast."

She wasn't lying about that. San Francisco's rental housing market was extremely tight, with even the shabbiest units snapped up the instant they were available.

The second Sarah disappeared Aurora shared her opinion. "I hate this place, Mom! Just like all the others."

The Perkinses had given Aurora time off, and for the past four days Mary Beth and her daughter had traipsed through apartment after apartment. Every place seemed too small and run-down, nothing like the spacious luxury they were accustomed to.

Unfortunately they no longer could afford luxury or time. In four weeks the house closed, with the new owners taking possession immediately. Dismal as it was, Mary Beth and Aurora had no choice but to find an apartment, and soon. "It's the best we've seen so far," Mary Beth said.

"I still hate it."

Anxious to secure a new home, start moving things, and put the past behind her, she tried to sell her daughter. "Look, it's clean and modern, and doesn't reek of smoke, onions, or cat pee. That counts for something, right?"

"Clean?" Aurora gestured at the grimy living room window that overlooked the parking lot, and shuddered. "It's totally gross. And the rooms are so little! Where will we put our furniture?"

"There isn't much left," Mary Beth reminded her. She'd sold off everything but the television, one sofa, the kitchen table and chairs, and her and Aurora's bedroom sets.

"I doubt my bed and dresser will even fit in 'my' bedroom." Aurora's mouth tightened into the stubborn line. "I am not living here."

Mary Beth stifled an exasperated retort. Truth was, her daughter's attitude was no surprise. Last Sunday she'd returned from Hawaii tanned and in good spirits—until she'd looked around and realized what the sale of their home meant. One glance at the boxes everywhere and she'd raced up to her room and slammed the door. Mary Beth understood and shared her daughter's pain. She'd longed to talk, and had hoped for another heart-to-heart. But no amount of coaxing had worked. Aurora hadn't come out of her room until the next morning. At breakfast she'd been silent, puffy-eyed, and miserable. She still wasn't talking much.

"We're running out of time," Mary Beth said. "If you don't want this place, we'll have to spend the weekend looking."

An impatient huff issued from her daughter's lips. "Did you forget that I'm taking care of Chloe all weekend?" For some reason she refused to meet Mary Beth's eye. "You'll have to go by yourself."

What was she hiding, Mary Beth wondered, or was she imagining things? These days she hardly knew. She sighed. "What if I find a place and need to sign the rental agreement right away? I don't want to make that decision without your approval. You want the final say, remember?" Aurora had insisted on that.

"I changed my mind. I'll never say 'yes' because no matter what we look at, I'll hate it." Aurora crossed her arms and raised her head defiantly. "You decide."

Fighting the urge to scream, Mary Beth nodded. "All right, but I want your promise you'll accept what I choose cheerfully and without a fuss."

"How can I, when I know it'll be awful? I hate this city and everybody in it," Aurora said through clenched teeth. "Couldn't we move to another state, where nobody knows us?"

"That's awfully extreme."

"You would say that." She stomped her foot, making the floor shake. "You never understand anything!"

Patience worn thin, Mary Beth silently counted to ten. "Why don't you try me?"

"I hate school. My life sucks!" Aurora shut her mouth, apparently unwilling to elaborate.

"The good news is, you'll be in a new school next year. High school. I'm sure that will make a world of difference."

"But that's ages away." Aurora hung her head. "I want to start over right now, in a brand new place." She pointed the toe of her flip-flop at a threadbare spot in the carpet. "As long as it's not here. Can we please go?"

They crossed the parking lot and headed for the car, Aurora silent and brooding. "I hate that Daddy did this to us," she said at last. Her eyes filled. "I hate Daddy, period!"

Her daughter had used the "h" word so many times, Mary Beth had lost count. Not that she blamed her. "Same here, yet I also love him," she acknowledged. Noting the me-too look on her daughter's face she shook her head and unlocked the car. They slipped into their seats. "It's so darned confusing."

Aurora nodded and tears spilled unchecked down her cheeks. This was when she usually ran upstairs to her room to cry in private. But in the car, she had no place to hide.

Mary Beth leaned across the bucket seat and pulled her into a hug.

"It's so not fair," her daughter sobbed against her shoulder.

"I know, honey, I know."

Mary Beth patted Aurora's back. After a moment

she sniffled and pulled away. She swiped the we
mascara from under her eyes and wiped he
smudged hands on her jeans.

Mary Beth started the car. "What do you say w
skip dinner and gorge on comfort food? I'll whi
up the cream cheese-mashed potatoes if you mak
the brownies."

Her daughter managed a shaky smile. "Okay."

As she pulled out of the parking lot, Auror
turned on the radio, for once keeping the volum
low. "Mom?"

"What, honey?"

"How did you know you loved Daddy?"

What an odd time for the question. "Well,
thought about him constantly, and wanted to b
with him all the time. He made me happy." Stuck i
rush-hour traffic, she studied her daughter. "Wh
do you want to know?"

"Never mind. You should take somebody wit
you on Saturday. Why don't you ask Ellie?"

Confused over the abrupt jump from subject t
subject, Mary Beth absently rubbed the space be
tween her eyebrows. "Joe is flying in from Montan
Friday night. He'll be here all weekend."

Ellie had come back from Montana with stars i
her eyes. Apparently her sister's neighbor,
rancher named Joe whom she'd known for year
and whose wife recently had died of cancer, ha
knocked Ellie off her feet. According to Ellie, the
talked on the phone every night for hours.

"Wow," Aurora said. "That sounds serious."

Way too serious and way too soon, in Mary Beth'
opinion. "Sometimes things work that way," she said
"I'm happy Ellie met someone." She only hoped he

friend wouldn't end up with a broken heart. Which she'd told her when she'd urged her to slow down. Ellie wasn't listening. "Maybe you should ask her about love. She wants us to meet Joe. We're invited to her place for brunch on Sunday."

"Mo-om." Aurora rolled her eyes. "I told you, I'll be babysitting."

"Fine. I'll go by myself."

A song heavy on the bass side started, and Aurora cranked up the volume. "This is my favorite song."

And the end of the conversation.

Lost in her own thoughts, Mary Beth navigated through the stop-and-go traffic on automatic pilot. Nearly an hour later she turned into their gracious driveway and rolled past the SOLD sign. How she detested that sign, a blatant reminder of the unwanted changes in her and Aurora's lives. Aurora bowed her head and squeezed her eyes shut, as if blocking the view could change things.

Her daughter's suffering hurt unbearably. Helpless against the pain, Mary Beth waited for the familiar rage to flare inside her. Instead fierce determination flooded her—to make a new home for her and Aurora, to make a new life. Right here in San Francisco.

That'd show Stephen's snobby friends. *Without money or a decent job? How naïve and stupid is that?* The negative thought lowered her spirits. Until she realized the voice in her head sounded like Stephen. *I'm not stupid. I'll figure out something,* she countered. Her silent self-defense felt good, as if she'd flexed a muscle that had been ignored and neglected.

Mary Beth pressed the garage door opener and waited for it to rise. Arguing with yourself meant

you were crazy, didn't it? She wanted to call Caro
line and ask, but couldn't just now, not whil
Aurora might hear. Though she no longer kept se
crets from her daughter, she wasn't ready to explai
the peculiar friendship with Stephen's other wife
Or to deal with the questions and new hurts tha
were sure to arise. She'd save the call for later, whe
Aurora was in her room.

She pulled into the garage. For now, there wa
only one thing to do—hold on to her new-found re
solve to make a new and good life. She glanced a
her daughter. "Boy, am I hungry. Ready to whip u
those cream cheese-mashed potatoes and brown
ies?"

To her own ears she sounded bright and cheer
ful. Aurora's puzzled expression was almost funny

"What are you so happy about?"

"Don't ask me how, but I know we're going to b
okay," Mary Beth said, testing her resolve by statin
the words out loud. "I can feel it."

Chapter Sixteen

When Mary Beth picked up the phone later that night to call Caroline, she heard a male voice.

"I really care about you," he said.

Mary Beth frowned. "Who is this?"

Aurora gasped. "What are you doing listening to my call, Mother?"

"What are you doing on the phone at eleven o'clock on a school night, and who are you talking to?"

"None of your business."

The boy cleared his throat. "This is Mike Edison, Mrs. Mason. It's my fault Aurora's on the phone so late. We'll hang up now."

Aurora had mentioned the name once or twice—one of her new school friends. Mollified by his polite tone and pleased that he cared about her daughter, Mary Beth relaxed. "Thank you, Mike, and good night, Aurora."

"Did I wake you?"

Caroline recognized the voice immediately. "No,

but I am in bed." Smiling, she sat up and flipped on the reading lamp. "I've been lying here, wanting to call you, but it's nearly midnight . . ."

"I know. I had to wait 'til Aurora went to sleep," Mary Beth said. "I started to call earlier, only when I picked up the phone, she was talking to a boy."

"A boyfriend?" Caroline snuggled into her pillow. "That's a new twist."

"Could be," Mary Beth said. "But she's not dating or anything—they're both too young. Anyway, I waited awhile after they hung up, to be safe. She doesn't know about our conversations. She wouldn't understand."

"Jax doesn't even know about Stephen, for the same reason."

"Oh, my gosh, I forgot about Jax. Did I wake her?"

"You won't believe this, but she's still sleeping in her own room. Ten nights and counting. Fingers crossed that she stays there," Caroline said, making an X with her fingers.

"Wow. You must be doing something right. I don't know about keeping Stephen's shenanigans a secret, though. Aren't you worried someone will tell her?"

The same argument Becca and Martin had made. Caroline frowned. "Aside from my family and Martin, no one here knows, and that's the way it'll stay. My sister, Becca, disagreed. We fought about it and now we're not speaking."

"I was an only child. You're lucky to have a sister," Mary Beth said in a wistful voice.

"You can have Becca." Caroline wasn't ready to make up with her sister, and Becca hadn't contacted her, either. She never made the first move after they quarreled—Caroline always apologized first. Not this time. She shook her head. "Jax will never find out."

"Oh, but secrets have a way of sneaking out and clobbering you. I learned the hard way, with Aurora."

"Jax is little. She doesn't need to know." Caroline bit her lip, wondering whether their difference of opinion would cause another fight. She hoped not because she needed to talk.

To her relief, Mary Beth merely sighed. "That's your choice, of course." She changed the subject. "I can't believe you convinced her to stay in her own bed. The candy bribes must be working."

"That and Martin."

"Ooh, that sounds intriguing. *He's* not in bed with you, is he?"

She sounded almost giddy. Caroline's face warmed. "Of course not! He ate dinner with us. That's what he wanted as payment for helping with the basement."

"Martin helped you with the basement?" Mary Beth paused and made a pleased noise. "Sounds like a budding romance to me."

The man had been so helpful, so cheerful, and so good with Jax, that Caroline was no longer certain about their relationship. "I don't know," she admitted. "That's why I wanted to talk to you tonight. I'm confused."

The light-hearted laugh that greeted her statement surprised Caroline. Puzzled, she frowned. "You sound different."

"I *feel* different," Mary Beth said. "For the first time in ages I feel clear and determined about my life. That's why I called."

Who knew, maybe she'd decided to drop the lawsuit. Hopeful, Caroline prodded her. "What's changed?"

"I'm not sure, but late this afternoon something shifted in my brain. Our lives suck, and I have no reason to feel anything but awful, yet I truly believe Aurora and I are going to make it through this mess. Even though she detests every apartment we look at. She thinks we should leave California and start over." Mary Beth paused, and Caroline imagined her shaking her head. "Despite her negative attitude and losing the house, and despite the sad fact that I can't find a decent job, I feel incredibly optimistic, actually excited to move into an apartment and start fresh. Aurora thinks I'm insane. Do you?"

So this wasn't about dropping the lawsuit. Caroline wasn't surprised, but she was disappointed. At the same time she admired Mary Beth's new outlook on life. "I think you're amazing. How did you turn your attitude around?"

"That's the strange part," Mary Beth said. "One minute I'm a mess. The next, I'm bound and determined to show Stephen's friends that I don't need them. Not that they'll ever know, unless Kevin mentions me. But *I* will. I hope to find an apartment this weekend, then do everything possible to turn it into a warm, cozy home."

She sounded so certain. Caroline envied her, for even though grandmotherly Faye Roberts was about to move in, she felt as if she were barely surviving. "I wish you could clone that positive attitude."

"You've got that new renter moving in on Saturday, right? And your lawyer has the hots for you. Sounds positive to me."

Caroline grabbed the spare pillow and hugged it.

"As wonderful as Martin is, beyond a handshake or two, he's never touched me." And never looked at her with more than friendly warmth. Certainly nothing resembling lust. She shook her head. "I don't think he's sexually attracted to me."

"Maybe he's waiting for a signal from you before he makes his move. Are you attracted to him?"

"Well . . ." Martin's face filled her mind. "He's not what you'd call good-looking, but he does have soulful brown eyes that could melt a person's heart. But to tell you the truth, sex hasn't been on my mind much lately."

"Mine either."

In the moments of silence that passed, Caroline wondered whether she'd ever want a man again.

"Tell me about the apartment," Mary Beth said at last. "Maybe you can give me some tips. Is everything ready for your new tenant?"

"Not yet, but it's coming along. I was up 'til midnight last night and worked late tonight, too. You wouldn't believe the mess Delia left. I spent hours just sweeping crud off the carpets so I could vacuum. I ended up renting a multi-purpose steam-cleaner, which I used on the carpets, the mattress and the rest of the furniture."

"I didn't know a person could rent a steam-cleaner. I used to hire out that work."

"Me, too," Caroline said. "Renting the equipment is a whole lot cheaper. Try your local grocery store or look in the phone book."

"Thanks for the info. I'll bet the place looks spotless."

"Not quite. Nothing can remove the burn holes in the carpet." For that, Caroline wanted to wring

Delia's neck. "But I picked up an area rug at Home Depot that covers the burn holes, and cleaned the drapes and throw pillows at a do-it-yourself dry cleaner. At least the cigarette smell is gone." She yawned.

"No wonder you're tired. Did you leave anything for Martin to do?"

"He patched the holes and painted quite a bit. I'll finish up tomorrow while Jax is in school. He let her help." Something Stephen never would have allowed.

"No kidding? This guy sounds like a dream. Does she like him?"

"She didn't at first. She point-blank told him she didn't want a new daddy." Caroline flushed, remembering. "I nearly died."

"I would've, too. How did Martin handle that?"

"His ears turned red. He didn't talk down to her or anything, just said he wasn't trying to be anybody's daddy, and explained about being my lawyer and friend."

He'd been honest and straightforward, and Jax had believed him. Caroline still marveled at that. For a man who had no experience with children, Martin was a natural. What a shame he didn't have kids of his own.

"After that, they got along fine. In fact, she followed him around like a duckling trailing its mother. She hasn't had an adult male in her life since my father went back to Florida. I hadn't realized how badly she needed one."

"Hmm. Maybe you should try sending Martin 'I'm interested' signals and see what happens."

"He probably wouldn't notice. And really, I'm not ready." She yawned again.

"I heard that," Mary Beth said. "You should get to sleep."

Caroline nodded. "Good luck apartment hunting, and thanks for calling. I enjoyed talking."

"Me, too."

Late Saturday morning, Mary Beth stood in the small dining room of her third apartment walk-through of the day. The neighborhood was decent, the brownstone building was small—only six units—and the dark wood trim, stucco walls and leaded-glass windows were charming. Even Aurora would like this place.

"I'll take it," she proclaimed. "Where do I sign?"

Marguerite, the thirty-something woman who had shown the unit, detached a form from her clipboard. "First, I'll need the completed application and a deposit. After that I'll run the credit check, and then—"

"Credit check?" Mary Beth interrupted.

Her face must have reflected her alarm, for Marguerite frowned. "Standard procedure for all prospective tenants. Is there a problem?"

Mary Beth refused to discuss her embarrassing personal finances with this stranger. "Um . . . I'm recently widowed. I don't have credit in my own name," she hedged.

"You can explain that to Wilhelm—Mr. Kirby—who owns the building, during your interview." She pulled a Palm Pilot from the pocket of her blazer and punched a few buttons. "Will two o'clock this afternoon work?"

"Interview?" Mary Beth frowned. "You didn't mention that, either."

Marguerite glanced at the stucco ceiling and shook her head. "I'm sorry I didn't tell you every little detail of our application process. If you want to live here, you have to meet Wilhelm. He lives on the top floor of the building, and doesn't allow just anyone to move in. If he likes you and thinks you'll fit in with the rest of the tenants, you get the unit. If he doesn't . . ." She shrugged.

"I had no idea. Are you sure that's legal?"

"As you know, this is a tight rental market," the woman pointed out, speaking slowly as if Mary Beth were a child. "Lots of apartment owners interview prospective tenants, so it must be legal. Will two o'clock work for you?"

The whole scenario bothered Mary Beth, but she wanted this apartment. With the interview several hours from now, she could go home, grab lunch, change into nicer clothes, and call Aurora, who was staying the weekend at the Perkins' house. "I'll be back," she said.

Only Aurora didn't answer the phone. She must have taken Chloe to the park. Mary Beth decided to call back after she signed the rental agreement. At exactly two o'clock, dressed in a tasteful but loose Dana Buchman dress, hair in a neat chignon, she sat demurely in Wilhelm Kirby's tiny, cluttered office on the main floor of the apartment building.

He wasn't much for conversation, and while he silently skimmed her application, she studied him. Small, thin, about sixty, with a comb-over and a mouth that puckered so, she wondered whether he'd been sucking lemons. Fish lips, she decided.

"You don't work?" he said, eyeing her as if she'd committed a crime.

Offended by his tone and disdainful expression, she straightened her spine. "I've been a homemaker since I married over twenty years ago," she explained, smoothing a hand over her dress in hopes of calling Mr. Kirby's attention to her designer clothes. "Recently my husband died. I am looking for work, but my skills are rusty at best." She offered a hopeful smile.

Mr. Kirby didn't seem to notice her outfit or her smile. Instead of offering his condolences, he continued to squint at the papers on his desk. "Your credit rating is terrible."

Mary Beth's face warmed along with her temper. Since she wanted the apartment, she tamped down the urge to tell off the judgmental jerk. What was it Ellie had said about karma? *Love and grace,* she silently counseled herself. "My husband left us with . . . debts," she explained. "But I just sold my home in Nob Hill. I'm good for the money."

Her assurance did nothing to ease the ridges of disapproval on the man's forehead. "How do I know you won't spend it on clothes or a new car?" He shook his head. "I can't rent to you."

In her worst moments, Mary Beth had never imagined being turned down. She wanted this place, as a matter of principle, if nothing else. "If it makes you rest easier, I'll ask my realtor to cut you a check directly from the sale proceeds."

"Doesn't matter." The awful man tapped his fish lips with his index finger. "I made up my mind before lunch, when I interviewed a nice young fella in the advertising business. He's the one I want."

Karma be damned. "Then why didn't you cancel our appointment, and save us both the time?" Mary Beth snapped.

His eyes widened. "I don't like your abusive tone. Get out of my office."

"With pleasure."

Head high, she marched out. Inside, she felt humiliated and depressed. She'd never been kicked out of any place. When she reached her car, she found a parking ticket under the windshield. Lovely. She stuffed it into her purse.

As she slid into the driver's side she noted the "Apartments for Rent" section of the paper lying on the passenger seat. Surely there must be one decent apartment in San Francisco with a landlord willing to rent to her on the spot, no credit check required. Mary Beth picked up the paper.

Chapter Seventeen

While Joe headed on foot to the corner bakery to pick up the croissants for Ellie's Sunday brunch, Mary Beth and Ellie bustled around the compact kitchen, making coffee, setting the table, and keeping an eye on the egg casserole in the oven.

"Now that Joe's out of the house, tell me what you think of him," Ellie said as she placed sausage links in a skillet.

"He seems wonderful." Mary Beth arranged three place mats, napkins, and silverware neatly on the table. "And anyone can see, he's crazy about you."

Ellie's joyous smile erased years from her face. "I'm madly in love with him." She left the sizzling sausages to fill three glasses with orange juice. "We're already talking marriage."

"Oh, honey." Mary Beth's eyes filled.

"Are those tears of happiness?"

"Happiness and a healthy dose of concern. As I said before, this is happening so fast." She set a jar of strawberry jam on the table. "I don't want you to get hurt."

"And as I told *you*, I'm a big girl." Wielding a cooking fork, Ellie tended the sausages, which smelled heavenly. "This should make you happy. We've decided to wait a year before we get married. That'll give Joe's kids time to get used to the idea."

Mary Beth nodded. "I approve. But aren't Joe's sons and daughter in their twenties—adults with their own lives?"

"They are. But they can't quite reconcile their neighbor's sister and their widowed father in a romantic relationship. When they realize how crazy Joe and I are about each other, they'll come around."

"I know you don't want to think about this, but I have to ask because life doesn't always have happy endings." An understatement, given Mary Beth's situation. "What if you and Joe don't work out?"

"That'd about kill me. But the truth is, I'd rather suffer a broken heart than go through the rest of my life without experiencing the happiness I feel now. This sounds corny, but until now I was merely existing. My life has become so much richer and brighter."

"That's not corny, it's wonderful." A breath of envy slipped from Mary Beth's lips. "I don't think I ever felt that strongly about Stephen."

"You loved him," Ellie said, pulling water glasses from the cabinet.

"At first I did." Mary Beth filled the glasses from the tap. "I certainly loved our lifestyle. I don't remember experiencing the deep joy you're feeling. If I did, it died long before Stephen. Maybe that's why he turned to Caroline."

Ellie snorted and turned the sausage. "He 'turned

to' Caroline because he was a two-timing, selfish bastard, period."

"You're right. I don't know why I said that. Stephen's behavior is not my fault—or Caroline's."

"At last she sees the light." Ellie shot her a triumphant smile. "Hallelujah and then some. Speaking of Caroline, what's the latest?"

"We're talking several times a week. I like her, Ellie, and she likes me. We're becoming friends—good friends." Shaking her head, Mary Beth sat down on a café chair. "Can you believe that?"

"I can, and I think it's wonderful. Grace and love make for good karma."

"Not when it comes to finding an apartment." Mary Beth cringed, recalling yesterday's humiliation. Though they were alone, she lowered her voice before describing the disastrous interview with Wilhelm Kirby. "I didn't realize landlords ran credit checks," she finished.

"Not all do. I've never heard of an interview process to get an apartment. I can't believe he put you through that when he'd already made up his mind." Ellie pointed to her ear and waved her finger in a circle. "Kirby sounds like a wacko to me. Consider yourself lucky to be rejected."

"Aurora said that, too." She'd finally reached her daughter at the Perkins house and had filled her in. "Of course she doesn't want to live in San Francisco. She wants to move out-of-state."

Mary Beth expected Ellie to laugh. Instead, she shrugged. "Not a bad idea. There's nothing much for you here."

"You're here, and this city has been my home all my life. I know where to buy groceries, where to get my hair cut, and where to have the car serviced." Not that she could afford the salon or the mechanic anymore. "I know the schools."

"I'll be moving to Montana in a year. The other stuff is just a matter of habit." Ellie turned off the stove. "There are decent grocery stores, salons, and schools everywhere."

"But I'm comfortable here," Mary Beth argued.

"Are you?"

Maybe not lately, but the thought of moving away seemed ludicrous as well as expensive. Besides, where would they go? "We're not leaving San Francisco."

"Fine, but you have only three weeks to find an apartment."

Mary Beth groaned. "Don't remind me."

"If worse comes to worse, you two can bunk here awhile," Ellie offered. "The sofa converts into a double bed."

Mary Beth imagined sharing a bed with her dramatic daughter. Talk about uncomfortable. "I'll keep that in mind. Meanwhile, if you hear of any vacancies that don't require a credit check, let me know."

"Will do, but if I were you, I'd put it out to the Universe," Ellie counseled.

Mary Beth rolled her eyes. "You know I don't believe in that woo-woo stuff."

"Even so . . ." Her friend shot her a why-not smile. "You need all the help you can get."

"True." Feeling silly, Mary Beth opened her arms. "Universe, I need a place to live." She glanced at Ellie. "What else should I do?"

Ellie shook her head. "Nothing. That was perfect."

* * *

The day after Faye Roberts moved in, Caroline invited her for Sunday morning waffles and bacon—a welcome-to-our-home breakfast.

Faye came to the table dressed in a modest navy polka-dot dress and low navy heels, which impressed Jax.

"Pretty," she commented. "How come you're all dressed up?"

"For church, of course." The woman glanced at Caroline's sweats and Jax's bunny slippers and terry cloth robe and frowned. "Why aren't you two dressed?"

"'Cause today is brunch day," Jax replied.

"What she means is, Sunday mornings I make a big breakfast," Caroline explained. "Then we laze around the house in our jammies. We've never been regular church-goers."

The new tenant compressed her lips. "I believe church is essential, Mrs. Mason, especially when one is raising children."

Caroline shrugged. "You're entitled to your opinion." In no mood to argue, she offered a warm smile. "Please call me Caroline."

"Very well, Caroline." Curling her thin lips into a semblance of a smile, Faye Roberts angled her chin at Jax. "My church has an excellent program for children. Would you like to come with me this morning?"

"Can I?" Eyes wide, Jax looked to Caroline.

"May I," Caroline corrected. The last thing she wanted was her tenant dragging her daughter to a church she knew nothing about. "No, thank you," she said.

"You heard the child. She wants to attend."

The child? "No," Caroline repeated. "I'm sure *Jax* would prefer to go to the park."

"Park! Park!" Jax shouted, pumping her spoon in the air.

Faye Roberts made a sour face. "I don't approve of wasting the Sabbath on frivolities. Idle time is the devil's workshop."

What had happened to the sweet lady who had signed the rental papers? Caroline did not hide her displeasure. "I didn't ask for your approval."

"It's not my approval you should seek. You want God the Father and his son, Jesus Christ, who died for our sins."

"Enough!" Caroline said, so firmly that Jax's jaw dropped. "Religion is personal," she added in a softer voice. "You're entitled to your opinion and I'm entitled to mine. End of subject."

"But—"

"If you want to get along here, you'll respect my wishes and drop the subject," Caroline warned. "Permanently."

The woman tsked. "All right, but you can't stop me from praying for you and Jax." She squeezed her eyes shut and bowed her permed, gray-streaked head.

Caroline told herself she didn't mind. A little prayer couldn't hurt—provided Faye Roberts left things at that. As long as she didn't smoke, steal food, play loud rock music, or invite men to stay the night, Caroline could handle a little religious fervor.

Aurora batted Mike's hand away from the inside of her thigh. "Don't," she said, but her weak protest didn't even convince *her*.

They were lying on the sofa in the Perkins's living room, the same as yesterday during Chloe's nap, and again last night. Mr. and Mrs. Perkins wouldn't be home from their weekend away until late, so Aurora had fed and bathed Chloe, then put her to bed.

Now the lights were out and Mike was practically on top of her. He made her body hum, and she no longer felt scared. She thought constantly about the things he did to her and could hardly wait for his touch and his mouth. But this was new.

"Why not?" Mike whispered, blowing warm air on her damp nipple.

Shivers of pleasure spiraled through her. Her blouse was off and so was her bra, and he was doing things to her breasts that made her restless and damp between her legs. She writhed against him and moaned softly.

"I can make you feel even better," he murmured, again sliding his palm toward her panties. "Open you legs, babe."

Suddenly lights flooded the room. "What's going on here?" Mr. Perkins asked in a stern voice Aurora had never heard.

Mrs. Perkins gasped, her mouth open in shock.

Hot-faced, Aurora darted behind Mike, using him as a shield while she jerked on her blouse and buttoned it and he pulled on his T-shirt. Never mind her bra, which he'd tossed someplace.

Mr. Perkins looked grim. "Stand up, son." As Mike pushed to his feet, the older man looked him over. "Just how old are you?"

"Eighteen," Mike said, straightening his shoulders.

"Old enough to know better. Ever heard of statutory rape?"

"Aurora's sixteen."

"No, she's fourteen," the older man corrected.

"No way." Mike shot Aurora a sideways look. "You said you was sixteen."

He loved her. Her age shouldn't change that. "Does it matter?" she asked him.

"Hell, yes." Mike tossed Aurora's bra at her, along with a dirty look. "I don't mess with jailbait."

Mr. Perkins's mouth tightened. "Get out."

His shaken wife opened the door. Mike couldn't hurry through it fast enough. Aurora stared after him. Why hadn't he stuck by her? God, that hurt. Heart aching, ashamed, and embarrassed, she hid the bra behind her back, while tears filled her eyes and overflowed. "I need this job. Please don't fire me."

"You should have thought about that before you shamed yourself in my living room," Mrs. Perkins said. "We trusted you, even took you to Hawaii. And this is how you repay us?"

She looked so disappointed that Aurora's tears turned into sobs. "I'm s-sorry."

Neither of them seemed to hear her. Mr. Perkins jerked his chin at the door. "I'll drive you home."

Mrs. Perkins silently handed Aurora her overnight bag, which she'd set by the stairs. She stuffed the bra into a pocket and plodded after Mr. Perkins to the Range Rover out front. No wonder she hadn't heard the garage door open. In the tense fifteen-minute ride home, neither of them spoke. Silent tears continued to roll down Aurora's cheeks, hidden by the night. She dabbed her eyes and swiped her nose with a tissue from her purse.

As her ex-employer turned onto her street, she bit her lip. "Are you going to tell my mom?"

"I expect you to do that. But since I don't trust you anymore, I'll call her and check. You have until Friday."

Losing Mr. Perkins's trust hurt most of all. As he pulled up the drive, Aurora felt about two inches tall.

Except for the porch and entryway, the house was dark. That meant her mom was asleep. Aside from the usual "I'm home," called out so her mom didn't worry, Aurora wouldn't have to face her until tomorrow. She heaved a breath of relief, because right now she couldn't handle a confrontation.

She opened the passenger door to leave. "Wait," Mr. Perkins said. "I haven't paid you."

Aurora hung her head. "I don't deserve any money."

"It's the last you'll get from me. Better take it." He pressed the bills into her hand. "Chloe really liked you," he said in a sad voice. "My wife and I always thought you were a great kid. Why did you do this, Aurora?"

She had no answer to that. She only knew she hated her life, hated her mom, and hated San Francisco. Most of all, she hated herself.

Exhausted, Caroline fell into bed near midnight. It was Wednesday, and for some reason eleven clients wanted changes on their websites right away. Striving to satisfy each client, she'd spent the whole day—except for the weekly meeting with Martin, which she'd cut short—and most of the evening, at her computer, stopping only to pick up Jax from school and fix dinner. As she had on Monday and Tuesday, Faye had joined them for dinner.

To Caroline's relief she hadn't mentioned religion or church since their stand-off on Sunday. Without the cloak of stiff disapproval she was the warm, grandmotherly woman who had signed the lease. Amazingly, she'd offered to entertain Jax tonight while Caroline worked.

Jax doted on the attention. She needed a grandma, and seemed to like Faye. So did Caroline. They were lucky to have her, she thought, smiling as she turned out the bedside lamp.

Before her head hit the pillow Jax screamed. The nightmares had stopped ages ago. Apparently they were back. Heart in her throat, Caroline hurried to her daughter's room.

Thanks to the nightlight Jax insisted on, Caroline padded forward without hesitation, her footsteps soundless on the thick carpet. "What's the matter, punkin?" she called out in a soft voice.

"Mama." Sobbing, Jax sat up and reached for her.

Hating the fear in her child's face, Caroline sat down on the bed, clasped the small body close, and rubbed her back. "Tell me all about it," she crooned, ready for a bad dream about Stephen.

Jax burrowed close, her small body trembling. "I d-don't want to go to h-hell."

"Hell?" Caroline frowned. She pulled back to grasp her child's narrow shoulders. "Where did you get such an idea?" she asked, gazing into Jax's frightened eyes.

"Miss Roberts said if we don't go to church, we're going to hell." Tears cascaded down Jax's cheeks.

"There's fire there, and we'll burn and it'll hurt a lot." She shuddered. "I don't want to go there."

How dare Faye Roberts put such an awful idea into a little girl's innocent mind! After pretending to drop the matter, too. The vile, devious woman ought to be slapped and then some. Furious, Caroline narrowed her eyes and tensed.

Jax's eyes widened in terror. The last thing Caroline wanted was to further scare her daughter. Mustering control, she tamped down her anger and forced a calming breath. "You're not going to hell," she said, tucking Jax's hair behind her ears. "Neither am I."

"But Miss Roberts said—"

"Miss Roberts is mistaken." Caroline plucked a tissue from the box on Jax's bedside table and wiped her little nose.

"Promise?"

"I swear," Caroline said, holding up her hand, oath-like.

Her daughter studied her soberly for a moment, then nodded. "'Kay."

Releasing a silent sigh of relief, Caroline smiled. "Think you can sleep now?"

Her daughter bit her lip. "Can I be in your bed?"

Caroline didn't want to start *that* again. "How about if I lie here with you until you fall asleep?" she bargained. "I'll leave your door open when I go, so if you need me, I'll hear you."

Thankfully, Jax settled for the offer. She lay down and closed her eyes. Within minutes her slow, even breathing signaled that she was asleep. Caroline tiptoed out. It was time to give Faye Roberts a dose of hell on earth.

* * *

Faye Roberts was either asleep or deaf. She didn't respond to Caroline's knocks on the door. Using both hands, she pounded hard, the sound almost loud enough to wake Jax.

"Who is it?" came a muffled voice.

As if she didn't know. "It's Caroline. I want to talk to you."

Seconds later the door opened. Curlers held in place with a black do-rag, Faye Roberts clasped the collar of her aspirin-pink robe and gaped at Caroline. "It's awfully late."

"I don't care." Caroline pushed into the living room.

"I can see your nipples through your nightgown." Faye compressed her lips. "I can't allow that kind of dress in here."

That stopped Caroline. She hadn't thought to put on a robe. "Then avert your eyes, because at the moment I'm too mad to care."

The steel-laced tone worked. Head bobbing, Faye kept her slightly widened eyes on Caroline.

"I asked you not to talk about religion, yet you proceeded to do so anyway," Caroline said. "I just came from Jax's room, where she was sobbing in terror. Why did you tell her she was going to hell?"

"Because she is, unless I save her. I can save you, too, Caroline. 'Repent ye therefore, and be converted, that your sins may be blotted out . . .' Acts 3:19."

The look of smug superiority on her face infuriated Caroline. "We don't want your kind of salvation."

Faye's disapproving gaze moved over Caroline's

nightgown, her mouth stern and hard. "Well, you need it."

Shaking in anger, Caroline went nose to nose with her. "You will not discuss religion, hell, salvation, or anything remotely related in front of Jax or me. Is that clear?"

Faye Roberts did not reply. Her eyes were unfocused and her lips moved silently. Caroline knew she was praying.

The woman was out of her mind.

"Steer clear of Jax," she warned, "or I won't be responsible for my actions."

She had no idea whether Faye heard her. Her lips continued to move. When Caroline opened the door and headed upstairs, she didn't appear to notice.

PART THREE

The Universe Provides

Chapter Eighteen

Shaken by the confrontation with her tenant, Caroline crawled into bed. In need of a friendly ear, she picked up the phone and called Mary Beth.

"Something really scary just happened," she said, leaning against the headboard.

"I was just about to call *you,*" Mary Beth said. "Tell me."

"You know that sweet older lady I rented to? Turns out, she's wacko—ultra-religious in a scary way. We had a talk about that Sunday, and I asked her to keep her opinions to herself."

"Sounds reasonable," Mary Beth said.

"I thought so, and I also thought we had an understanding. Well, I was wrong. Tonight she told Jax we're headed for hell. Scared her so badly, she woke up screaming." Recapping the situation fired up Caroline's temper again, and her voice shook as she finished. "A few minutes ago, I marched downstairs and confronted her. Do you know what she did?"

"I can't wait to hear," Mary Beth murmured.

"Stared into space, muttering prayers as if I

weren't there. As if she were in some weird trance."
Caroline shivered.

"Jeez Louise. That *is* scary."

"I didn't know what to do, so I left her apartment, climbed into my bed, and called you."

"I know what *I*'d do—kick her out, same as you did Delia."

"Believe me, I'd like to. Unfortunately, she signed a six-month lease."

"Talk to Martin. If he's half the lawyer you claim, he'll find a loophole."

"That's a good idea," Caroline said, cheered at the thought. "I knew calling you would help." When she and Martin had met earlier today, she'd filled his ear with good things about Faye. This would shock him. "Trouble is, if there is a loophole and Faye goes, I still need a tenant." She rubbed the back of her neck, which was knotted with tension. "What is it about me that attracts weird renters?"

"Good question," Mary Beth replied. "Ellie would say, karma."

"What in the world does karma have to do with this?"

"If you've been mean or hurt anyone lately, this is your payback."

"Before tonight the only person I treated badly was Delia, and she deserved it. In return, she trashed my apartment. I call that 'revenge.' Faye terrified my daughter, and when I confronted her, she didn't even hear me." Caroline snorted. "I call *that* 'bizarre,' and I say, baloney on Ellie's theory."

"I don't really believe in the karma thing, either," Mary Beth said. "Not with the things that have happened over the past five months. I can't have behaved that badly toward other people. Certainly not Stephen."

In no mood to discuss him, Caroline changed the subject. "How's your apartment search going?"

"Not so well. That's what I wanted to talk to you about. That, and Aurora. Something's going on with her. She's not sleeping well and has started eating dinner in her room again. When I try to talk to her, she won't open up. I'm really worried about her."

"Maybe you should reconsider counseling."

"I'm starting to think so, but I don't exactly have the money." Mary Beth was quiet a moment. "Maybe it's this apartment business," she said. "It certainly has me upset. Do you know that since Saturday I've found three places for us to live?"

She sounded less than excited. Caroline frowned. "Three? Last time we talked, you couldn't find a thing. This sounds like good news. I'm guessing Aurora doesn't think so."

"That's not the problem. Every landlord pulls a credit report. With my bad rating, no one will take a chance on me."

Caroline sympathized. "I didn't run credit reports on Delia or Faye." Martin hadn't mentioned that, and she certainly hadn't thought of it. "Surely there's a landlord in San Francisco who doesn't care about your credit."

"Not with the housing shortage we have."

"You could move to Bainbridge Island and live with Jax and me," Caroline suggested, surprising herself. *Wouldn't that be a disaster.*

Scornful laughter greeted her suggestion. "I'm not that hard up."

"Neither am I. I don't know why I offered. Forge I asked."

"I definitely will."

When Mary Beth fell asleep after the conversation with Caroline, she dreamed that she lived i Caroline's house. "Ridiculous," she said when sh woke up.

Yet crazy or not she couldn't shake the idea fron her mind. As soon as Aurora, who was in her usua foul mood, slammed the door behind her Thursday morning, Mary Beth phoned Ellie. "You wan to hear something wild? Last night Caroline suggested we move in with her."

Ellie sucked in a breath audible even through th phone line. "What'd I tell you about the Univers providing?"

"This wasn't what I had in mind. All I wanted wa a landlord who doesn't do credit checks."

"Isn't that exactly what you got? Are you going t take her up on the offer?"

"Live with Stephen's other wife? I don't think so.

"You told me yourself that you and Caroline ar becoming good friends, that she's the only one wh truly understands what you're going through. can't think of a better roommate for you."

"You're as nuts as Caroline," Mary Beth said. " intend to find an apartment before Monday or di trying. If that means lowering my standards . . ."

She shuddered at the thought. But with less tha three weeks to find a new home she was desperate The Universe had better provide a better alternative than moving in with Caroline.

* * *

Amazingly, Thursday morning Jax awoke happy and rested. In the light of day she seemed to have forgotten the Faye Roberts' induced fears about burning in hell. Caroline hadn't. She'd slept badly, her insomnia fueled by anger at Faye and fear over her odd behavior. She definitely wanted the religious zealot gone—if Martin could find a loophole in the lease. First thing in the morning, she phoned his secretary, Jean, and asked for an appointment, the sooner the better. Jean squeezed her in, and after she dropped Jax at school, she drove straight onto the ferry and then to Martin's office.

He stood to greet her, his eyes lit with pleasure and his smile warm. "I didn't expect to see you again so soon."

Her heart did a funny flip-flop, which she decided must be indigestion. Never mind that the yogurt she'd eaten didn't cause indigestion. She was not falling for Martin.

Perceptive as he was, he noticed her discomfort. Immediately he sobered. "Is everything okay?"

Caroline shook her head. "It's Faye," she said, taking a chair. "I want her out."

"What?" Looking puzzled, Martin sat down behind his desk. "Didn't you tell me yesterday that she was exactly what you wanted—a clean-living grandma-type?"

"Yes, but was I wrong." Caroline told him everything, starting with breakfast on Sunday. "She disrespected my wishes and frightened Jax," she finished, angry all over again. "Then she scared *me.*" She explained what had happened in Faye's apartment. "I

truly think the woman is crazy. The people who gav
her glowing references must be, too. She must go
Problem is we signed a six-month lease." Carolin
pulled the folded document from her purse an
opened it on the desk. "Mary Beth said you'd know
what to do."

"You talked to Mary Beth about this?" Marti
asked, one eyebrow arched as he picked up th
lease. "I thought she was hard-headed and you were
mad at her."

"We got past that."

Ignoring the lease, he settled back in his chai
"What else did she say?"

Caroline couldn't detect a hint of derision or sar
casm in his tone. She didn't understand the relie
that brought, but she relished it. And felt incredi
bly lucky to have Martin in her life. "She was as ap
palled as I am, and agrees that Faye must go. Sh
says if you're any kind of decent lawyer you'll find
loophole that will get me out of this lease."

"She did, huh?" Martin's mouth twitched. "She'
right about the loopholes. These generic lease
probably wouldn't hold up in a court of law. Let m
re-read the thing, though."

Hands clasped in her lap, Caroline waited as h
scanned the lease. This morning his hair was neatl
combed. The instant she noticed, his fingers rifle
through it, causing tufts to stick up. Now he looke
normal.

Suddenly he glanced up. "What are you smiling at?

"Nothing." She gestured at the lease. "Did yo
find a loophole?"

"If she wants out, too, no problem. You'll want t
prorate the rent and refund some of it. Same wit

the damage deposit. But if she decides to stay, and if she pays the rent on time and takes reasonably decent care of your property, you're stuck with her. That *would* stand in a court of law."

"Oh."

Caroline didn't have the money for a refund, but that wasn't going to stop her. She could easily sell the Persian rug in the back guest room—without informing Martin or Mary Beth, of course. Anything to get rid of Faye Roberts.

"Is there time for a hypothetical question?"

"I always have time for you," Martin said, looking into her eyes.

Her heart did another happy leap. "Suppose Mary Beth and Aurora moved in." Mary Beth had turned down the offer, but she might reconsider.

Her lawyer's usually implacable expression vanished under a wide-eyed, incredulous look.

Caroline laughed. "I've never seen you so surprised."

"This is more than surprise, it's cause for concern." Solemn, he leaned forward. "The woman is suing you for one point three million dollars. If that's not enough to stop you, she certainly won't agree to pay rent. How will you cover your bills?"

"Mary Beth doesn't want me to lose the house," Caroline said. "If I do, she'll never collect her money. She'll be more than happy to pay rent. I think."

"You've decided she deserves her money?" Martin frowned. "That changes everything."

"Not really. I still think she's asking for way too much, and I want to continue fighting her on that."

"So hypothetically, you want to live together while

you sue each other?" Martin asked, stroking his chin. "That seems crazy."

"Well, it isn't." Caroline leaned forward to make her point. "I happen to know that most of Mary Beth's friends have dropped her, she doesn't have a job, and she's having trouble finding a place to rent. All good reasons to relocate and start over. And since I need a housemate. . . . Forget 'hypothetical,'" she said. "Her moving in with me makes perfect sense." She intended to repeat the same line of reasoning to Mary Beth.

"You've thought a lot about this." Steepling his hands under his chin, Martin regarded her for a while through slightly narrowed eyes. "You're sure this is what you want?"

"Absolutely. Of course I'll have to convince her, and you should talk to her lawyer."

"I will, but let's not rush into anything just yet. Best wait until you settle things with your tenant."

Caroline nodded. Everything hinged on Faye.

As Caroline walked into her kitchen after the meeting with Martin, Faye stood waiting, hugging a worn bible to her chest.

"You didn't come back after dropping Jax at school," she accused. "I've been waiting for you."

Wondering whether she planned to use the book as a weapon, Caroline kept her hand on the back-door knob. "Good, because I want to talk to you, too." Faye's gaze darted to the table, and good manners forced Caroline to offer refreshment. "Please sit down." She moved into the room. "Would you like a cup of coffee?"

"No, thank you." Mouth pinched, Faye took a chair, setting the bible on the table in front of her.

"Well, I would." In need of something warm to hold onto—kicking out a tenant, especially a crazy one, was hard on the nerves—Caroline poured the remains of the breakfast coffee into a mug and warmed it in the microwave.

Faye was silent until she sat down. Then she folded her hands over the bible. "You said you belonged to a church. When I moved in here, I thought I was moving into a house of righteous believers." Disapproval darkened her face. "You lied to me."

"We *are* believers," Caroline said firmly. "Just not in your particular way. And speaking of lying, you agreed not to preach at me or my daughter."

Faye raised her head defensively. "I told you, I was trying to help. But you won't listen. The devil has you in his clutches, Caroline. You're a daughter of Satan, and so is Jax." She picked up the bible, cradling it like a child. "I cannot live in such a house."

"You're saying you want to break your lease?" Never in her wildest imagination could she have imagined this. She couldn't even pretend to be sorry. "When are you moving out?"

"Today. My mover friends are waiting for my call."

Barely able to suppress a "yahoo!" Caroline nodded. "I suppose you'll want a refund on part of the rent. It'll take me a few days to get the money."

"I can wait for that," Faye said. "I just want out."

Chapter Nineteen

"Mom?"

Mary Beth jerked awake. It was still dark outside. She shot a glance at the bedside clock—five-thirty A.M. Startled, she sat up. "What's the matter?" She flipped on the reading lamp, blinking in the sudden light.

Dressed for the day, biting her lip, Aurora swallowed. "I need to tell you something."

"Now?"

Aurora nodded. Never had she voluntarily awakened and dressed so early, especially on a Friday, when she was tired from the long school week. And she did look tired. Dark smudges hung under eyes that were red with fatigue. She refused to meet Mary Beth's gaze.

Alarmed, Mary Beth patted the bed beside her. "What's the matter?"

Her daughter shook her head and stayed where she was, as if she couldn't bear to move one step closer. "I got fired from my babysitting job," she said in a low voice.

"Fired?" Mary Beth echoed. Puzzled, she frowned. "But Mr. and Mrs. Perkins took you to Hawaii. They left you with Chloe all last weekend. The whole family loves you."

Shoulders slumped, head bowed, Aurora shook her head. "Not anymore."

Mary Beth had seen her daughter mad. She'd seen her lost to grief. But she'd never seen such dejection. Curious—why had Aurora lost her job?—and wanting to comfort her, she offered a sympathetic expression. "I'm sorry, honey." Again she patted the bed. "Why don't you sit here and tell me what happened."

Shaking her head, Aurora stayed where she was. "You won't want me near you when you find out what I did." Her teeth raked her lower lip and her hands locked together at her waist.

A range of scenarios played through Mary Beth's head. Theft? Drugs? Alcohol? Dear God, had her daughter stolen jewelry or money, or turned to mind-altering substances to cope with her burdens? She tried a reassuring smile, but couldn't quite manage it. "Tell me."

"It's really, really bad and you're gonna hate me," Aurora said. "But that's okay, because I already hate myself." At last she made eye contact. "I let a boy come over while Mr. and Mrs. Perkins were out. They caught us."

"Boy? What boy?"

"Mike."

"The one on the phone the other night? I had no idea you two were seeing each other outside school."

"We aren't, not anymore." Aurora tugged angrily at a spike of hair. "He doesn't go to my school, or any school. He's eighteen. I met him at the mall."

Eighteen? The mall? "What are you doing with a boy that age?" That her daughter had lied hurt terribly. Forget about doling out comfort. Mary Beth narrowed her eyes. "You little sneak."

Aurora's mouth twisted in pain. "You can yell at me later, Mom. Please, I need to tell you everything."

There was more? Uncertain she wanted to know, but at the same time more than curious, Mary Beth nodded.

"I thought he loved me, but all he wanted was . . ." Aurora's lower lip trembled. "Sex."

Mary Beth gasped. "You and Mike had *sex*?" She'd hunt him down and throttle him.

"No!" Tears filled the girl's eyes. "But he wanted to."

Thank God. Relief spilled from Mary Beth in an enormous breath. Until an ugly thought niggled into her brain. "Did he hurt you?"

Her daughter shook her head and swiped her eyes. "But we were on the couch when Mr. and Mrs. Perkins came home. That's why they fired me. Mr. Perkins will be calling you today to make sure I told you." She stared at the floor. "Now you can yell at me."

Mary Beth could only guess at her daughter's humiliation. Poor girl seemed to have punished herself enough. "I'm not going to yell," she said. "I just wish you'd told me the truth about Mike. Maybe I could have helped."

"How?" At last her daughter flopped down at the foot of the bed. "You'd just get mad like you did a few minutes ago. You'd tell me he was too old and not good enough for me."

"And I'd be right, wouldn't I?" Aurora conceded with a nod, and Mary Beth continued. "Why did you get involved with him?"

"I told you before, he didn't judge me for what Daddy did. Unlike everybody else he was *nice* to me."

More fallout from Stephen's deception. "There are some people who love you regardless of what your father did," Mary Beth pointed out. "Ellie, for one."

"I'm talking about school." Now the tears were gone, replaced by bitterness and anger. "You don't know how awful it feels to walk down the halls, knowing all the kids are looking and whispering."

Mary Beth had felt just as bad walking into Jones, Westin and Hawkins. She completely sympathized. "Well, school will be over in a few weeks, and we'll be living someplace else."

"But I might run into kids I know, and they'll still treat me like I have some horrible disease. Couldn't we please move someplace where nobody knows us, and start over?" Aurora sent Mary Beth a desperate look. "Could you at least think about that?"

"We can't just pick up and leave town," Mary Beth argued. "Where would we go?"

To Caroline's house on Bainbridge Island, a voice in her head replied as clearly as if someone had whispered in her ear.

"Bainbridge Island?" Aurora gaped at her as if she were out of her mind, and she realized she'd spoken out loud. "Isn't that where *they* live?"

Mary Beth had no idea why she'd thought of living on the island, when a few days ago she'd firmly nixed the very suggestion. "You're right," she said. "It's a ridiculous idea. But Caroline invited us to move in, and remember, half their house belongs to us."

"How could she ask us to live with her?" Aurora

made an indignant sound. "We hate her, and she hates us. She must be crazy."

Time to come clean with her daughter. Mary Beth smoothed the satin border of her wool blanket. "Since you were totally honest me, I need to tell you that Caroline and I talk all the time. Believe it or not, we've become good friends."

Her daughter's eyes widened. "I know you don't have friends here anymore, Mom. But *her*?" She gave her head a dismal shake. "You're even more mixed up than I am."

"Maybe so, but I can't find a decent job, and with my bad credit we can't get into an apartment, either. Give me one good reason to stay in San Francisco."

"Ellie," Aurora said. "You don't want to move away from her."

"Before the year is out, she'll be living in Montana," Mary Beth replied. "Caroline runs her own graphic design business, so she at least earns something, but she's having money problems. She needs to rent out part of the house to make the mortgage payment. I think we should seriously consider living with her."

"You mean, we'd pay rent?" Aurora looked thoroughly confused. "I thought she owed *us* money. Isn't that what your lawsuit is about?"

Mary Beth nodded. "It's complicated, honey. If Caroline doesn't collect rent, she can't make the mortgage payment. Then she'll be forced to sell, like us. Her mortgage is big like ours, and most of the sale price would go to pay it off. Then we'd never get our money. But if we rent from her, she'll be able to hold on to the house, and eventually we'll get the money she owes us." Mary Beth eyed Aurora. "Does that make sense?"

Fiddling with the back of her hair, her daughter mulled that over. "I guess. But I still think living with Daddy's other wife is a lame idea. I vote, no."

"Nothing is decided yet." But the more Mary Beth thought about it, the more moving into Caroline's house appealed to her. Of course, that weird, religious tenant could decide to stay on, or Caroline might've changed her mind.

Mary Beth hoped not. She itched to call and find out, but it was way too early.

She would have to wait.

"I drop Jax at school, walk through the kitchen door, and you call about moving in." Cupping the phone between her ear and shoulder, Caroline headed for the kitchen table. "I can't believe this is happening."

"Believe it," Mary Beth said.

"Your timing couldn't be better. Faye will be gone by the end of the day, and I was about to place an ad in the paper."

"Ellie says it was supposed to happen this way—the Universe providing and all."

"Could be." Caroline fiddled with the salt and pepper shakers in the middle of the table. "But if this is going to work out we need more than woo-woo stuff. We should set some ground rules."

"Absolutely. You go first."

"I don't want Jax to know about Stephen."

"But Aurora and Jax are half-sisters," Mary Beth said. "Don't you think—"

"This is non-negotiable. Jax is finally adjusting to life without Stephen. I won't have her upset all over again."

"I've said this before, but I feel compelled to repeat it. You're making a mistake. Take it from me, who learned the hard way. I hid the truth from Aurora for one little week and she still hasn't forgiven me."

"Yes, but she's a teenager. Jax is only seven." Ready to fight for her daughter's peace of mind regardless of the consequences, Caroline narrowed her eyes at the art deco tea kettle sitting on the stove. "If you tell her, you're gone."

She meant that, too—just ask Becca. The thought of her sister put a hollow feeling in Caroline's chest. Who knew why the was thinking of Becca just now. *She* certainly didn't think about Caroline. According to her father, who talked with both women weekly, Becca always asked about Jax but she never mentioned Caroline. She didn't seem to care that they weren't speaking, and the indifference stung. Caroline frowned. "Nobody talks about what Stephen did. Is that clear?"

"All right, already," Mary Beth muttered. "I won't say anything. But what *are* you going to tell Jax about us?"

The sixty-four million dollar question. Caroline hadn't a clue. "I don't know yet, but I'll think of something. When I do I'll let you know." That settled, she eased back in her chair. "Here's another ground rule. The mortgage payment is due the first of each month and I can't afford any late fees. I'll need your check on time."

"No problem. Once the house closes I'll have

enough for at least for the first few months. After that . . . I'd better find a decent job. Hear that, Universe?"

"I'll ask around," Caroline offered, already doing a mental sift through a list of people to contact.

"Thanks. I'm willing to try anything, and I don't mind starting at the bottom and working my way up. As long as my paycheck covers the rent and food, so no minimum wage positions. If possible I'd like health insurance, too."

"Got it. Your willingness to start at the bottom? That's a big change in attitude," Caroline said.

"You get turned down enough, you have to adjust. Besides, if I truly want to move on with my life and start fresh, I'd better be willing to compromise."

Maybe she wanted to compromise and start fresh in other ways, too. Caroline leaned into the phone. "Dare I ask whether you've had a change of heart about the lawsuit?"

"I want my money, so the answer is no. That's *my* ground rule. Oh, and I think my rent payments should be added to my share of the equity. I want that in writing."

A fair enough idea, Caroline decided, though Martin might not agree. But one point three million was way more than Mary Beth deserved. Caroline compressed her lips. She refused to let Mary Beth have anywhere near that much.

And there was the sticking point, the reason for the lawsuits and counter-lawsuits that made this whole moving in together idea absurd. Yet she wanted their living arrangement to work. "I'll talk to Martin," she said. "He and Kevin can hammer out the details."

Mary Beth made a noise that sounded like a cross between a groan and a laugh. "Kevin already thinks our friendship is weird. When he hears about us living together he'll think I've lost my mind. Aurora certainly thinks so. She's against this whole thing. Ellie is my only ally."

"Besides me. How soon can you get here?"

"The house closes in two weeks, and Aurora's school lets out a week later. She hates that place but I want her to finish, so we'll pack a U-Haul, drive it to Ellie's, and commute from her place until then. Hmmm . . ."

Caroline heard pages turn and imagined Mary Beth checking the calendar.

"I'd like to be settled in by Aurora's fifteenth birthday, which is June first. If we drive ten hours a day, we should make it in two days. We'll leave San Francisco the last Saturday in May."

"Perfect. To reach our house you'll need to catch a ferry."

They spent a few minutes discussing ferries, and Caroline gave her the website that listed the summer ferry schedule and fares. "I'd like to bake Aurora a cake," she offered. "What kind does she like?"

"That's very sweet of you. Her favorite is chocolate cake with coconut-brown sugar icing. I'll email the recipe."

"That'd be great. See you in a few weeks."

Chapter Twenty

"I know you disapprove," Caroline told Martin the following Wednesday. They were in their usual spot at the bustling Starbucks, and had spent most of their time reviewing the details of the living arrangement Martin and Kevin had worked out.

"I never said that."

After five-and-a-half months she knew that while Martin the Friend candidly shared his personal opinions, Martin the Lawyer did not. Right now he was in lawyer mode, his expression carefully neutral.

She couldn't stem a knowing smirk. "You sound like a diplomat, but you can't fool me. You still think it's crazy."

His mouth toyed with a grin. "You have to admit, what you're doing is completely unconventional. Risky, I'd say."

"I'm willing to take the risk because this feels right, if that makes sense. Mary Beth and I have been through the same emotional wringer. We connect on many levels."

"Many levels, huh? That sounds metaphysical."

Caroline hadn't mentioned Ellie's "the Universe Provides" theory. He'd probably laugh. "All I know is, we're both excited about this move. Mary Beth needs a job, though, so if you hear of anything . . ."

Martin rubbed his chin. "What kind of work?"

"Anything that pays decently and doesn't require much in the way of experience. She hasn't worked since college. Doesn't have a degree, either."

"That'll make finding decent wages tough," he said. "But I'll put out the word."

"Thanks." Using her napkin, Caroline swiped the crumbs from the table onto her empty muffin plate. "I wish I knew what to tell Jax about all this."

"You mean you haven't told her?"

Now he looked and sounded like Martin the Friend—a slightly disapproving friend.

"When the time is right, I will," Caroline said, sounding defensive to her own ears. "I'm still working on what to say." She noted his questioning look and set her jaw. "It definitely won't be about how Mary Beth and I are connected, so don't pressure me to change my mind."

"Your choice." Martin picked up his cup and slanted it in salute. "Good luck."

She relaxed. "I appreciate your not lecturing me on the dangers of keeping my daughter in the dark."

"And make you mad at me?" His mouth twitched. "Can't have my favorite client angry."

"I'm your favorite?" She couldn't help smiling. "Is that good or bad?"

"Good. Very good. Caroline . . ." He shifted in his seat. "I need a favor."

The whole time she'd known him, he'd never once asked her for anything. She'd done all the asking and all the taking. Eager to pay him back at least a little, she propped her head between her fists and gave him her full attention. "Name it."

"One of my clients, a guy named Ted Flannagan, is hosting a dinner party Saturday night. I need a date. And since we're friends, I thought . . ." His ears reddened endearingly. "Will you come with me?"

She'd never seen him so flustered. She liked this man a great deal. Smiling, she nodded. "I'd be happy to—if I can find a sitter for Jax. I haven't used one since Stephen died."

Mainly because of the expense, which Caroline couldn't afford.

"You find the sitter and I'll pay," Martin offered, as if he'd read her mind.

She shook her head. "I can't let you. You've already done so much for me."

"Your coming to this dinner party is a big deal to me, well worth the price of a babysitter. Heck, I'd pay four figures just to get you there."

Caroline shot him a sideways look. "Why?"

"So I'll have a comfortable friend to talk to."

She liked that he found her comfortable. "I'm guessing you don't enjoy socializing with this particular client. So why waste your evening with him?"

"I don't mind Ted. He's a good client. It's parties I dislike."

"They're not my favorite activity, either."

"Then I owe you doubly for helping me out." Martin flashed a grateful smile. "I'm definitely paying for that sitter."

Caroline opened her mouth again to argue, but he cut her off. "Look, we both know that right now, money's tight for you. If it makes you feel better, I'll add the cost of the sitter to your tab."

Since she intended to pay him somehow, someday, she gave in. "Okay," she said. "Should I dress up?"

"I'm stuck wearing a suit and tie, so you probably should."

"No problem." Luckily she had more than a few dressy outfits. Last year's styles, but decent all the same. "Should I ride the ferry over and meet you someplace?"

"Heck, no. I'll pick you up." Martin glanced at his watch. "Better get back to the office." His chair scraped the tile floor, but he waited for Caroline to stand first.

As they exited the coffee shop his hand touched the small of her back. A little thing that pleased her.

"I'll pick you up Saturday night at seven," he said before he headed for the elevator to his office.

A date with Martin. Caroline practically floated toward her car. Suddenly the May sunshine seemed brighter. She couldn't stem her excitement or ignore the scared feeling in the pit of her stomach.

Was she ready to start dating, and was it wise to go out with her attorney? The very question caused her to snicker. Oh, that was rich. A man in a business suit walking toward her gave her an odd look, and she flattened her lips.

Dating her attorney was nothing new. The man she'd married had been her lawyer for ten-plus years, though that had cost her dearly.

On the ferry ride home she stayed in her car and continued to mull over her pending date, wondering what Mary Beth would think about this turn of events. She'd probably read more into the situation than she should, and then start in with probing questions, the same ones Caroline was asking herself.

The boat docked. Deep in thought, she waited her turn behind dozens of cars, then drove down the ramp. Maybe she'd keep this date thing to herself. After all, it was only a get-together between friends.

Really, there was nothing to tell.

"Thanks for bailing me out tonight," Martin said as he pulled into Caroline's driveway.

The moon was barely a sliver in the star-studded sky, and though the welcome lights winked along the dark driveway and yard, shadows hid his face. She thought he might be smiling.

She smiled, too. "I enjoyed myself. Ted Flannagan and his friends are nice, and the food was great."

"You weren't bored out of your mind by all that business talk?" Chuckling, he parked in front of the garage, beside the sitter's car. "You need to get out more."

This was the first Saturday night in months that she'd left the house without Jax. She hadn't realized how badly she needed a night out. "I really didn't mind the business talk, because I wasn't expected to contribute."

"Good point. But Flannagan's endless bragging about the 'killing' he made on the stockmarket last week . . ." Martin unhooked his seat belt. "The man may be my client, but he's also full of hot crap."

"You mean he's not one of your favorites, like I am?" Caroline teased.

"You're at the top of the list."

The warmth in his voice thrilled and worried her—they were supposed to be *friends.* She simply wasn't ready for more than that. Was she?

Martin exited the car. He opened her door and helped her out. In easy silence they ambled up the brick walkway to the front door. Motion lights flashed on, turning the night bright as day.

"Would you like to come in?" she asked.

"I'll pay the sitter. Then I should go."

Ten minutes later, the eighteen-year-old sitter paid and gone, they stood alone in the entry.

"Thank you for inviting me tonight," Caroline said. "I really did have fun."

"Me, too."

Martin's gaze homed in on her. She didn't miss the heat in his eyes. Her body responded, suddenly warm and alive. Would he kiss her?

Caroline wouldn't stop him. Tingling with anticipation she lifted her face.

He leaned toward her and brushed her cheek, his lips skimming lightly over her skin. She caught a whiff of pine soap and man before he backed away.

Sharp disappointment stabbed her, but she pasted a carefree smile on her face. She opened the front door. "Next time you need a date for a boring dinner party, I'm your woman."

"So you *were* bored." His mouth quirked.

"Good night, Martin. I'll see you Wednesday."

Later in bed, as she reviewed the evening, she decided she'd misinterpreted the warmth in his eyes. Otherwise he'd have grabbed his chance and kissed her mouth instead of her cheek. He definitely wasn't interested in her as more than a friend.

That really was for the best, because she wasn'

ready for anything more. Except, that was a total lie. At some point without her realizing it, her feelings for Martin had grown beyond friendship. Given that she'd lost Stephen nearly six months ago, that seemed awfully fast. But her heart didn't seem to care, and since Martin didn't share her feelings, nothing would happen anyway.

What mattered were her deep, warm feelings. She wasn't dead inside, after all.

Weeks ago she'd told her father, *I think I'm going to survive.* Now she knew for certain that she was truly on the mend.

Leaning across the sink in Ellie's tiny powder room Aurora stared into the mirror. Even though yesterday was her last day of middle school—yay!—she didn't look any different. Same spiky black hair, same zit on her forehead, same slightly oversized nose. People said she had a heart-shaped face, but Aurora thought her cheeks looked fat. And her eyes were a little too close together, just like her father's. Ick. She hated having his eyes because she hated him for ruining her and her mom's lives. That was why she wore black eye liner, to make them look different from his. She turned sideways, checking out her breasts in the mirror. A few days from now she would turn fifteen, yet her body looked twenty.

She'd sure fooled Mike. For a moment her world turned dark. After the disaster at the Perkins' she'd never heard from him again.

Aurora told herself she didn't care, but her pained reflection said otherwise. She didn't like to show her feelings, especially around her mom, who tended to want to talk, but usually ended up lecturing instead. Bo-ring.

She forced a smile that looked as fake as it felt. Not that her mom would notice this morning. She was all wrapped up in moving. Now that their house belonged to strangers Aurora didn't mind that they were leaving. She was relieved she'd never see the snotty kids who once had been her friends. But Bainbridge Island was the last place she wanted to go. Living on an island sounded remote and isolated. Who wanted that, and who wanted to live with her father's other family? Not Aurora.

Yet in a few minutes her mom would force her into the ugly U-Haul. Barely masking a scowl she trudged into Ellie's small living room in time to see her mom wipe tears from her eyes.

"I'll miss you so much," she told Ellie, who also was teary-eyed.

"Once I move to Montana I'll be only seven hours' drive away."

"A drive we'll both make often," Aurora's mom said. She glanced at Aurora. "My turn to use the powder room."

The second she closed the bathroom door, Aurora cast a pleading look at Ellie. "Can I stay here with you?"

Ellie shook her head, then slung her arm around Aurora's shoulders and pulled her into a sideways hug. Aurora smelled her flowery cologne. "Though I love you like my own, that'd never work out. You wouldn't like living with me. I work long hours, rarely cook, and I hog the phone talking to Joe every night. You've been here a week, so you already know that this little apartment is way too crowded for more than one person. More important, your mom would be miserable without you." She raised an eyebrow at Aurora. "You know that, don't you?"

"I guess," she grumbled, though lately her mom seemed more excited about Caroline than her. "But I'd rather sleep on your hide-a-bed forever than live with *them*."

"How do you know that? You've never even met Caroline and Jax."

"I don't want to, either. I hate them." Aurora cringed. "I don't see how Mom could be friends with Caroline."

"Because she realizes that none of what happened was Caroline's fault. She didn't know your father was already married with a daughter any more than your mom knew about her. In that way, she and your mom are kindred spirits. And don't forget, you and Jax are half-sisters." Ellie smiled as if that pleased her. "Family is important, and you don't have much, hon, so be thankful you get to know and live with yours."

"Thankful?" Aurora wrinkled her nose in distaste. "Some family. They're not what I would choose."

"None of us gets to choose our relatives."

"Caroline won't even let us talk about what Daddy did. She thinks Jax is too young to understand, so we have to pretend we don't know. That means that even if I want to, and I don't, I'm not allowed to treat Jax like a sister. How lame is that?"

"I agree that Caroline's making a big mistake with this secrecy business, but right or wrong, she believes that hiding the truth will protect Jax from more pain and confusion," Ellie said. "At least that's what your mom says."

"Protect? If either Mom or I mention what Dad did or that Jax and I are related, Caroline will kick us out. We'll have to watch everything we say." Aurora rolled her eyes. "I don't know if I can stand to live like that, and I think Mom is crazy for saying she can."

"Do it anyway, for her sake. She needs a friend and she needs support. Who better than a woman going through the same grief and misery? For your mom and Caroline to move past the bitterness and hatred they once felt takes a great deal of maturity. I think it's wonderful."

Aurora wanted to be mature, too, but this? She remembered the time she'd called Caroline's house and Jax had answered, and then, when Caroline had called back. She'd told her mom they sounded nice, but she had no intention of liking them or stupid Bainbridge Island. She crossed her arms. "Maybe I'll run away."

"You're way too smart for that," Ellie said. "You know your mom doesn't deserve the pain and worry that would cause. You're all she has."

"That's not true. Now she has Caroline and Jax, too." Feeling bleak Aurora stared at her black flip-flops and black toenails.

"Look at me," Ellie ordered in a voice that couldn't be ignored. Aurora grudgingly obeyed. "I want you to promise you won't run away." The way she looked at Aurora reminded her of a teacher expecting a bad student to do better. "If things get really awful, talk to your mom. If you can't talk to her, call me. But don't make your life worse by running away." She searched Aurora's face. "Promise me."

"Okaaaay."

"Atta girl." Ellie smiled, but not for long. "There's one more promise I want from you. Give this move a chance. You just might be surprised by what you find."

Aurora wasn't about to do that. Bad enough she was forced to move to an island. She'd promised not to run away, but she hadn't promised to keep her mouth shut. If life grew unbearable she'd tell Jax the truth and let Caroline kick her and her mom out. That she could do that gave her a feeling of power.

Her mom came out of the bathroom looking both sad and excited. "If we want to get there and settled in before your birthday, we'd better leave now."

"You go on," Ellie said, winking at Aurora. "We'll be down in a jif."

Humming, her mom grabbed her suitcase and headed out the door.

When she was gone, Ellie opened the coat closet and pulled a small, foil-wrapped box from the top shelf. Beaming and sniffling again, she handed it to Aurora. "Happy birthday early, kiddo. You're turning into a lovely young woman, and don't you forget it."

With all the packing and moving, Aurora was sure her mom's friend had forgotten her birthday. The warm words and thoughtfulness touched her heart. Tears threatened to fill her eyes, but she refused to cry. Blinking furiously, she clasped the gift close. "Thank you, Ellie."

"My pleasure." Ellie blew her nose. "Now, don't

open that 'til June first, okay? And promise you'll give the move a chance."

Aurora nodded to the request, and said a silent *no* to the promise.

She hefted her suitcase and they took the elevator to the ground floor. They headed for the side street where their U-Haul was parked. Her mom's car was hooked to the back, making it impossible to park in the guest slot of Ellie's building.

It was a foggy morning, but that would soon burn off. Standing by the U-Haul, Ellie opened her arms. "I need a hug." Aurora did, too, and she stepped into the embrace. Then Ellie hugged her mom one more time. "Drive safe and be happy," she said. "Call me from the road and when you get there."

"Will do." Her mom stepped up and into the driver's seat, and Aurora did the same on the passenger side.

Ellie blew kisses at Aurora, and mouthed the words, *remember your promises.* Busy with her seatbelt, she pretended not to see.

No way was this move going to be anything but pure disaster. Her mom was nuts, and so was Ellie. Somebody had to use common sense and keep a distance from the enemy. Aurora would.

PART FOUR

A New Leaf

Chapter Twenty-one

The last Saturday in May Caroline drove Jax to a birthday party for Bobby Greenleaf, a friend from class. While Jax squirmed with excitement, Caroline stewed. She hadn't yet told her daughter about Mary Beth and Aurora—hadn't figured out exactly what to say. But time was running out, and there was no more putting this off.

"Two new people are moving in tomorrow," she said, glancing at her daughter.

The smile faded from Jax's face. She blew the bangs off her forehead, then tightened her little mouth. "I don't like tentants."

"Tenants," Caroline corrected. "This is a mother and daughter, and they'll be our housemates, not our tenants. Sleeping upstairs, eating with us and sharing the whole house." Jax was listening, so she went on. "They're nice and I know you'll like them. Aurora, that's the daughter, turns fifteen on Tuesday. I thought we'd have a nice birthday dinner and bake her a cake. You can help me make it *and* lick the bowl," she added, playing on Jax's sweet tooth.

"'Kay," her child said, sounding pensive. "But what about Aurora's mom? Won't she want to make the cake?"

"Mary Beth doesn't mind at all. She even told me what kind of cake Aurora especially likes—chocolate with coconut-brown sugar icing."

"Yum!" Jax rubbed her stomach and licked her lips. After a few moments she frowned. "I know about Mary Beth. She didn't come to Daddy's funeral, and you got mad. If you're mad at her, how come you want her to live with us?"

Caroline's jaw dropped. She hadn't once uttered Mary Beth's name within hearing distance of her daughter. The only time her name had come up was when Becca had mentioned it after the funeral almost six months ago. Apparently her daughter had a mind like a steel trap—just like her father.

A good memory was a definite asset, but at the moment, Caroline wished her daughter were more forgetful. Stifling a groan she signaled and turned onto Bobby's street.

"How come, Mommy?" Jax persisted.

"I never expected her at the funeral." Which was true, but no real answer.

"Uh-huh, you did. I remember, 'cause when she didn't come, you got mad and fought with Aunt Becca and she and Uncle Hank and my cousins went away. You said Mary Beth was busy and that she lived in California. Why is she moving here?"

How to explain? "Because we need help paying the bills and so does she," Caroline summarized. "So we decided to live together."

Jax absorbed the information, fiddling pensively

with the scrunchie on one of her pigtails. At last her brow smoothed and she nodded that she understood. Caroline let out a relieved breath.

"If you're not mad at Mary Beth, why are you still mad at Becca?" she asked a moment later.

Caroline's stomach started to churn. Bobby's driveway was a few yards away, and she slowed and signaled. "Um, we're almost at the party. Can we talk about this later?"

"I want to talk to Meg and Molly," her daughter pushed, her eyes big and accusing. "When are you going to make up?"

This was the second time in a month that Jax had brought up her cousins, whom she obviously missed. Caroline felt bad about that, even guilty. But not guilty enough to call Becca first. As she pulled into Bobby's driveway she opened her mouth to make excuses, but Jax plowed ahead.

"If you tell Aunt Becca about Mary Beth, maybe you won't fight anymore."

"I'll think about it." Which was an out-and-out lie. She wasn't telling Becca anything unless she called and apologized.

Caroline braked to a stop. Thanks to Bobby's mother, who greeted Caroline and welcomed Jax, and the yard full of kids in birthday hats who called out to Jax, Caroline was saved from more anxiety-producing questions. God only knew what her daughter would have asked next.

No doubt something complicated that needed more than a *yes*, *no* or *maybe later*. Caroline didn't know how to answer without revealing what Stephen had done. The very thought of trying to explain bigamy to her sweet, innocent daughter made her ill. She set her jaw. Not gonna happen.

She waved as Jax and her friends skipped happily toward a picnic table laden with party favors and gaily wrapped gifts. She watched as her daughter deposited Bobby's present with the others, then donned a party hat.

As she drove home she wondered whether she'd made a mistake after all, inviting Mary Beth and Aurora to move in.

Well, there was no way to take back the offer now. By dinner tomorrow they'd be here.

Mary Beth tapped the U-Haul brake and squinted at the handsome stained-wood mailbox with the gold-edged, black numbers. "This must be it."

Aurora stared out her window without speaking, apparently lost in the music spewing from her iPod and the giant firs offering peek-a-boo glimpses of the elegant homes beyond. Mary Beth couldn't see her face, but the stiff shoulders and tension were impossible to miss.

Except for one heated exchange, her daughter hadn't said more than a dozen words since they'd left Ashland, Oregon, their half-way point, at dawn. Which, counting stops for lunch, gas, leg stretches, and a thirty-minute ferry boat ride to cross Puget Sound, had been close to ten hours. Surely by now she must be sick of listening to music.

"Ignoring me isn't going to change things," Mary Beth had pointed out after about an hour of silence this morning.

"I know that, Mother. But why should I talk, when you don't care what I say?"

"Give me a break," Mary Beth had snapped. "You know darned well that every time you open your mouth, I listen. I think I've done a heck of a good job of it, too. So don't tell me I don't care."

"Ha!" Her daughter had crossed her arms and narrowed her eyes. "I hate sitting in this uncomfortable U-Haul, and I hate where we're going. If you cared, you'd turn around and drive someplace else."

"It's a little late for that."

"See?" Aurora snickered. "You just proved that you don't care at all. Now leave me alone."

Her dark expression and pink cheeks warned Mary Beth to back off. She had enough to think about, and Aurora needed to cool down. So Mary Beth had kept her mouth shut.

But now . . .

Behind them a car honked. Excited, nerves on end, and stomach clenched, Mary Beth signaled, pulled over as far as she could, and waved the impatient driver around the U-Haul. Reaching over she tugged off her daughter's earphones. The faint strains of some male band singing about love floated toward her. "If you peek through the trees out my side, you can see the house. Looks like lots of glass and wood."

Without so much as a glance in the right direction, Aurora shrugged.

Mary Beth tried again. "I have to admit, I'm nervous about this." She bit her lip. "I could use your support."

Maybe it was her pleading tone that finally grabbed her daughter's attention. At last she turned to face Mary Beth, her eyes glinting with a steeliness so like Stephen's. "I will never support this move."

Feeling very much alone, Mary Beth turned up a long, winding driveway flanked by flowering rhododendron bushes and fir trees that cast long, afternoon shadows. Moments later she braked to a stop in front of a detached three-car garage stained the same fawn color as the house and mailbox. Through the twenty-foot space between the garage and the large, stunning house she saw a rolling lawn in need of attention, and the ocean beyond.

She knew Stephen had spent lavishly on Caroline and Jax, yet this first glimpse of their beautiful home wrenched her heart. The pain so sharp, she wondered whether she'd made a mistake coming here.

Aurora gasped as if she'd been stabbed. "Look at this place. I can't believe Daddy bought it for *them*."

"Well, now a big piece of it belongs to us." Or would, once they won their lawsuit. There was no time to say more, for the front door opened, and Caroline stepped through it.

She was as pretty as Mary Beth remembered, her blond hair tied back at the nape, the snug jeans and T-shirt showing her long legs and slim, shapely body. A young girl, no doubt Jax, peeked from behind her.

Unease settled like ice in Mary Beth's gut. Aurora was right. They shouldn't have come. Suddenly Mary Beth wanted desperately to back out of the driveway and speed back to San Francisco.

Offering a nervous smile, Caroline herded her daughter toward the U-Haul, leaving Mary Beth with no option but to climb out and greet them.

* * *

They're here. Heart in her throat, more nervous than she could ever remember being, Caroline fixed a smile on her face and approached the grimy U-Haul.

Even Jax seemed to sense her sudden trepidation. Rather than dart ahead to greet the newcomers, as was her usual way, she held fast to Caroline's hand, her little fingers warm. Caroline's were cold as ice, the balmy air and afternoon sun failing to warm her.

Clearly worried, Jax frowned up at her. "Are you okay, Mommy?"

Caroline dearly wished her daughter was someplace else for this meeting, but this was Memorial Day weekend and most of her friends had taken advantage of the long weekend by leaving town. "I'm just fine," she lied.

Mary Beth was out of the truck now, looking every bit as nervous. It had been nearly six months since Caroline had seen her. She'd lost a good twenty pounds and badly needed a haircut. But then, so did Caroline. Regular hair appointments were a luxury beyond either of their budgets.

Aurora was still in the truck, but Caroline was too focused on Mary Beth to care. "Hello," she said shyly.

"Hi." Mary Beth didn't even try a smile.

For a long moment they eyed each other, both wary and uncomfortable. *This is a huge mistake,* Caroline silently acknowledged. She thought she saw the same sentiment reflected on Mary Beth's face.

Then Jax stepped forward and broke the ice. "I'm Jax and I'm seven years old."

Mary Beth's eyes widened in shock. "My God, she looks just like Aurora at that age."

A statement bordering dangerously on the connection between the two families. If Jax started in with the questions . . . Tensing, Caroline shot Mary Beth a murderous look. *Watch your mouth or else.*

Mary Beth's eyes widened still further. Mouthing "sorry," she stepped back. "Um, nice to meet you, Jax."

Caroline's daughter nodded, then pointed to the passenger side of the truck. "Is that Aurora?"

"Yes, it is." Mary Beth gestured for her daughter to come out. When the teenager refused, her voice rose. "Aurora, you get out of the truck this instant!"

The passenger door opened, and the unhappy girl reluctantly slid out.

She was a pretty girl with Stephen's eyes and coloring, a punkish hairdo, and a surly look that reminded Caroline of Delia.

Taken aback by her hostile expression, Jax shrank behind Caroline.

"Don't worry, she's nicer than she looks," Mary Beth said. "Where are your manners, Aurora? Say hello to Caroline and Jax."

The girl shot her mother an furious look. Then scowling, nodded toward Caroline. "Hi." No smile, and no eye contact.

"How come you don't like us?" Jax asked.

Afraid of what she might answer, Caroline widened her eyes at Mary Beth, who shifted uncomfortably.

"She does like you, Jax. She's just . . . shy."

Aurora glanced at the pale blue sky and shook

her head. "Why lie to them, Mother? Jax is right. I don't like them, and I don't like being here."

Jax looked shocked and upset. Caroline's protective hackles rose. "She didn't mean that, honey," she said, squeezing her daughter's shoulder and shooting Aurora a dirty look.

"That was rude," Mary Beth agreed. "Please accept our apologies."

Mary Beth's daughter was even more antagonistic than Caroline had imagined. More than ever she wished she could undo her offer and send them away.

Because she couldn't, she led Mary Beth toward the house. "The boys I hired to help move your furniture should be here soon." Martin had lined up three college boys, the son of a colleague and two friends, to carry the heavy stuff, for the bargain price of sixty dollars. "Meantime, how about a tour?"

Chapter Twenty-two

Aurora sat cross-legged on the thick, pale blue carpet in her bedroom, listening to A Fall Out Boy on her iPod. Caroline and Jax were downstairs working on dinner, and her mom was next door unpacking her stuff, humming the way she used to when she cleaned, cooked, or did chores. Aurora couldn't stand listening to that, or the drawers opening and closing as her mom put away her things. She was settling in fast, and that made Aurora want to throw up. So she'd put on her earphones and cranked up the music. If she closed her eyes, she could almost forget she was here.

The only decent part of this whole dumb move were the college boys who had carried the furniture upstairs to their rooms. But aside from a few warm smiles they hardly spoke to Aurora, and once they'd set up her and her mom's beds and brought up the rest of their stuff, they'd left. Her mom expected her to unpack, but Aurora wasn't sure she wanted to—now or ever.

Back against the wall, she glanced around what

was supposedly her bedroom. Boxes were stacked everywhere. Since this bedroom was almost as big as the one she'd slept in all her life, her stuff would fit easily. No window seat, though, but there was a big window that faced the backyard and Puget Sound. The view was different from home, where the window overlooked a smaller yard and gazebo, and the trees and rooftops of other houses.

Everything here was color-coordinated, just like her old room, only different colors. Dark blue drapes with tiny white and burgundy flowers matched the throw pillow on the striped blue cream and burgundy armchair, and also the strip of wallpaper that lined the walls just beneath the ceiling. Her canopy and bedspread totally clashed, but all the same, it was a nice room . . .

Aurora caught herself and frowned. So what if the house and setting were beautiful. She hated it!

Caroline was young and really pretty. Her mom should feel inferior and jealous, but she didn't seem to. Well, Aurora was angry enough for the both of them.

Suddenly Jax peeked into the room, her mouth moving. She wore her hair in pigtails that reminded Aurora of Pipi Longstocking, a character from a kids book. She was cute and funny and likeable, but she was Caroline's daughter. That meant Caroline had had sex with Aurora's father. Gross. Even grosser, he did it while he was married to her mother. Aurora thought she might barf.

"I can't hear you." She slipped off her earphones.

"Mommy says to tell you dinner is ready," Jax said, seemingly oblivious to Aurora's scowl. "Your room is across from mine. Isn't that awesome?" She strolled in without asking, taking in the boxes and mess with her big blue eyes. "How come you're sitting on the floor?"

Aurora thought about ordering her out, but changed her mind. A better idea was to tell her about their father. That would get her and her mom kicked out fast, and they could move someplace else. She shrugged. "I like sitting on the floor."

"Me, too."

Jax flopped down beside her and crossed her legs. What was she trying to do, copy every move?

"You sure got a lotta stuff," she commented.

"Not as much as I used to. I sold most of my CDs and DVDs, and I gave away lots of stuffed animals and books."

"We sold some of our stuff, too," Jax said. "We're broke."

"Us, too. That's why we moved in with you, to split expenses."

"Uh-huh. Your birthday's in two days," the little girl said, "and my mom bought coconut for the frosting." She licked her lips. "And we bought you a present. But I can't tell what we got you, 'cause it's a surprise."

The last thing Aurora wanted was a cake and present from Jax and her mother. Now she felt guilty about telling Jax about their dad. "Great," she muttered.

Jax's face fell. "You don't like birthdays?"

"Sure I do. I just didn't expect to celebrate mine *here,* where I don't have any friends." She didn't have any friends left in San Francisco, either, but Jax didn't need to know that.

"I'll be your friend."

As if. When Aurora didn't respond, the little girl changed the subject. "What grade are you in?"

"I start high school in the fall."

"Wow," Jax said, mouth opened in awe. "I'm in first grade, and next year I'll be in second. I have two more weeks of school, and then, summer vacation. Yahoo! Mommy says—"

"Don't you ever shut your mouth?"

Jax did just that. For about one second Aurora enjoyed the silence, but the little girl's hurt look made her feel crappy. She decided to tell Jax about their father some other time.

"I'm kidding," she said. "What were you saying?"

In search of Jax, who was supposed to call Mary Beth and Aurora to the table but hadn't, Caroline headed upstairs. She was probably in Aurora's room, staring at her with stars in her eyes. One glance at the Goth-looking teen and Jax was captivated. Aurora didn't care, though. If the chip on her shoulder grew any bigger, she'd fall over. This move couldn't be easy for her, and Caroline had decided to cut the girl some slack.

Sure enough, she heard Jax's voice floating clearly from Aurora's room.

"Molly and Megan are my cousins," she said. "When they visited they used to sleep in here. But now I guess they'll stay in the basement. If they ever visit again." She let out a dejected sigh. "I don't get to talk to them anymore 'cause Mommy and Aunt Becca are mad at each other. They had a fight about your mommy."

"My mom? What are you talking about?" Aurora asked.

Mary Beth, who no doubt heard the exchange too, left her room and joined Caroline in the hall. They hadn't seen each other since a quick walk through the house, both of them uncomfortable and guarded. Now they exchanged nervous glances—what would Aurora say? Would she mention Stephen?—and suddenly the strain between them morphed into a different kind of tension.

"Your mommy didn't come to the funeral for my daddy, and they were mad," Jax explained. "My daddy died."

"Yeah, I know. I—"

"There you are, Jax," Caroline interrupted before Aurora said something she shouldn't.

Mary Beth gave her head an apprehensive shake. "I thought she understood your rule," she muttered in a voice too low for Jax to hear. "I'll talk to her later."

Forget about giving Aurora a chance to settle in. "How about now," Caroline returned in an equally low voice. "Just let me get rid of Jax. Dinner's ready," she said, focusing on her sweet little girl. "Did you forget to tell Aurora and Mary Beth?"

"No, Mama." Jax shook her head. "I told Aurora and I was gonna tell Mary Beth, only Aurora and started talking."

"That's nice," Caroline said, "but our casserole is getting cold. Go wash up, punkin."

Jax scrambled to her feet. "Come on, Aurora, let's wash our hands."

Looking less than thrilled, Aurora also stood.

"She'll be along in a minute," Caroline said, stopping the teenager with a look. "You go on."

The moment her daughter scampered into the bathroom, Caroline crossed her arms. "There are rules in this house, which your mother assured me you knew."

The guilty look on Aurora's face told Caroline that she knew exactly what she'd almost revealed.

"I expect you to behave yourself and watch what you say," Mary Beth said, softly but sternly. "Is that understood?"

Aurora opened her mouth, but at her mother's pointed frown shut it and gave a resentful nod.

"Excellent." Caroline released a relieved breath. Hungry and ready to forgive she lightened her tone. "I'm sure you're both starved. Let's eat."

"Not me I'm skipping dinner," Aurora announced. "Now please get out of here."

"Again, I apologize for my daughter," Mary Beth said hours later.

She and Caroline were nestled in twin pale yellow leather chairs in the cozy den, sipping wine and talking the way they had on the phone. The earlier discomfort between them was all but forgotten. She liked the house and liked owning part of it, and was happy she'd come.

"I know, and I feel for you," Caroline said. "That's one belligerent teenager." She tucked her feet under her the way she probably had every time they'd talked on the phone.

"Not always. Aurora doesn't handle change well.

In time she'll adjust. I'm just relieved we stopped her from telling Jax anything."

"So am I."

"I slipped up, too, when I first saw Jax. She and Aurora look so much like sisters. . . . That caught me completely by surprise, and I mentioned their resemblance without thinking. I'm sorry. It won't happen again."

"It had better not." Caroline stared pensively at the massive, empty fireplace in the corner. A moment later she glanced at Mary Beth, a stricken look on her face. "If you noticed the resemblance, other people will, too."

A likely possibility. Sensing Caroline's trepidation, Mary Beth bit her lip. "Was our moving in a mistake?"

Without a moment's hesitation Caroline shook her head. "I'm delighted you're here," she stated, the warmth in her eyes underlining the words. "But keeping the truth from Jax and everybody else will be a real challenge, much harder than I—"

"Mommy?" Jax said, suddenly ambling into the room. "I can't sleep."

Mary Beth noted the panicked look on Caroline's face and read her thoughts. What had Jax heard?

"Come here, punkin." Caroline drew her daughter onto her lap and tucked her shoulder-length hair—no pig-tails now—behind her ears.

Rubbing her eyes, Jax nestled close.

Mary Beth felt a nostalgic pang. At seven, Jax was almost too big for her mother's lap, but still willing to cuddle. Aurora barely tolerated a kiss on the cheek.

"Maybe you need to read me another chapter of the Amelia Bedelia book. Since tomorrow is Memorial Day and no school, I think we could swing that," Caroline said, resting her chin on her daughter's head.

For a long moment, Jax contemplated the offer. Then, setting her jaw exactly as Stephen had and Aurora sometimes did, she pulled out of her mother's arms. "No reading."

Her wide, solemn gaze fastened on Mary Beth, and Mary Beth knew exactly what she'd overheard. Explaining this mess wasn't going to be easy for Caroline. It was also private, which was fine with Mary Beth. She wanted to be someplace else, anyplace but in this room, sharing the pain that was sure to come. She tried to telegraph a message to Caroline, but with her head bent toward Jax she didn't see.

"If you don't want to read, how about a glass of warm milk?" Caroline offered.

Looking at her mother now, Jax shook her head. "I heard what you said, Mommy. You always say, tell the truth. So why are you keeping the truth from me?"

Caroline froze, paralyzed by dread. She wasn't ready for this. Her gaze flew to Mary Beth, who looked equally unsettled.

"What do you mean, punkin?" she asked.

"Mary Beth said me and Aurora—"

"Aurora and I," Caroline corrected on automatic pilot while her mind raced. How was she going to explain?

"Should I leave?" Mary Beth asked, sounding hopeful.

Needing her friend's support, Caroline shook her head. "Please stay."

"Mary Beth said Aurora and I look like sisters," Jax said, steering them back to the subject. "And you said, keeping the truth from me was gonna be hard." Her brow furrowed. "Lies are bad, so why are you telling me one?"

Mary Beth was watching her with a wide-eyed I-warned-you expression. Martin had warned her, too, and so had her father and Becca. Now Caroline wished she'd listened. Or at least prepared something to say.

Because want to or not, it was time to tell her daughter the truth about Stephen. With a heavy heart she sat Jax on the footstool opposite her so she could make eye contact as she explained.

"Your daddy loved you very much," she began.

Jax nodded.

"He loved me, too. But he also loved Mary Beth and Aurora. They were his other family."

"I don't get it." Her daughter scratched her head. "How could he have two families?"

This was the tricky part. Caroline looked to Mary Beth for help.

She nodded and joined in. "He wasn't supposed to, but he did anyway."

The simple explanation was perfect. Caroline sent her friend a silent nod of thanks.

Brow wrinkling, Jax angled her head. "Is that why you were so mad at Daddy after he died?"

"Partly," Caroline said. "What he did hurt us, and also hurt Mary Beth and Aurora."

Her daughter's grave expression let her know she understood.

"Is he in hell now?" Jax asked.

He definitely should be. Spreading her arms, Caroline shrugged. "I don't know."

"Do you hate him?"

Yes and no, but why go into that? Caroline shook her head. "Neither should you. Because no matter what he did, he loved you. And one really good thing came out of this." She glanced at Mary Beth. "I made a new and wonderful friend, and you have a half-sister—Aurora."

"She's my sister?" The confusion on Jax's face faded, replaced by amazement and delight.

That her seven-year-old brain had assimilated the information so easily was a marvel. A huge weight dropped from Caroline's shoulders, and she couldn't stem a relieved smile. Wait 'til Martin heard about this. And Becca. . . . But she couldn't tell her sister, since they weren't speaking to each other.

Looking equally relieved, Mary Beth exhaled loudly. "I think I'll tell Aurora that the rule has changed."

"Please invite her to come down and join us," Caroline suggested.

"I always wanted a sister," Jax said after Mary Beth left.

"And now you have one."

Caroline waited for more questions, but her daughter was blessedly silent. Probably too tired to think of anything.

Ten minutes later Mary Beth returned without Aurora. "She's busy unpacking," she said, giving her head a dismal shake. Translation—Auror didn't care or wasn't interested.

One step at a time, Caroline told herself. Eventu ally Aurora would grow comfortable here. Now th: she could openly act like a big sister, maybe she' warm up to Jax. That would be nice for both girls

She took her daughter's hand. "It's late. Wh don't I tuck you in one more time?"

"Do I have to go to bed?" Jax asked, yawning "There's no school tomorrow, 'member?"

"I know, but we've had a big day, and we're a tired. Tomorrow we'll follow Mary Beth to drop o the U-Haul. Then we're going show her an Aurora around the island. Then we'll take a ferr to Seattle and drive around downtown. *Then* we'r making Aurora's cake." Caroline pretended to mo her brow. "You need a good night's sleep for a that."

"I get to lick the bowl, right?"

Caroline nodded and pulled Jax toward th stairs. This time she didn't argue.

Chapter Twenty-three

Jax clapped her hands. "Get ready to sing, 'Happy Birthday.' Aurora's cake is coming!"

Her enthusiasm for everything really bugged Aurora, especially tonight, with everyone making a fuss over her birthday.

They were seated around the dining room table in a room as formal as the one in Nob Hill but with a view of the Sound. Jax was across from Aurora, and their moms sat at the ends. Except right now Aurora's mom was in the kitchen, getting the cake. She acted as if she'd lived here forever, even had a job interview in the morning. And it had only been two days.

Moving slowly, her mom carried the candle-lit cake into the room. Everyone except Aurora burst into song, their voices slightly off-key. Her mom placed the cake in front of her. Sixteen candles—the extra one "to grow on"—danced merrily atop the coconut-brown sugar icing Aurora loved. This cake looked exactly like what her mom baked her every year, only this time her mom had emailed the recipe to Caroline, and *she* had made it. Her mom acted like that was a big deal, and so did Caroline.

Both pretended they hadn't yelled at Aurora for something she didn't even say. All day yesterday they were warm and friendly as Caroline drove them around the island, which wasn't so small and isolated after all. They were just as nice in Seattle, and Jax had been all bubbly and cute, calling her "my sister" and wanting to hold hands. As if!

They were trying to make Aurora like them and like the Northwest. That never would happen. The island was woodsy and pretty, and Seattle seemed like a cool place, but too bad. The house and everybody living here, including her mom, disgusted her. But her mom didn't care, and Aurora had made up her mind that from now on she'd keep her thoughts and feelings to herself. Which meant she wasn't talking much these days, but really, that was nothing new. She'd been keeping quiet on and off for close to six months now, but her mom still worried when it happened, which was the whole point. If she worried enough, maybe they'd leave.

Tonight no one seemed to notice her silence. Throughout dinner, they'd all chatted and laughed and acted as if everything was fine.

"Make a wish and blow out the candles," Jax instructed, sounding like a miniature grownup.

Smiling, they waited for Aurora to blow out the candles. Closing her eyes, she wished she could disappear and end up someplace else, where nobody knew her and life made sense.

She opened them to a burst of applause and trails of smoke from the extinguished candles. Despite herself she was excited about the presents sitting on the buffet—all three of them. She wanted the cake, too. But she refused to show her feelings.

"Do you want to cut the cake?" her mom asked, extending the cake knife toward her.

Aurora shook her head. Though she itched to jump up, grab a gift and tear it open, she pretended she didn't care.

"When can she open her presents?" Jax asked.

Silently Aurora thanked the girl.

"Good question," Mary Beth said. "Aurora honey, why don't you do that before we have our cake?"

Caroline brought her the wrapped packages, all different sizes.

"Open ours first," Jax said, bouncing in her seat as if she were about to explode.

Aurora didn't want to open theirs at all, but she wasn't about to hurt Jax's feelings. She was a little kid. She couldn't help what had happened.

With everyone watching Aurora carefully slid off the ribbon, then removed the tape from the wrapping paper and meticulously unfolded it. She could feel her mom's curious stare and knew she wondered why Aurora wasn't ripping it away as she usually did. Well, she wasn't the same dumb girl anymore.

"Lavender-scented bath oil," she said. Since she hated baths, a totally lame gift.

Jax nodded and did another little bounce. "And powder and lotion, too, so you'll smell extra good. Mommy wanted to get the lemon set but I picked this one."

Her words earned an adoring smile from her mother and a fond grin from Aurora's mom. Aurora felt left out of their small circle. She longed to be part of it—until she reminded herself that she didn't.

"How thoughtful," Aurora's mom said, shooting her a look.

She'd have a fit if Aurora didn't act pleased "Thank you so much," she added in her polite voice.

Next she reached for Ellie's box, again carefully removing the bow and paper.

"There's a card, too," her mom reminded her Their custom had always been to read cards out loud and then pass them around for everyone to see.

This was a plain, white note card with a handwritten message. "To a girl with a heart of gold and a soul as rich as pearls," Aurora read.

Caroline made an appreciative sound, and her mom swiped a tear from her eye. "That's my Ellie, she said, sniffling. She looked at Aurora, love shining on her face. "She's right, too."

Unbidden and unwanted tears stung Aurora's eyes. Horrified, she hastily blinked them back.

"Open it," Jax coaxed.

Inside was a quarter-sized gold heart necklace outlined in tiny pearls—her birthstone—hanging from a delicate gold chain.

"It's beautiful," Aurora breathed before she remembered . . . she wasn't showing her feelings "Can we call Ellie later?" She'd thank her and beg the woman to take her in.

"You bet," her mom said. "Put it on, honey."

The chain was long enough that she could easily pull it over her head. The heart dangled a scant inch over her breasts.

They all oohed and ahhed, especially Caroline.

Why were they acting like they cared?

"Aren't you gonna open the present from your mom?" Jax asked.

Aurora shot her an of-course-I-am look. She opened the square package the same careful way. Inside was a velvet box, and inside that, a watch she'd wanted, an expensive Ashford with a pink face and hot pink band.

Aurora loved it. "We can't afford this," she said, glancing at her mom, who smiled.

"A girl only turns fifteen once. I splurged."

Aurora took off her old Swatch and placed the new watch on her wrist. It looked great. "Thanks, Mom," she said, forgetting to hold in her enthusiasm.

Her mother's eyes shone. "You're welcome, honey."

It was so easy to make her happy. Aurora felt guilty for treating her so mean. Then stupid for feeling guilty. Turning fifteen was emotional and really confusing.

"When can we eat the cake?" Jax asked.

"Aurora's the birthday girl," Caroline reminded her. "When she says it's time." She slanted her chin at Aurora.

Aurora was dying to eat cake, but she managed a sedate nod. "Now's good."

Jax clapped, Mary Beth grabbed the cake knife, and Caroline set the plates nearby.

"I splurged too, and bought Godiva vanilla ice cream, so hang on." She dashed into the kitchen and returned with two pints, an ice cream scoop, and a happy gleam in her eye. "Who wants some with their cake?"

"Me! me!" Jax shouted.

"I know you do, punkin. I meant the birthday girl."

Caroline pulled the top off one small container and looked at Aurora. "How many scoops for you?"

With the bundle of enthusiasm across the table it was hard to stay remote and calm. Aurora meant to ask for one small scoop as a way to show she didn't care. But as she met Caroline's warm gaze, her brain forgot. "Two big ones," she said, licking her lips.

By mid-morning the following day, Aurora had yet to come out of her room. No sounds issued from behind her closed door, and Mary Beth figured she was sleeping in, as teenagers do. If nobody bothered her she'd sleep half the day.

"Honey?" She knocked on the door, waited a moment, then opened it and peeked in. "Are you awake?"

Still in bed, her daughter groaned. "Now I am."

"It's a beautiful day." Mary Beth strode toward the window and opened the drapes. Sunshine flooded the room. "Don't you want to get up?"

"What for? I don't have anything to do."

She needed something to keep her busy all summer. At fifteen she wasn't old enough to work a regular job, and Mary Beth couldn't afford to send her to camp or art or drama class. Maybe the parents of some of Jax's friends needed sitters. She made a mental note to ask Caroline. For now . . .

"You have plenty to do." She gestured at the boxes cluttering the room. "They don't unpack themselves. And what about exploring the beach? You haven't done that yet."

Stony-faced, Aurora sat up and crossed her arms over her chest. "No, thanks."

After last night the hostility surprised Mary Beth. With Caroline so warm, and Jax excited and utterly adorable, the entire evening had felt like a family celebration. Even Aurora had succumbed—though her actions were more reserved than usual. Mary Beth had assumed she was starting to adjust. Apparently she'd assumed wrong.

Striving to re-kindle a better mood, she smiled. "Wasn't your birthday party fun?"

Aurora shrugged. "Not really."

"Not really?" Mary Beth settled her hands on her hips. "What kind of answer is that?"

"One dumb birthday party isn't going to change things, Mother. I still hate it here. When I talked to Ellie last night I begged her to let me live with her, but she said no." She shot Mary Beth a hostile frown. "Why did you wake me up?"

Mary Beth couldn't get over her daughter asking Ellie again if she could move in. Ellie had filled her in on the phone a few days ago. But asking a second time? Fed up, she aimed a no-nonsense look at her daughter. "You're stuck here, Aurora, so you may as well accept that."

Naturally she rolled her eyes. Mary Beth pretended not to notice.

"Now, I'm about to leave for my job interview. Caroline took Jax to school, and is running errands. So you'll be all alone."

"Good." Yawning, Aurora finally really looked at her, her gaze traveling from the loose but presentable suit, upward. "Who did your hair?"

"You like it?" Mary Beth patted the glamorous French twist at her nape. "Caroline fixed it."

"Huh." Her daughter seemed unimpressed. "What's the job?"

"Well, it's a company located in Seattle, called Boone's Messenger Service. Messengers on bicycles deliver legal papers and things around the downtown area."

"Bicycles?" Aurora shook her head in disbelief. "I can't see you doing that, Mom."

Mary Beth laughed. She hadn't been on a bike since college, and was sadly out of shape. "I don't think Boone Everett, the man who owns the company, wants a bicyclist. Apparently he needs someone to handle the phones and pay bills—things I can do."

"I hope you get this one."

"Me, too, so think good thoughts. After the interview I'll be meeting Caroline and her attorney, Martin, for coffee, so I probably won't be home for several hours."

"Are you sure you want to have coffee with her attorney?" Aurora asked, her face and tone disapproving, reminding Mary Beth so much of Stephen, she cringed.

"Since he's the man responsible for getting me this interview, absolutely."

Truth was, Mary Beth couldn't wait to meet the man Caroline constantly talked about. Yes, he was responsible for countersuing her, but that aside, he sounded like a good man. Even more interesting, Caroline had gone out with him once, and wanted to again.

Aurora looked unconvinced so she tried to explain.

"Lawyers who are enemies in court meet as friends to play golf all the time. Why shouldn't I do the same?"

"If that's what you want."

Ignoring the I-think-you're-nuts smirk was tough, but if she started an argument she'd be late for the interview. "You're sure you'll be okay by yourself?" she asked.

"Geesh, Mother." Aurora rolled her eyes. "I'm fifteen years old. I'll be fine."

Defiance glinted in her eyes, and a prickle of unease shivered through Mary Beth. She quickly dismissed it. Aurora was in her usual bad mood, that was all. Sooner or later she was bound to settle in.

Boone's Messenger Service was just south of downtown Seattle, within walking distance of the ferry, and on a one-way street Mary Beth's Mapquest search had failed to identify. She could have left the car on the island and walked onto the ferry, saving money and precious minutes. Instead, by the time she exited the boat, found a place to park and hurried into the one-story building, she was five minutes late.

And way over-dressed, if the jeans-clad, black "I Survived the Ride Around Mt. Rainier in One Day" T-shirted male working the phones was any indication.

He was talking into a phone headset, typing on the computer keyboard and working a walkie-talkie—all at the same time. He glanced at Mary Beth and held up a finger, signaling that he'd only be a moment, then pointed at the lone chair across from his desk.

As she took her seat he pressed a button on

the walkie-talkie and leaned toward it. "Jason, you there?"

A masculine voice squawked over the walkie-talkie. "Yeah, Boone."

So this was Boone Everett. While he and the man traded comments, Mary Beth studied him. He looked to be in his mid-forties and was trim and fit, no doubt himself a bicyclist. His rust-colored hair was threaded with gray and pulled into a neat ponytail, but his trimmed, rust-colored goatee was free of gray. He looked nothing like the clean-shaven, custom-suited men she was used to, but she thought him attractive.

Suddenly a second phone line rang. Still juggling the one line and the man on the walkie-talkie, his eyes flashed panic. Mary Beth jumped up and hurried toward a small office off this bigger room, where another phone sat on a desk. She pushed the blinking light on the phone panel and snatched up the receiver. "Boone's Messenger Service."

Without missing a beat, Boone swiveled around, grinned and threw her a thumbs-up.

"This is Cory Everett," said a young voice. "Who're you?"

"Mary Beth Mason." The computer on the desk flashed a screen saver of Boone without the gray in his hair, a pretty young woman, and a boy about Jax's age, who must be Cory. Mary Beth smiled. "I'm here to apply for a job."

"I hope you get it, because Sylvia quit and my dad needs help. Can I talk to him?"

Mary Beth glanced through the door. Boone was hard at work, his fingers flying over the keyboard as he spoke into his headset. "Um, he's really busy."

"I need to ask him something. Could you put me on hold and tell him it's me?" She found the hold button and pressed it.

"Who is it?" Boone said, holding his hand over the mouthpiece.

"Cory."

He nodded and quickly finished the call. Mary Beth didn't want to eavesdrop on the conversation between father and son, so she stayed in the small office. Still, she overheard every word Boone uttered.

"You spent the night at Matthew's last week. Why don't you invite him to our house this time?" He listened. "Pizza at the arcade, huh? Can't this wait 'til I get home tonight?" Again he swiveled toward Mary Beth and waved her into the room. "I have an interview waiting."

By the time she re-seated herself across the desk he'd disconnected.

"That was my son," he said.

"I thought so."

"You have kids?"

She nodded. "A fifteen-year-old daughter."

"Cory's ten, going on thirty."

Mary Beth could relate. "Aurora, too."

"You mean this I-know-better-than-you phase lasts *five years*?" Boone Everett groaned, though his eyes, a nice sky blue, lit with humor.

"Or longer. Lately she's gotten worse. Maybe because her father recently died."

"I'm sorry," Boone said. "Cory lost his mom, too, a few years back. She died in a car accident after we divorced."

"That's awful. Stephen had a heart attack." No need to reveal the rest of the sordid story. "I brought a résumé for you, Mr. Everett," she said, hoping he wouldn't notice that all her experience came from short bursts of volunteer work for the garden club and various cultural events.

"Call me Boone," he said. "Otherwise I sound like my father."

"You can call me Mary Beth." As he skimmed her résumé, she held her breath and prayed.

After an all-too-brief few moments, he set the paper aside. "I don't need to look at this. You obviously know how to answer the phone. I need a dispatcher, someone who can handle stress and still be customer-friendly. My last dispatcher quit without notice to follow her boyfriend to Kathmandu, and I'm in a real bind." He paused to eye her. "You're not the kind of woman to run off and leave a guy in the lurch, are you?"

"I'd never do that," Mary Beth said. And meant it.

Boone nodded, then leaned toward her with an apologetic look. "The pay isn't great."

"How much?" she asked, bracing for the worst. Which was a shame, since she really needed a job and liked Boone Everett. But she couldn't afford to settle for minimum wage.

"Twelve dollars an hour, with health and dental benefits after ninety days. But," he said hurrying on as if he feared she'd turn him down, "business is booming, and I have plans to grow both here and nationally. If things work out between you and me, I guarantee your position will grow along with the company, with raises along the way. Who knows, in a few years you could be vice president with stock options and a fat salary." He sat back and stroked his goatee. "You up for that?"

Above minimum wage? Health benefits? Exactly what she wanted. She could hardly believe her luck. *Thank you, Universe.* Another positive was the location. "I certainly am," she said, sending up a silent cheer.

Who knew, she might be able to take evening college classes along the way and finally earn her degree. But that was something to think about later. For now, she was going to kiss Martin Cheswick.

"Can you start tomorrow, say eight?"

If he'd asked her to show up at five A.M., she would have. "I'll be here."

"Good. We don't dress up around here," Boone said, "so wear jeans."

Chapter Twenty-four

Sitting between Mary Beth and Martin at thei
regular Wednesday table, Caroline heaved a menta
sigh of relief. It wasn't every day your attorney an
the woman he was suing met for sandwiches an
coffee. Though Martin had assured her he coul
put legal differences aside for this meeting, she'
worried all the same. For nothing, as it turned ou
Buoyed by her job offer, Mary Beth had greete
him with heartfelt gratitude. In turn, Martin dre
her out, asking about her hobbies and Aurora, hi
interest in both charming her. A skill that no doub
contributed to his success as a lawyer.

That and keen intelligence. And warm brow
eyes. And an endearing smile. He was a very speci
man, indeed, and Caroline liked him more tha
ever. If only he felt the same . . .

"Earth to Caroline." He waved his hand in fro
of her.

"Sorry," she said. "I was thinking about Ma
Beth's great news."

"That *is* good news. Well, time for me to get ba

the office." He nodded at Mary Beth. "Congratations again Mary Beth. Good meeting you."

She beamed. "And you. Thanks again for getting e that job."

"All I did was arrange the interview. You did the st."

"I did, didn't I?" Her shoulders straightened, and e looked pleased with herself. "This happens to my night to cook. I'm fixing a batch of mouthatering fried chicken. Would you like to join us?"

The invitation caught Caroline by surprise, and e knew she looked it.

Martin glanced at her, his eyes questioning. oping he'd join them, she held her breath. To er disappointment he offered an apologetic smile. etter not. Until next week," he told Caroline.

Shaking her head she watched him amble away. Vhat a guy, huh?"

"He's everything you said he was." Mary Beth udied her curiously. "Why the glum face?"

"You invited him to dinner and he turned you own. That's as good as saying he doesn't want to e me outside our weekly get-togethers."

"Not true. The way he looks at you and hangs on ur every word? The man really likes you."

"As a friend." Chin in hand, Caroline sighed. "I ant more."

"So does he. I'd bet my first week's salary on at."

"You'd probably lose it. He sure hasn't acted on s feelings."

"Maybe he's afraid. Stephen's only been gone six onths . . ."

"Clichéd as it sounds, that seems like a lifetime.

In the past six months I've changed more than the whole thirty years before." Caroline shook h head in amazement. "When I think back to wher was in January . . ."

"I know," Mary Beth said. "We've both evolved much that I hardly recognize either of us. If th makes sense."

"It does to me. Though I'm probably the or one who understands."

"Maybe he doesn't realize how much you' changed." Mary Beth leaned forward and gestur Caroline to do the same. "Here's the solution your Martin troubles. Help him understand. If were me, I'd straight out tell him how I feel and from there."

"You would?" The idea both excited and scar Caroline. "I don't know. That seems awfully ris What if you're wrong and he doesn't want wha want?" She imagined that dismal scenario ar frowned. "Can you imagine how awkward th would be?"

Mary Beth dismissed the argument with an imp tient gesture. "Did you not hear what I said? T man is wild about you. Go talk to him."

"I'll think about it," Caroline said, crossing h arms over her chest.

"What's to think about? March yourself up to office right now."

"He's with a client."

"So wait until the client leaves."

"But I need to catch the ferry and get home s can pick up Jax."

Mary Beth checked her watch. "You have thr hours, but if you want, I'll bring her home."

"Thanks, but I prefer to do that myself," Caroline said. Bolstered by Mary Beth's certainty about Martin, she made a snap decision. "I think I will go up to his office. Maybe Jean, his secretary, can fit me in between clients."

"Atta girl, Caro."

Caroline stared at her. "Nobody calls me Caro except Becca and my dad. It's a family thing."

Mary Beth grinned. "Guess that means we're family."

"I guess it does."

Jean Ballard, Martin's fifty-something secretary, hung up the phone and smiled at Caroline. "He says go on back. You have about thirty minutes."

"Thanks."

Caroline's stomach clenched and her hands felt clammy. She wished she'd ignored Mary Beth and caught an early ferry home. But since she was here she would do this: tell Martin how she felt. Now, before she lost her nerve.

He came around his desk to greet her. "I didn't expect to see you again so soon."

"I know you're busy, but I forgot something, and it can't wait." She closed the door behind her.

"Oh?" He looked concerned. "Is this about Mary Beth?"

"No." She walked straight to him. "It's about us." Cupping his warm face between her palms, she coaxed his head down and kissed him. A deep, passionate kiss that revealed her true feelings.

Martin hesitated a moment. Then growling,

wrapped his arms around her and kissed her back. Her world tilted and her bones went soft.

When they broke apart his heavy-lidded eyes were dark and hot. "Wow."

"I like you, Martin," Caroline said. "A whole lot."

"I like you, too." He shot a brief, sizzling gaze at her mouth. "But . . ."

Caroline's spirits sank. "But what?" she asked, almost afraid to find out.

"There are . . . mitigating factors."

Oh God, he was involved with someone else. "I didn't know," Caroline said, feeling like a fool. "You never said anything and I assumed . . ." the words trailed off.

Martin frowned. "What in hell are you talking about?"

"Your girlfriend. It's good that you have someone, Martin, because you're too special to live life alone."

His jaw dropped. Then he chuckled. "You're crazy, you know that? I don't have a girlfriend. I haven't since Leila died."

Relieved and then sad, Caroline nodded. "You're still pining for her. I should've guessed."

"I got past that long ago." Martin stared into her eyes, his face unreadable. "I'm more than ready to be with someone. You, on the other hand, must miss Stephen. I know he was a jerk but it's only been six months."

"I'm over him," Caroline said. "I can't explain why that happened so quickly, but each of us heals differently, some faster than others." Puzzled, she frowned. "If it's not your wife, and you don't have a girlfriend, what exactly *are* the mitigating factors?"

"First, I don't know if you're ready for what I want."

His eyes were warm and intent, and Caroline's heart lifted. "Why don't you tell me and I'll let you know."

"A relationship. Lively conversation. Spending quality time together." Holding her gaze he lifted her hand, turned it over, and kissed the sensitive underside of her wrist. "Hot sex. I want all of that with you, Caroline. I just wasn't sure you were ready."

The feel of his lips on her skin made concentrating difficult. She let out a dreamy sigh. "That's exactly why I'm here now—because I'm ready. I want those things, too. With you."

The pleased, sexy smile that lit his face brightened the room. "Well then, we have a whole different problem."

"Jax," she guessed, suddenly feeling sick. She tugged her hand from his. "I thought you liked her."

"I'm crazy about her. This is something else."

"Mitigating factor number two?" she guessed.

He nodded and gestured for her to take a seat, then sat in the swivel chair behind his desk. "You're my client. It's unethical for us to be romantically involved. If we start this thing, you'll have to fire me. Or we can wait until you and Mary Beth settle your differences."

"I don't want to wait," Caroline said. She gave him a sideways look. "Haven't we been dating all along? Meeting every Wednesday without fail, even when there's no business to discuss? You came all the way to Bainbridge Island when I was sick, and again to help with the apartment. You ate dinner with Jax and me. And you took me to that party."

"True." Martin's big brown eyes warmed. "And a
of it as friends, not lovers."

"Lovers," Caroline repeated, dizzy with the sounc
"I guess that means you're fired."

"Then you're dropping the lawsuit? Are you sur
about that?"

Caroline had grappled with the question for
full month, mentally tinkering with what sh
wanted and what she felt Mary Beth deserved. "
still think Mary Beth wants way too much, but I'n
willing to compromise if she is," she said. "The ba
news is, that means you might not earn your fee
Don't worry, though, I'll figure out a way to pa
you."

Martin shrugged. "I knew the risks when I too
you on. You don't owe me anything."

Regardless of what he said, she still meant to pa
him. Eventually. "Anyway," she said, "I should tal
to Mary Beth before I make a decision."

"As your lawyer, I concur."

She bit her lip. "I guess this means we can't mak
out now, huh?"

"Unfortunately, no. But I'm a patient man. I'v
waited years to find you. I can wait awhile longer.
He grinned. "First time in my life I'm happy to los
a client."

Chapter Twenty-five

Burdened with her tiny shoulder purse and a bulging backpack—all the luggage she wanted to carry—and fifty dollars she'd filched from her mother's sock drawer, Aurora headed for the front door. She'd lived up to her promise to Ellie to give this move, Caroline and Jax a chance. She still wasn't happy. Despite the birthday dinner and gifts, she couldn't bear to live here. She glanced down at her purse. A corner of the note she'd written her mom, explaining everything, stuck out of the front zipper pocket. Before she walked away forever she'd read it one more time, then leave it someplace where her mom would be sure to find it.

For a moment she felt guilty. She didn't want to hurt her mother. And the party last night *had* been nice. Caroline and Jax were trying their best to make her feel welcome. It could never be enough. Aurora felt like an outsider and knew she always would.

Now that her mom had Caroline and Jax she'd

be fine without Aurora, and hardly would miss her. She'd miss her mom, though. Aurora swallowed.

Sunlight streamed through the windows, making the house look light and airy. This really was a gorgeous place. Not old and classy like their home on Nob Hill, but classy all the same.

The weird thing was, now that she'd made up her mind to run away she felt sad. She hated it here, so that made no sense, but since her dad's death, everything confused her.

The phone rang. Though Aurora knew it wasn't for her, she couldn't ignore it. Maybe Ellie had changed her mind. . . . She dropped her backpack and purse by the front door and raced into the kitchen to answer it. "Hello?" she said breathlessly.

"Is this a babysitter? I'm looking for Caroline," said a woman, her clipped tone making her sound cold and stuck up.

Aurora tossed the attitude right back. "Caroline isn't here, and I'm not a babysitter, not for Jax, anyway."

"Well, who are you?"

The rude tone irked Aurora. "Aurora Mason. Who are *you*?"

"You and your mom moved in already?"

She didn't say anything more, but Aurora sensed the disapproval.

"This is Becca, Caroline's sister. Will you tell her I called?"

"Okay." Aurora hung up and went in search of a pen and paper. At least that was her intention. But her mind was full of her plans to leave, and she quickly forgot.

She wandered to the living room and stood in

front of the floor-to-ceiling window that faced the ocean. Glistening wavelets danced on the surface of the water, and in the distance a ferry boat glided slowly past. Her mom was right, it was beautiful out there. She ought to at least stand on the beach before she left forever. If she hustled there was time for a quick walk before her mom or Caroline got home. Then she'd hitch a ride to the ferry terminal and head for Seattle and the Greyhound bus station.

Aurora returned to the kitchen and headed out the back door. Instantly she smelled the sea. As she walked through the backyard she noted the leafy trees, flowering bushes, and all kinds of colorful flowers. But the weeds that clogged the gardens were about to smother the flowers. Something a gardener probably handled when her dad was alive and paying the bills. From the look of things Caroline was no gardener. Aurora's mom was. Maybe she'd weed and clean up the mess.

A swing set and climbing bars filled one corner of the big yard. Aurora imagined Jax laughing and gliding through the air, pigtails flying behind her. She was a cute little girl, and seemed to like being Aurora's baby sister. She didn't care that she was part of their father's *other* family. Aurora cared a lot, and told herself Jax wasn't really a sister, not one she could accept. Yet at the thought of never seeing the freckled face again, she felt emptier and sadder than before. Pushing the unwanted feelings aside she hurried toward the beach.

Along the water, even with the June sun beating down, the air was cool. Aurora shivered and pulled her hooded sweater close. She was the only person around, which fit her solitary mood. With no idea where she was going, eyes on the beach and deep in thought, she strode forward, her sneakers churning up the sand.

Where would she go when she left Washington? Because she'd decided to leave the state and—

"Watch where you're going."

Aurora looked up in surprise. "Sorry," she said. "I didn't see you."

A girl about her age shrugged, the tiny gold hoop in her right nostril glinting in the sun. "It's okay. I do that sometimes, too—look at the ground when I'm thinking. I'm Simone."

"Aurora."

Simone brushed red-orange bangs off her face with her fingerless-gloved hand. "I've lived on this beach all my life and I know everybody around here. I've never seen you before."

Aurora's turn to shrug. "My mom and I just moved here from San Francisco. Is 'Simone' French?"

The girl nodded. "My mother's from Giverny, home of Claude Monet."

She pronounced the words with a perfect French accent.

"Butch," Aurora said. Which was the hippest word she knew for "really neat."

"The town is awesome," Simone said. "But my mom totally bites. Last year she left me, my older sister, and our Dad for someone else. Another woman." She stuck two fingers in her mouth and pretended to gag herself.

"That sucks," Aurora said. "My family's all screwed up, too. My dad died awhile back, and we ound out he had two families at the same time. He vas a bigamist." She spat out the word.

"A lesbian and a bigamist." Shoving her hands nto the rear pockets of her hip hugger jeans, imone shook her head. "With parents like that, we *ave* to be friends."

"Know what sucks even more?" Aurora said. "My nom and I moved here to live with the other family."

"Get out." Simone's jaw dropped. "Which house?"

Aurora glanced around and realized she'd valked a long distance. She could no longer see the ouse. "It's down the beach a ways."

"What's the name of the family?"

"Same last name as mine. Mason. Caroline and ax Mason."

Simone's heavily made up eyes widened. "I know hem. Claudine—that's my sister—used to baby-sit ax all the time. She did again a few weeks ago. Mrs. Mason likes her because she has her own car. Jax is uch a cute kid."

"I know. We're half-sisters," Aurora proclaimed, orgetting she didn't want to be related to Jax.

"Awesome. What grade are you in?"

"I just graduated eighth. My fifteenth birthday vas yesterday."

"No way! Mine, too. Mass butch."

"Mass butch," Aurora said at the same time.

Laughing, she and Simone hooked pinky fingers nd pulled.

"You going to Bainbridge High next year?" Simone sked.

"I don't know. Are you?"

Simone nodded. "My sister's a senior there. Hard lasses, but lots of cute guys. We could ride the bus together, and when I get my license, I could pick you up. There's my house." She pointed to a big glass-front home a dozen yards away. "Want to hang out in my room?"

Aurora decided to put off running away for now. She nodded. "Sure."

Mary Beth hummed as she drove up the driveway. From landing a decent job to meeting Martin, this had been a terrific day. She couldn't wait to tell Aurora about her new job. In the mood to celebrate, she'd stopped at the grocery to pick up another carton of ice cream for the leftover birthday cake and a bottle of merlot for her and Caroline. She hoped things went well for Caro this afternoon, and that she'd been right about Martin.

Caro and Jax truly felt like family, and you didn't sue family. Mary Beth was considering dropping the lawsuit—provided Caroline agreed to a fifty-fifty split of the equity in this house and the other assets still tied up in the lawsuit. She'd discuss the matter tonight with Caro.

Juggling the groceries and the house key she managed to open the back door. A smattering of Rice Krispies on the table and the open dishwasher door let her know Aurora had eaten. But there was no sign of her. "Aurora?" she called as she set the grocery bag on the counter.

No answer. Her thoughts on her daughter, Mary Beth put away the perishables. She was probably in her room listening to music on her iPod. Given the glorious day, moping about in her room all day was plain silly, but Mary Beth's spirits were too high to let that bother her. Sure that her good news would brighten Aurora's mood, she headed upstairs with a light heart. Smiling, she knocked on her daughter's door, waited a beat, and then barged in.

"I'm back, and wait 'til you hear—"

She stopped. Aurora wasn't in her bedroom. From the boxes still taped shut she hadn't unpacked a thing, though her closet doors were open. She'd left her iPod on the desk, and her computer was off. She wasn't in the bathroom either, or in any of the other rooms upstairs.

Mary Beth figured she'd decided to explore the beach. That was okay. Great, in fact. The news about the job could wait a while longer.

She changed out of her good clothes, then headed downstairs again to mix the breading for the chicken. As she reached the main floor her gaze landed on Aurora's backpack beside the front door. Her very fat backpack. What had she put in there? Her purse lay next to it. Mary Beth didn't recall seeing either there this morning. Odd. She scratched her head.

She noticed the slip of paper that stuck out of the front pocket of the purse, and for some reason a bad feeling chilled her. she slid the paper from the pocket, unfolded it, and began to read.

Aurora had run away. Gasping, she dropped the letter. Dear God.

Covering her mouth with her trembling hand, she bit back a cry and ran through options for leaving the island. For a person without a car there was only one way off the island—by boat. She'd call the ferry terminal and find out if they'd seen Aurora. Trouble was, there were terminals at opposite ends of the island. She'd call both, she decided as she hurried to get the phone book in the kitchen. She realized she had no idea what her daughter was wearing, or which ferry she'd caught. Or how she intended to pay the fare.

Wait a minute. Wouldn't Aurora take her things with her? Thoroughly confused now, Mary Beth frowned out the kitchen window, which faced the back yard and ocean.

There was Aurora, strolling through the back yard as if she'd never even considered leaving. In lockstep beside her walked a girl with dyed orange-red hair, wearing tight black jeans, a black hooded sweater, and a snug black belly shirt just like Aurora's. They were talking nonstop, gesturing excitedly, and laughing.

Relieved that her daughter was here where she belonged, Mary Beth exhaled. Then she bristled. How dare her daughter laugh when she'd just given her mother a heart attack! Mouth set, fists on her hips, foot tapping the tile, she waited by the door.

Seconds later it opened. "Mom." Aurora started, clearly not expecting to see her. "I didn't think you'd be home so soon. Um, this is Simone. She lives down the beach, and her sister sometimes babysits Jax."

"Hi, Mrs. Mason," Simone said.

"Hello, and excuse me while I straighten out some things with my daughter." Mary Beth turned toward Aurora. "I read the note you wrote. So you're planning to run away."

Simone looked surprised, meaning she didn't know.

"You went through my purse?" Aurora flushed, a tell-tale sign of anger. "God, Mom."

"Don't 'God' me. I did what I had to do. I saw your backpack by the front door. You weren't around and I was worried. Are you planning to run away?" she repeated, folding her arms over her chest to hide her shaking hands.

"I was." Aurora chewed her bottom lip. "But I changed my mind." She glanced at Simone. "It's not so bad here, after all."

Hours later, Mary Beth sat with Caroline in the den, sipping the merlot she had bought. The night-time ritual of discussions over wine was becoming a pleasant habit she relished.

"I can't believe what Aurora almost pulled," she said. "I think I aged a decade this afternoon.

"Be grateful she took that walk on the beach and met Simone."

Mary Beth was profoundly thankful. "I'm relieved she made a friend, even if she does have red-orange hair and a ring in her nose."

"Despite appearances, Simone is a nice girl. Aurora dyes her hair, too."

"You're right."

"She really isn't a bad kid," Caroline said. "And she did return the fifty dollars she borrowed."

"Stole," Mary Beth corrected. "But you're right, she gave it back before I noticed it was gone. I suppose that's a positive. Now if we can find a way to keep her busy and out of trouble this summer. . . . She needs a job. Any ideas?"

"Not off the top of my head. I'll mull that over."

"Maybe Martin will know of something. He certainly helped me." Mary Beth leaned forward and arched her eyebrows at her friend. "Speaking of Martin, what happened this afternoon?"

Caroline's beaming face told her what she wanted to know.

She grinned. "I was right, wasn't I?"

Caroline nodded. "He wants a long-term relationship, Mary Beth. Only he refuses to get romantically involved while he's my lawyer. According to him, that's unethical."

"I do love an ethical man." Mary Beth patted her heart. "But you need a lawyer."

"Maybe I don't. Seems silly to sue each other when we're practically family."

"Funny, I've been thinking the same thing," Mary Beth said.

"What'll it take for us to reach a friendly agreement?"

Swirling her wine glass, Mary Beth considered the question. Did she really need one point three million dollars plus the additional equity from her portion of the monthly mortgage payments? Taking so much from Caroline and Jax no longer seemed important. Yet she and Aurora deserved something. "What if we split everything straight down the middle? That seems fair."

"Exactly what I told Martin this afternoon," Caroline said.

"Then we're agreed? That was easy." Suddenly Mary Beth felt lighter than she had in ages. "Feels good, too."

Caroline laughed. "Sure does. Let's toast to dropping our lawsuits."

They clinked glasses and finished their wine.

"I'll phone Kevin first thing tomorrow," Mary Beth said.

"Well, I'm calling Martin tonight. I can't wait to tell him that once this is settled, he's fired."

"Then you two can get hot and heavy," Mary Beth said, shooting her friend a wicked smile.

"I can hardly wait." Caroline rubbed her hands together. "Will that bother you? Since you're not involved with anyone."

Mary Beth wasn't ready for romance, and didn't think she would be for a long time to come. She shook her head. "Right now, I just want to start my job, pay my bills, and keep my daughter on the straight and narrow. I don't think I could handle anything more." She glanced at her watch. "Heavens, it's nearly eleven o'clock. I want to get a good night's sleep so I'll be at my best tomorrow."

"And I'd better call Martin before it gets too late." Caroline blew her a kiss. "Wishing you sweet dreams."

With their money issues at last resolved, Mary Beth thought she just might have some.

Late the following afternoon, when the phones at last stopped ringing, Mary Beth heaved a relieved breath. Her first day at Boone's had been hectic. She felt like a fish on dry land, a really stupid fish. So many mistakes.

She'd accidentally cut off a client by pushing the disconnect button instead of 'hold'. She'd given a messenger the wrong instructions and twice had let the phone ring until the machine clicked on—a huge no-no—but she'd been trying to work the

walkie-talkie, type into the computer, and talk int
the phone at the same time. Boone had made i
look easy, but it wasn't. Then she'd mistakenl
erased a client's file. This afternoon she'd inter
rupted Boone with questions that wouldn't wai
while he was meeting with a marketing exper
named Katie Ventura, a hot-shot young woman wit
an MBA and an expensive suit.

At five fifteen they were still in Boone's office, th
closed door muffling their conversation. Mary Bet
knew the meeting was running late because she'
interrupted Boone too many times. Her shif
ended at five. She could leave, but first she wante
to talk to Boone. She'd rather he fired her face-t
face than over the phone.

Dread filled her—she *needed* this job—but th
way she'd bungled things, she deserved to lose i
Fidgety, she straightened her desk.

At last the door opened and Boone ushere
Katie through it. When he saw Mary Beth sitting a
her desk he raised his eyebrows. "What are you stil
doing here?"

"Um . . ." Not wanting to discuss her inadequacie
with anyone but Boone, Mary Beth glanced at Katie

"I'll let myself out," she said. "Good night, Mar
Beth. I'll be in touch, Boone."

He nodded, then focused on Mary Beth. "I can'
afford to pay you overtime, so go home. I'll see yo
tomorrow."

"You're not going to fire me?"

"Why would I do that?"

"Because I made so many mistakes."

Boone chuckled and sat down in the chair Mar
Beth had used during yesterday's interview. "Yo

did fine. This isn't your average office. Lots to learn at a breakneck pace, but you're a smart woman and I know you'll catch on fast. So don't quit on me, please. I need you."

It had been a long time since anyone had needed her, and decades since she'd been called smart. Mary Beth felt as if she'd grown a foot taller.

She was going to like working here.

Chapter Twenty-six

"Tomorrow is the last Friday of school, 'cause we get out next Wednesday," Jax said at dinner Thursday night.

Wanting everyone to eat together, Caroline had waited for Mary Beth before serving the meal. Now they were grouped around the kitchen table—even Aurora—sharing conversation and food. Family.

She thought wistfully about her blood relatives. Clearly Becca wasn't going to call her first. As usual it was up to Caroline to end the standoff and re-establish contact. It was time and she would do that soon, she decided. Their father would be overjoyed, and so would Jax.

"Bet you're excited about summer," Mary Beth said to Jax.

She nodded. "I'm gonna play with my friends and go swimming and stuff." She glanced shyly at Aurora, who was seated across from her. "Will you come to school with me tomorrow?"

Caroline and Mary Beth exchanged looks, both wondering what Aurora would do. Since meeting imone the previous day, her attitude had improved. But with teenagers you never knew. Caroine held her breath, hoping Aurora would at least e nice when she turned Jax down.

"What for?" Aurora asked with less hostility than ormal.

"Show and tell," Jax said. "I want everybody to neet my sister."

A grudging smile bloomed on Aurora's face. Show and tell, huh. What time would I have to et up?"

"What time, Mommy?"

"Well," Caroline replied, "School starts at nineen, and we always leave at eight-fifty."

"Would I be stuck there all day?" Aurora asked.

"I could wait for you and bring you home."

Aurora shrugged. "Guess I'll go, then."

As enthusiastic replies went, it wasn't much. Jax lidn't seem to care. Overjoyed, she wriggled in her eat and clapped her hands. Caroline exchanged a elieved glance with Mary Beth.

"I haven't found my alarm clock yet," Aurora aid. "Could you wake me up, Mom?"

"If you don't mind getting up at seven. That's vhen I'll be leaving to catch the ferry for work," Mary Beth said with pride.

After her first day on the job she seemed tired ut pleased with herself. Caroline was happy for er, and looked forward to hearing about the day ater, while they sipped their wine.

"No, thanks." Aurora wrinkled her nose. "That's oo early."

"Mommy wakes me at seven forty-five. She can vake you, too," Jax said.

"Okay."

That settled, everyone was quiet for a while, bu
with their lasagna. Suddenly the phone rang. Ca
line and Jax didn't take calls during dinner and i
nored the sound. Aurora jumped up.

"We're eating," Mary Beth said. "Let it go
voicemail."

Aurora looked stricken. "But what if it's Simon
She said she'd call tonight."

"Call her back later."

"Okaaaay." The girl sat back down. "Oh, I forgo
she said, glancing at Caroline. "Your sister called

"Becca?" Caroline's fork dropped to her pla
with a clatter. "When?"

"Um, yesterday. I think."

"You think? Why didn't you write it down?" Ma
Beth said with exasperation. "You know you're su
posed to."

"So-rry."

Caroline was too stunned to care about the bic
ering. *Becca called.*

Her eyes wide, Jax stared at her mother. "Do
this mean you and Aunt Becca aren't mad ar
more?"

"I'm all through with anger." Caroline kn
she'd never feel as close to Becca as she did Ma
Beth. But they were sisters by birth and th
counted for something.

"Can we call her tonight?"

"It's two hours later there—too late tonight. B
sides, Aunt Becca may be working at the restaura
with Uncle Hank."

Jax's disappointment was hard to ignore. "I'll ta
to her first thing in the morning, before we lea

for school," Caroline promised. "We'll arrange a time for you and your cousins to talk."

"Yes!" Jax pumped her fist in the air, looking and sounding like a teenager. "I can't wait to tell them about my sister."

Five weeks passed, and suddenly it was July eleventh, what would have been Mary Beth's twenty-first wedding anniversary. Sitting on the ferry on the way to work, watching the water churn and froth as the huge boat glided toward downtown Seattle, she waited for the pain and emptiness and anger that had been with her on and off since January. She felt nothing more than a minor twinge of sadness. Stephen's death had been a blow and his betrayal a bitter knife in the heart, but the dark feelings had all but faded. Like Caroline she was through with anger.

She thought back over the past seven months and all that had happened to bring her to this point. Life wasn't the same as it had been a year ago. The old "friends" were gone and the full-time housewife and doormat a distant memory. Making the money stretch was a struggle, but she was a stronger woman and a better person with so much to be thankful for.

In the distance another ferry passed by, headed for Bainbridge Island. Her home. Mary Beth smiled and continued to count her blessings.

Aurora was adjusting slowly but surely to the island and her new family. Twice a week she babysat a girl from Jax's class. The rest of the time she spent with Jax and the friends Simone had introduced her to. They were a nice group of kids who had accepted her without judgment.

Mary Beth, too, had made a close friend who had become the sister she'd always wanted. She also had an adorable second daughter, which was what she considered Jax, a good job with room to grow, and no more lawsuits to deal with. Kevin had been shocked at that, and horrified that she and Caroline had moved in together, but then he'd been in shock since Stephen had died.

The ferry tooted loudly and a female voice on the intercom announced the impending docking in downtown Seattle.

As Mary Beth stood and made her way among the commuters and tourists toward the exit, she knew without a doubt that she would be all right. More than that, she was going to thrive.

The Universe had provided, and life was good.

Please turn the page for an exciting sneak peek of
Ann Roth's newest novel
coming in early 2008 from Zebra Books!

Chapter One

Saturday

Margaret Lansing was carefully dropping lichen extract onto a sterilized chromatography plate when the phone rang. Startled out of a deep concentration, she jerked. The contents of the capillary tube dribbled across the plate, ruining it. "Dammit!" she muttered. "I'll have to make a new one."

A few feet away, Bruce Cropper, the other PhD working on the project, frowned. "Who in hell would call the lab on Saturday night?"

"Probably a wrong number."

"Let's hope they figure that out and hang up."

They couldn't afford the interruption, not with Hassell Pharmaceuticals pushing them for results. Shutting out the distraction, or trying to—the darned phone rang at least ten times—Margaret returned to her work, which required care and focus. This was why she and Bruce had turned off their cell phones, to avoid unwanted intrusion.

Not that anyone would call her on a Saturday

night. Bruce, she didn't know. They never discussed those things.

By the time she finished the plate the annoying *Rrring! Rrring!* started again. Bruce shrugged. Margaret wasn't so unflappable.

"All right!" Carefully setting aside the capillary tube she slid from her stool with her lips compressed.

"Whoever they are, I don't envy them talking to you mad," Bruce said. His grin softened the words.

He was an attractive man, and the smile was contagious. Margaret strode across the white linoleum floor in a better mood.

The phone, a dingy yellow wall model that had seen better days, was at the far end of the lab, and by the time she snatched the receiver from its cradle she was slightly winded. "Margaret Lansing."

"Hello, Maggie," said a kindly, masculine voice she hadn't heard in years.

No one had called her "Maggie" since she'd turned eighteen and moved to Seattle fifteen years ago. People here called her Margaret or Dr. Lansing. "Dr. McElroy? Is that you?"

"Yes, it is. I tried to reach you at home and on your cell. Lucky your mother carries your lab number in her purse."

"She does?"

She'd never used it, but then she never called Margaret, period. Susan expected her daughters to do the calling.

Certainly Dr. McElroy had never phoned. He hadn't been her doctor since high school, so there was no reason to. Fearing bad news, Margaret leaned against the white plaster wall and bowed her head

She noted that her summer-weight slacks were creased from sitting so long, and idly smoothed her hand over them. "What's happened to Mother?"

"There's been a car accident."

Margaret could hear the doctor's heavy breathing, as if he were struggling with the news. "And?" she prodded, gripping the phone.

"Your mother . . . she died."

"What?" Too shocked to fully absorb what she'd just heard, Margaret sank onto the floor. "When? How?"

Bruce stood, his face a mask of concern. Warning him off, Margaret shook her head and stared at her lap.

"She was broadsided by a pick-up truck. Some teenage boy from out of town, passing through. Wasn't his fault, though. According to eyewitnesses and Officer Washburn, your mother ran a red light because she took her attention from the road and leaned down. Suzette was sitting in the passenger side, and we think she must've slipped off the seat . . ." Doctor McElroy stopped and cleared his throat. "I'm sorry, Maggie."

"Suzette. Naturally." Feeling oddly disconnected, Margaret couldn't cry. But her sinuses ached and felt swollen the way they did when the weather was about to change. She squeezed the bridge of her nose. "My God."

Doctor McElroy made a sympathetic sound. "Would you like me to call your sisters?"

"No, I will." Margaret hadn't talked to either one in nearly six months, since Christmas. She dreaded sharing the grim news, but someone had to. Better she than their old family doctor. "It'll take me five

hours to drive over, but if I leave in the morning I'l
be there by midafternoon," she said. "Rose lives i
Sacramento and Quincy's in Las Vegas, so they ma
not show up so fast."

"As long as you all come home, Maggie. Anythin
you want me to do?"

"Start calling me Margaret. And please get hol
of Mrs. Overman. Ask her to make up the beds, an
leave the key under the mat."

"You know we don't lock our doors in Shado
Falls, Magg—Margaret. Mrs. Overman is over at th
house now, getting it ready for you girls."

Her mind spinning, Margaret hung up. He
mother's death still hadn't hit. She stared numbl
at the receiver and pushed to her feet with a sigh.

Bruce hurried forward. "You look as white as
lab coat."

"My mother was killed in an accident tonight.
Saying it felt horrible.

"I'm sorry."

His hands curled and opened at his sides, an
she knew he wanted to comfort her. He'd asked he
out several times, but she'd always turned hin
down. Lately he'd stopped asking. Odd that nov
feeling numb as she did, she wanted a hug. Sh
wouldn't ask, though. What if she lost control?

Margaret didn't like to share her feelings. That wa
how you got hurt. Besides, this was too personal t
share with a coworker. To hold herself together sh
relied on what always worked—focusing on practica
issues and decisions. "I'll need a week off, starting t
morrow," she said. Even that was too long away fron
the lab, but with a funeral, the house, and who kne

hat else to deal with, she didn't have much choice. ;an you handle things without me?"

"Don't worry about a thing. Just take care of ɔurself. I'm real sorry, Margaret."

Tears gathered behind her eyes. Unable to speak, ıe nodded.

The next decision was more difficult. Who to call rst: Rose or Quincy? Margaret wasn't close to ither one, and hadn't been in what seemed forver. By age seemed fair, and Rose was older than uincy by eleven months. Unfortunately, both had nlisted numbers that were neither stored in Mararet's sharp memory nor programmed into her ell phone. They didn't talk often enough for ither. She would have to drive home, when what ıe wanted was to stay here with Bruce and escape ıto her work.

"Go on, Margaret," he said, shooing her out.

She grabbed her purse and left.

With a heavy heart Rose Abbott trudged from the athroom and returned to the living room. Danny adn't moved from the sofa. He was flipping ırough the latest *Enology Today* magazine and ating the popcorn she'd made for their Saturday ight movie-fest.

On the TV screen the *Sideways* DVD they'd been atching, paused while Rose used the facilities, ıowed Paul Giamatti, his expressive face frozen in ıdness. How fitting.

"Ready to watch the rest of the movie?" Danny ɔssed the magazine onto the end table, but it didn't

quite make it and landed on the floor. Ignoring th:
he shoved a handful of popcorn into his mouth.

The buttery aroma that five minutes ago h:
made her mouth water now sickened her. Sl
picked up the magazine and set it on the rack b
neath the table. She remained standing.

"I started my period," she said, slipping her an
hands into the lace-trimmed pockets of her favori
dress, which she'd sewn from Laura Ashley fabri

Her husband's round, friendly face fell before l
caught himself. "That's okay, honey." Grabbing
napkin from the pile on the coffee table he wip
his hands. "We'll try again next month."

He'd been saying that for nearly two years no
They both had.

"I'm not getting any younger," she said, soundi
shrill to her own ears. With reason. At thirty-o
her biological clock was ticking right past the b
childbearing years.

"Maybe it's time to make an appointment wi
Rachel Grant, that fertility doctor Mike and Lin
used."

Rose recalled the cadre of questions Linda h:
had to answer, and the myriad tests that left no s
crets untold. The very thought terrified her. Wh
if Dr. Grant somehow could tell what had ha
pened in college? She'd want to tell Danny. Tl
panicky feeling Rose hated but couldn't igno
squeezed like a boa constrictor. *No!* She couldn
Wouldn't. No matter how badly she wanted a chil

Oh, the irony. Here she was, a Home Ec teach
who couldn't create the home she longed for.
woman who loved her husband, but sometim
hated him, too, who was honest but afraid to t

ıe truth. Her life was one big contradiction. If that idn't make her her mother's daughter . . .

"It'd be easier if you got tested first," she argued, nowing that Danny wouldn't and that she was safe. or now.

Predictably, his jaw tightened. "We've already discussed this, Rose."

She crossed her arms. "Grow up, Danny. Findıg out if your sperm count is low is not a threat to our masculinity."

"I don't need any test to know I'm fine," he insisted, looking threatened all the same. Now his rms, too, were crossed. He studied her through arrowed, accusing eyes that spoke volumes.

You're the faulty one.

Rose feared he was right. The sins of the past and ll that. Guilt and remorse churned in her gut, twin lagues she'd harbored for twelve years. Between ıe panic and the regret she sometimes thought he'd go mad. "I don't want to talk about this," she napped. "I'm going to bed."

The ringing phone startled them both. Rose lanced at her watch. It was nearly eleven o'clock n a Saturday night. Nobody called this late, even n a weekend.

Danny stretched toward the end table and picked p. "Hello." He listened. "Maggie," he mouthed to ose. "It's been a long time, *Margaret.*"

Both Rose and Danny thought the formal name, hich Maggie insisted they use, pretentious. What as wrong with plain old "Maggie"? And why call ow? She sent Danny a curious look.

Equally puzzled, he shook his head. "Rose is right ere. Hang on." He handed over the phone.

Forgetting she was mad at her husband Rc
sank onto the arm of the sofa. "Hello, Margaret.

"Mother's dead," Margaret said in her usual r
nonsense fashion.

"Mother is dead?" Rose repeated, exchangin
shocked look with Danny. "But she's only fifty-o
and really healthy." *Physically, anyway.*

"I know."

She heard Margaret sniffle and her own eyes fill

Danny scooted over and held out his arms. S
batted him away. "What happened?"

"Car accident. A kid passing through to
plowed into her."

Despite the tears running down her face, Rc
couldn't feel much quite yet. "A kid." She sho
her head. "Was he drinking?"

"Not that I know of. Apparently Mother was
fault. She ran a red light. Something about leani
down to pick up Suzette while she was driving."

"Of course Suzette would be involved," Rc
muttered.

"Exactly what I said," Margaret replied.

"Suzette." Danny rolled his eyes and snickerec

"When did this happen?"

"Earlier this evening."

"Who called you?" *Why didn't they call me inste*
Jealousy reared its ugly head. Petty in light of h
mother's death, but Rose couldn't help her fe
ings. After all, she was the middle child. What w
Margaret's brains and Quincy's stunning beau
the invisible one.

"Dr. McElroy. I suppose he contacted me becau
I'm the oldest. I would've called sooner, only I w
in the lab and didn't have your number with me

That her own sister didn't know her number by heart stung. Even though Rose rarely called Margaret or Quincy, she knew their numbers. "Does Quincy know?"

"Not yet. I'm about to call her."

At least she knew before Quincy. That felt good. Also small-minded and awful. Here she was, gloating over knowing first, when their mother was dead.

It finally sank in. *My mother is dead.* Pain welled in Rose's chest, filled her heart, and clogged her throat. Crying noisily, she tumbled from the sofa arm into Danny's embrace. His solid warmth comforted her, and she burrowed against his chest.

"I'm leaving for Shadow Falls in the morning," Margaret said. "How soon can you get there?"

She swiped at her eyes. "I'll book a flight out as soon as we hang up." The plane trip from Sacramento to Seattle took nearly three hours. From there she'd need a car to get to Shadow Falls, a five-hour drive that crossed the Cascade Mountains. "But summer school starts a week from Monday, and the kids and district are depending on me, so I can't stay long."

"Me either."

Susan is dead. *Mama.* A name Rose and her sisters had been forbidden to use since their father had run off with a blond bimbo.

Rose raised herself from Danny's chest and slowly shook her head. "I can't believe this."

"It hasn't sunk in for me, either," Margaret said, sounding tired and sad.

Fresh tears rolled down Rose's cheeks. Danny handed her a paper napkin. She dabbed her eyes and crumpled it in her fist.

"Mrs. Overman is making up the beds," Margaret said. "You and Danny can sleep in Susan's room."

Danny barely knew their mother. They'd met exactly twice: at their wedding four years ago and again at Thanksgiving that same year. The worst holiday of Rose's life, which said a lot. That her sisters agreed said even more. She hadn't been back to Shadow Falls since, and neither had Margaret or Quincy.

Rose didn't want Danny with her, not now. Maybe in time for the funeral. "Um, Danny won't be with me."

He looked confused and hurt. She covered the mouthpiece. "You can't afford to miss the enology conference in San Francisco." Which started tomorrow. "Just come for the funeral." Sniffling and wriggling off his lap, she stood. "I'll be okay."

"If that's how you want it," he said, pouting like a little boy.

Now was no time to worry about soothing his feelings. She carried the phone into the kitchen. "I suppose I should call Quincy," she mused to Margaret. "We can meet in Seattle and rent a car for the drive."

"Oh, that sounds fun. You'll probably kill each other before you leave the airport."

Which could happen, since she and Quincy were as different as cotton and Lycra. Margaret was permanent press. None of them got along. Now their bitter, self-absorbed mother, whom they all hated was dead.

How empty that felt.

"Even if we fight the whole time, sharing a rental car is a good idea," Rose insisted. "I'm calling her."

"Fine, but give me ten minutes to break the news.

* * *

Breathing hard, Duke rolled off Quincy. "That was great."

If you liked men interested only in satisfying themselves. Quincy pasted a fulfilled smile on her face. "It sure was."

Duke, who was old enough to be her father, pulled her tight against his flabby side. She tried not to grimace. Every night for the past two weeks he'd shown up at the Blue Dove, the cocktail lounge where she worked. Or had until her boss had fired her earlier tonight. A drunken customer had pinched her behind one too many times, and she'd lost her temper and slapped him.

Barely able to pay the rent and other bills as it was, especially since Chuck had moved out, she was in a world of trouble now. Quincy hated being alone. So when Duke, who'd witnessed the whole thing, grabbed her hand and said, "Come on, Doll Baby, let's go someplace," she had.

He'd treated her to dinner, which was sweet. Trouble was, instead of eating he guzzled gin and tonics. Her second husband had been an alcoholic, and Quincy wanted nothing to do with another drunk. Before she finished her dinner salad, she'd decided to ditch Duke.

Yet here she was, in bed with him, and as lonely as ever. Without a job and broke to boot.

Disgusted with herself and her life, she pulled out of his arms. She'd clean up and grab a robe. Then she would send him home. "Be right back, Sugar."

Knowing he was watching, she fluffed her red

hair and sashayed her perfect rear end across th
room. The wrong thing to do when she wanted hi
gone, but after her face, her body was her best fe
ture, and she simply couldn't stop herself.

She was out of the bedroom and halfway to th
bathroom down the hall when the phone ran
That it was after eleven on a Saturday night was n
big deal. This was Las Vegas and the night was ju
beginning. Quincy pivoted around, returned to th
bedroom and snatched the phone from the dresse

"This is Quincy," she said, putting a purr into he
voice. She winked at Duke, whose eyes wer
clouded with booze and lust, and again parade
toward the hallway and bathroom.

"It's Margaret. Did I wake you?"

"Who's that, Doll Baby?" Duke hollered.

"Are you kidding?" Of all the people to call no
when she'd lost her job. Quincy forced a laugh.
have company, Mags, and he's hung like a—"

"Quincy, please," her sister said.

Margaret hadn't been laid in years. Quincy coul
hear the contempt in her voice. Or was it jealous
Either worked for her. She grinned. "Sorry abo
that, Mags."

"My name is Margaret."

She sounded as if she were gritting her teet
Getting to her was fun, and so easy. "What in th
world are you doing up at this hour on a Saturd
night?" Quincy asked.

If Margaret heard the dig—outside her work wi
lichen—*lichen*, for God's sake—she didn't have
life, she didn't let on. "Mother's dead."

Quincy's smile faded. "No way." She carried th
phone into the bathroom. "What happened?"

"Dr. McElroy said it was a car accident. Her fault. She drove through a red light. Witnesses say she was leaning down, probably distracted by Suzette. Some kid driving through town smacked into her."

"Wow." Overwhelmed, Quincy sat down on the toilet. "Suzette, huh?" She shook her head. "So Mama's favorite caused her death. How fitting."

"Baby Doll?" Duke called out.

Quincy covered the mouthpiece. "Shut up!" She kicked the door closed—which since the bathroom was small was easy to do from the toilet—and returned to Margaret. "I'll have to ask my boss for time off," she lied. "He won't let me take more than a week." She could barely afford that. "What's the plan?"

"There isn't one, yet, but we're all busy with our own lives, so we'll get things done fast. We can decide how to do that when we're together. I'll be driving to Shadow Falls in the morning. Rose will fly in as soon as she can. You should, too. She mentioned the two of you renting a car at the airport and driving over together."

"Rose and me alone in a car for five hours?" Despite her grief, Quincy laughed.

"Well, it does make sense from a practical standpoint."

Practical. That was Rose. Margaret was, too, and look where it got them? One sister spent her life isolated in a lab and the other taught Home Ec to high-school kids and was married to a man without an ounce of imagination. Bo-ring. Quincy was the only one who enjoyed life to the fullest. Though at the moment, "enjoy" seemed a tad exaggerated.

My mother is dead. As lousy a mother as Susan was,

her passing hurt unbearably. Tears gathered behind Quincy's eyes. Her chest felt heavy and way too full. Or was it empty? She couldn't wait to send Duke home and bawl like a baby. "I'll make a plane reservation right away," she said.

"You might wait until you hear from Rose, so you can coordinate. She'll probably call as soon as we hang up."

Despite her grief and fierce need to cry, Quincy changed her mind about sending Duke home just yet. She wanted him all hot and bothered when Rose called. Just to get her goat.

After all, she had a reputation to uphold.

About the Author

Ann Roth lives in the greater Seattle area with her husband and a crotchety cat who rules the house. After earning an MBA, she worked as a banker and corporate trainer. She gave up the corporate life to write; and if they awared Ph.D.s in writing happily-ever-after stories, she'd surely have one.

For a list of ten financial tips every woman should follow and a discussion guide for *Another Life,* visit www.annroth.net.